"The Event is like the Beverly Hillbillies meets the Real Housewives of New York City, only it takes place in Creek Water, Missouri. Once again Whitney Dineen pens a story that is comparable to outrageously hilarious events you could picture in a romantic comedy movie. This is an excellent book which needs to be picked up to become a Big Screen hit!" *-AJ Book Remarks*

"Emmie's big city life clashes with her small-town roots in this winning, hilarious romantic comedy." —*USA Today Bestselling Author, S.B. Babi*

"Whitney Dineen never ceases to amaze me with her penchant for writing original and engaging stories. The Event is all that and more. Do yourself a favor and download this sweet book fill with Southern charm and laugh out loud moments. You won't be disappointed." *-Jennifer Peel, Author of My Not So Wicked Boss*

"Funny, quirky, heartwarming, small town drama. I love the way Whitney sucks you into the story so easily. From the first line and throughout the entire book, I found myself smiling and laughing and swooning. I didn't want this story to end!" *-Becky Monson, Author of Just a Name*

Also by Whitney Dineen

Romantic Comedies
Relatively Normal
Relatively Sane
Relatively Happy
She Sins at Midnight
The Reinvention of Mimi Finnegan
Mimi Plus Two
Kindred Spirits
Going Up?

Thrillers
See No More

Non-Fiction Humor
Motherhood, Martyrdom & Costco Runs

Middle Reader
Wilhelmina and the Willamette Wig Factory
Who the Heck is Harvey Stingle?

Children's Books
The Friendship Bench

The Event

Whitney Dineen

The Event
By Whitney Dineen

https://whitneydineen.com/newsletter/
33 Partners Publishing

ACKNOWLEDGMENTS

The journey of writing a book is much like climbing Mt. Everest. It *sounds* like such an exciting adventure, it *feels* like the right thing to do, and your creative muscles are begging for the challenge. So, one morning you put on your best writing outfit (pajamas), sit down at your computer and crack your knuckles in a "you're going down" kind of way, and then you unleash the beast (that sounds so wrong, sorry.)

You write and write and write for hours, days, weeks on end while the voices in your head spin, weave, and otherwise release your epic from the confines of your imagination. It's a heady rush for sure.

When the last word is typed, your whole body is covered with the sheen of your efforts, your muscles ache, the relief is so great all you want to do is cry. Then you look down to see how far you've climbed only to realize you're barely halfway up the mountain. Then you really do cry.

The worst part of finishing a book is that you don't finish at the peak. You're only midway, hanging off a sheer wall with one little toe grip keeping you alight. You've gained five snacking pounds during the climb, and you're pretty sure your toe is going to snap off from the extra load if you don't get that boost to keep you going.

Just when you're sure all is lost, and you're destined to be another climbing/authoring casualty, the first Sherpas arrive! I am fortunate to have many Sherpas on my authoring climb. They keep me motivated, encouraged, challenged, and excited. My dedicated troop includes:

My mom, Libby Bohlen, who pops into my office every four hours like clockwork to see if I have something new for her to read (she reads as I go) and my husband, Jimmy Dineen, who does the first edit once the book is through. Their efforts get me off the wall and semi-securely situated on a skinny ledge that may certainly still break off, sending me into the abyss, but for the moment is enough to catch my breath.

Enter my beta reader Sherpas. For this book, they were the fabulous authors Becky Monson and Jennifer Peel. Becks and Jen always carve time out of their VERY busy lives to read and advise. When they're done, I go back to the drawing board for the second run. When I'm sure my book can be no better, I look down, then up, and realize I'm finally closer to the summit of my climb than the valley below, so I keep going.

My Sherpa editor, Celia Kennedy, is next. Celia thinks I'm funny/talented but not so much so that she lets me get lazy. No, sir. She's been known to say things to me like, "What does this even mean?" "Yeah, no, this won't work at all." and my personal favorite, "Why are you even writing this book?" But through her tough love and knowledge of the path, she gets me within spitting distance of my goal. I'm often bloodied from this portion, but I'm also invigorated and fully charged to finish. Celia ALWAYS demands my best. She makes me a better writer.

When the book is as tight as can be, it goes off to my proofreading Sherpa. Paula Bothwell is the ideal proofreader because she also offers editorial comment, which I greatly value. She's the first fresh eyes on the best version of my book. Once Paula adds her two cents and I invariably make changes, it's off to Sandy Penny for the final polish.

Once the book is proofed, it goes out for blurbs and editorial reviews. This varies from book to book, but this time around, authors Becky Monson, Jennifer Peel, Sherly Babin, Diana Orgain, Melanie Summers, Kate O'Keeffe, and AJ Book Remarks have my back. Additional fabulous Sherpas on my journey include Tracie Bannister, Annabelle Costa, and Virgina Gray. In the world of editorial reviews, Chick Lit Central's Sara Stevens always makes sure to read my latest and help get the word out—invaluable and beloved Sherpas, all.

My assistant Sherpa Karan Eleni picks up all the crazy slack like getting my newsletters sent out, my website updated etc., so I can keep writing more books. So really, Karan, we all thank you for that!

Once all of these steps are complete, my Big Daddy, Hollywood Attorney Sherpa, Scott Schwimer, gets hold of the book. He reads it on vacation in Mexico, then sets out to find the best and smartest movie studios/producers to get my baby up on the Big Screen (either the one in your living room or the movie theater."

Finally, finally, my book gets published and you, my lovely reader Sherpas get your hands on it. All of the previous legs of the journey would be for naught without you. Your reviews, recommendations of my work to your friends, and your lovely emails are what makes me want to climb this mountain again and again, and I thank you with all my heart.

Chapter One

In my esteemed, but obviously biased opinion, Creek Water, Missouri, population 14,012, is the armpit of the world. Scratch that, it's a ripe pustulant boil on the butt of the Northern Hemisphere. If it weren't my hometown, and I weren't desperate for employment, I'd have never considered moving back. Ever.

I just got off the phone with my Uncle Jed—the *Beverly Hillbillies* reference is not lost on me—and he's offered to make me manager of a new commercial venture he and my other uncle Jesse (yes, like *Full House*) are starting up in the old warehouse district. The revitalization of Creek Water continues as my former peers have discovered that it's cheaper to live at home and not go out into the real world like I did. Problem is, I got myself into a tiny bit of trouble in the real world.

I was driven in my formative years to prove that I could make something of myself without any backing from the illustrious Frothingham family, of which I am one. I was sick to death of people thinking everything was handed to me on a silver platter just because of my last name. So, I worked hard to get excellent grades in school, and I earned myself a scholarship to college. After graduation, I moved to New York City, determined to leave my small-town, small-minded roots behind. Things were going great too, until *The Event.*

I worked as head buyer for Silver Spoons Enterprises in Manhattan, an exclusive gourmet/kitchenware boutique chain on the Eastern Seaboard. I was stationed at our flagship location on East Seventy-Third Street.

The Event was the corporate dinner dance at the Metropolitan Museum of Art, where all the bigwigs gathered to pat each other on the back and recognize top-performing employees. I thought I was a shoo-in for the Demitasse Award, honoring the most creative contribution to the company during that fiscal year. I was personally responsible for the whole "Linens for Dinner" campaign, which promoted the idea that both urban and suburban millennials only use cloth napkins to dine, thus not only cutting back our carbon footprint by lessening paper waste, but also adding a touch of elegance to our lives. We sold more linens that year than in the previous ten years combined. It was *that* successful.

So there I sat in my way too expensive dress—I splurged because I knew how important it was to make a good impression on the executives *and* because it was the perfect little number to accept my honor in—when Jameson Diamante announced the nominees for the Demitasse.

There were only three of us—me with my linen campaign, Juliet Smithers from the Southampton store for her "Drink More Wine!" crusade, and Allison Conrad from Atlanta for her "Pretty Please, Y'all" call to reinstate formal invitations on engraved card stock.

Why don't we just kill the planet, Allison, with all the trees we're going to murder for your cause?

I was poised on the edge of my seat ready to throw my hands across my heart and gasp something along the lines of, "What? Me? My word, I'm so surprised!" I'd imagined how I'd get up and show off my six-hundred-dollar understated elegance to the whole room.

Jameson announced, "This year's decision was not an easy one to make, with all three ladies greatly contributing to our brand, but in the end, we chose the contender who was responsible for the most innovative campaign."

Here's where the chain of events gets a wee bit cloudy. I could have sworn he'd called my name, so I stood up as planned, but my good friend and table-mate Lexi says that isn't what happened at all. Apparently, old Jameson had called out Allison's name, and she and I both went up to accept the award. How deforesting the planet is innovative, I do not know. I did hear through the corporate grapevine that Allison had gone to Jameson's hotel room with him before the ceremony like a Kardashian auditioning her new sugar daddy. But I digress. Back to *The Event.*

I grabbed the silver spoon out my fellow nominee's hand and proceeded to give my speech. All of it. Which for some reason I was allowed to do. It was a beautiful speech. I thanked my mother for her graciousness and manners, and I thanked my grandmother for teaching me how to fold dinner napkins into swans. I was about to thank Silver Spoons for having the wisdom to hire me, when Allison grabbed the Demitasse out of my hand. I may have chosen that moment to snatch it back and hit her over the head with it—obviously not very hard as she never pressed assault charges, thank God.

It's all conjecture really. All I can say for certain is that I hastily fled the ceremony, trotting down all eight hundred thousand stairs of the Met in four-inch heels, in a cloud of disgrace and disappointment. I took a cab to a nearby bar, where I proceeded to drink my body weight in tequila before waking up in an unknown apartment in Brooklyn.

Tequila and I have a sordid past. One incident of over consumption resulted in my belting out my karaoke version of "I Will Always Love You"—the Dolly Parton version, not Whitney Houston's—so poorly I'm sure ears bled; another found me French kissing a giant stuffed frog before throwing up on it; and the last time, before the Brooklyn incident, was when I urinated in my sorority sister's shoe because I was so drunk I couldn't find the bathroom. Now I can add "indiscriminate behavior" to the list.

Let me just say, I'm not loose by anyone's estimation. I believe in using linens at every meal, for Pete's sake! But the truth is, I spent the night with a stranger and if he wasn't Armie Hammer from that movie *Hotel Mumbai*, because that's who I thought he looked like, then I have no idea who he was. To make matters worse, we apparently didn't use any protection. I soon discovered that I, Emmaline Anne Frothingham, of Creek Water, Missouri, was going to become a mother at the tender age of twenty-eight.

Chapter Two

The reason I'm so bitter about my roots is because when I was eight years old my daddy, Reed Frothingham, died, and the whole town of Creek Water—with the exception of our family—acted like Mama and I were leeching off my uncles for our survival. Which is simply not the truth. We were left a decent-sized inheritance, not huge as most of the family money was spent during my grandparents' generation—we have the sterling-silver snail tongs to prove it—and my uncles didn't start making good investments until after I'd become a half-orphan. It is by surname alone that we aren't considered nouveau riche.

Mama and I had enough money to keep our house and pay our bills, but she had to go back to work so we could have the extras. She kept the books for the uncles and, in that way, managed to stay part of the family business, which, as I mentioned earlier, has become revitalizing Creek Water. Mama didn't invest any of our money because she worried that risking it might send us to the poor house. My uncles didn't have a good track record at the time.

I *needed* that scholarship to Duke as there simply was not enough money to pay for that caliber of education any other way.

Yet, no one acknowledged my hard work, and instead, treated me as though I was using money I wasn't entitled to. Every time Mama and I did something extra, like go shopping in St. Louis, some busybody would inevitably say, "Your uncles are so good to y'all!"—completely negating our ability to take care of ourselves. The uncles tried to set them straight, to no avail.

This is why I was determined to get out and make something big out of my life. I was going to prove once and for all that I was more than a charity case.

Of course, that was before I'd accepted the gift of a stranger's swimmers and decided to bring new life into this world. I continued working at Silver Spoons through most of my pregnancy. I worried that after *The Event* they might try to find a way to let me go. But if I was pregnant, they couldn't do so without fear of a lawsuit. I told my boss about my situation as soon as I found out. I realize that was a little manipulative on my part, but Gloria Gaynor and I, we're survivors.

When I told Lexi, her response was, "Emmie, how in the world are you going to have this baby? You can't raise a child alone in New York City."

My response was simple, "I made my bed, now I'll have to lie in it." But to tell you the truth, I was nowhere near the martyr I made myself out to be. When I lay with my feet in the stirrups at the doctor's office and heard a heartbeat coming from inside my body, one that wasn't my own, it was *insta-love*. I don't judge what other women do or do not do with their reproductive systems, but mine was making a person, and I wanted to know everything about who she would become. (I just knew she was a girl.)

"You need to go back to that apartment and let that man know he's going to be a father. He'll have to pay you child support," Lexi said very practically.

I probably should have, and maybe even would have, had I taken note of his address. The truth is, I was still drunk when I woke up and all I could think to do was hightail it out of there before I had a witness to my walk of shame. I had absolutely no idea how to find the father, so I decided to forget he existed.

After going to my doctor to make sure I was disease-free—I'll never put myself in *that* situation again—I settled down and tried to enjoy my pregnancy. In my eighth month, Silver Spoons decided to cut my position, claiming they couldn't afford a senior buyer and two junior buyers, so they offered me six months' severance to go away. I probably could have sued them for wrongful termination, but I was fat and tired and all I wanted to do was lie on my couch and watch classic romantic comedies until my baby was born. So, that's exactly what I did. Thank goodness too, as Faye came twenty-six days early. Frothingham babies historically like to show up to the party ahead of schedule.

Chapter Three

"Who's the prettiest baby in the whole world?" I hear my mama, Gracie, ask in her soft Southern drawl. She's making duck faces at Faye, while I unpack my daughter's things in the spare room. One thing is for certain, Mama loves my precious girl, and doesn't seem the least bit concerned about her lack of a daddy.

I'd always dreamed of naming a daughter Faye after my maternal grandma. I certainly didn't think my last name would still be Frothingham, though. The alliteration alone would have turned me off the idea. But, being a single mother in my hometown, I cannot realistically expect to have any more children. I'm pretty sure they spray painted a scarlet letter on my backside when Faye and I crossed the city limit line, or more accurately, when we crossed the tracks to the right side of town, where the Frothinghams live.

Mama carries the baby around while saying, "This here girl is as sweet as shoo-fly pie. I could just eat her up."

"Are you sure you don't mind watching her while I go meet with the uncles?" I ask.

"I might never let you pry her out of my arms!" She snuggles her giggling five-month-old bundle. "Isn't dat right, little missy?"

Faye squeals in delight. I love this tiny person so much I'd cut off my foot and sell it for groceries if I had to. Luckily, I don't have to. What I do have to do is go meet with my uncles about the job they used to lure me home. While I'm grateful for their kindness, I feel like I'm taking a giant step into the past by considering it.

Once they found out about Faye, they said, "Emmie, get back here where you belong! We can't let you raise a Frothingham in that big city all alone." As much as I expected the citizens of Creek Water would judge my indiscretion, I knew my family would be nothing but supportive. I am more thankful than I can say.

I truly did think of staying in New York City, but the thought of handing off my baby to a total stranger to raise while I worked hellishly long hours to support us did not seem appealing in the least. Not to mention the fact that I saw Armie Hammer lookalikes everywhere I went and couldn't help but wonder each and every time if he was Faye's daddy.

Don't worry, I googled the actor's whereabouts on the night of the conception and discovered he was nowhere near Brooklyn. More's the pity. So, I lived out the length of my severance and then gave notice on my apartment before shipping my worldly possessions home.

*****

Uncle Jed's wife, Auntie Lee, is the first to greet me when I walk through the door of Frothingham Brothers. She's sitting at the reception desk addressing notecards when she looks up to see who's invaded her space. "Emmie!" She jumps up and dances around me like I'm a maypole and she's vying for queen. "Look at you. Welcome home, honey." She hugs me so hard she nearly pops the stuffing out of me. Then she holds me at arm's length and declares, "Will you just look at those boobies?"

I'm still breastfeeding Faye, so my regular B-cup has jumped to a D. You'd think I was a walking sideshow the way she's ogling me. Uncomfortable, I tug up the already modest neckline on my sweater dress and say, "Hey, Auntie Lee." I give her a kiss on the cheek. "I'm here to see Uncle Jed and Uncle Jesse."

"Honey, they're waiting for you in the big office. They're just finishin' up a meeting with the contractor. You might as well go on in."

I steel myself for this step back in time and wish there were a way to stop my racing heart. I tentatively knock on the door and Uncle Jesse booms, "Get in here."

It sounds like he's expecting someone else, but I open the door anyway. My uncles nearly tackle me to the ground when they rush me and give me great big hugs. I'm not sure who's saying what, but there's a lot of "Girl, look at you!" and "Finally, our Emmie's home!" and excited sentiments like that. It's nice to be the recipient of such a warm welcome. Their support combined with my postpartum hormones brings tears to my eyes.

But before I can start blubbering, Uncle Jed pulls back and says, "You remember Zachary Grant, dontcha?"

I turn to see a tall, shockingly gorgeous man with sparkling green eyes get up off the sofa and walk over to greet me. My god, Armie Hammer lookalikes are everywhere. Ever since the night Faye was conceived, I've been bombarded by them.

Zach's metamorphosis is so astonishing I would have never

guessed he was the same boy I knew in high school. Of course, a lot can happen to someone in a decade and apparently has in his case. Gone is the gangly teenager with braces and acne. He's been replaced by a virtual movie star. That Mother Nature sure is a wonder.

Zach lets his gaze stray to my bosom before meeting my eyes and saying, "Hey, Emmie." He smiles shyly, almost expectantly.

I flash back to the time he asked me to the spring dance at the club his senior year in high school. I was a sophomore. I said no because, well, it was at the club. Mama and I weren't members at the time, and I didn't want to draw any more attention to myself. The less those nasty gossips saw of me and Mama, the better. Unfortunately, I never explained that to Zach.

"Hi there, Zach," I say back.

I feel like he's waiting for something more, like maybe an apology for turning him down without an explanation. I know I hurt him because he went out of his way to never speak to me again. Seriously, he'd be walking down the hall at school, lay eyes on me, and turn around and go the other direction just to avoid me.

I segue into wondering if apologizing after all this time would even be appropriate. He'd probably think I was pretty stuck on myself to think he even remembered.

Uncle Jed explains, "Emmie and Faye have just moved back home and Emmie's going to work on the new project with us. Isn't that exciting?"

Zach clears his throat and attempts to nod, but looks more like a bird pecking at some crumbs. "Ah, yes? I guess." He's not selling his enthusiasm in the least. Then he asks, "Who's Faye?"

"My little girl," I answer, squaring my shoulders, ready to do battle, even if it is only for a judgmental lift of the eyebrows.

I might as well have said my pet giraffe considering how surprised he looks by this news. "You're married?"

Uncle Jesse quickly says, "No, our little Emmie lost her fiancé to friendly fire in the Middle East."

Say what? I look at him in complete shock. My daddy's brother just puts his arm around me and continues to say, "It's been what, a year now since Armand died? We're all still so shaken up by it."

I can't seem to force any words out of my mouth. First of all, apparently my whole family knows about my infatuation with Armie Hammer. I only ever told my mama, but it seems the news has traveled. And secondly, my what?

Uncle Jed reads my mind or my expression and pipes in, "Your auntie Lee has gone ahead and told folks about him, honey. There's no shame in having a precious baby with your fiancé. It's not your fault he died before the wedding."

My head starts whirring like the spin-cycle on a washing machine. *So that's how they're playing it.* I should have known they wouldn't want a Frothingham bringing a bastard child home without an acceptable explanation. As mad as I am, I decide to perpetuate the lie, at least temporarily, until I decide how to play this long-term. Plus, I need the job.

I smile at Zach as though I'm forcing it through thick layers of sadness. "It was such a tragedy."

"How long were you two together?" he asks.

I answer, "Three years," at the same time Uncle Jed says, "Two years, if you can believe," while Uncle Jesse contributes,

"Just a year, but still it's so hard."

For crying out loud, if we're going lie, we should get out stories straight first. I try to make sense of this farce by saying, "We had our first date three years ago, got engaged two years ago, and he's been gone for a year." *God rest his soul.*

Zach looks at us in the same way I imagine he'd look at the Three Stooges after one of their ridiculous skits. Then he says, "I guess I'll see you all at the warehouse tomorrow morning." I swear he shoots me a dirty look on his way out the door.

As soon as he leaves, I turn on my uncles and demand, "What the heck was that all about?"

Chapter Four

Uncle Jed starts, "Honey, it was your auntie Lee's idea. She thought it best. You know how the ladies at *the club* can get when anything out of the ordinary happens."

Those club ladies are a menace. Ever since I was a little girl, I've been intimidated by their judgment. Part of me wishes I could just tattoo a big "Screw You" on my forehead and meet them for tea some afternoon. I could bring my poor fatherless child and discuss the benefits of nipple piercings. Not that mine are, mind you, I'm so boring I only have one hole in each ear, but still, if they're gonna gossip so much, I might as well give them a reason.

"What do those club ladies have on you, Uncle Jed?" I demand. "You got some extra kids of your own out there they know about?"

"You watch your tongue, young lady," Uncle Jed chokes out as Uncle Jesse snickers in the background.

Uncle Jed is the oldest brother at fifty-five, my daddy would have been fifty-two, Uncle Jesse is the family surprise at only forty-two.

Uncle Jed explains, "There's just certain ways things are done here, and folks expect the ring before the baby, otherwise they assume you're trash."

I arch an eyebrow, and he continues, "Not that *we* think you're trash, honey. Good lord, it's not like any of us waited until we got married, we just didn't have any accidents."

Uncle Jesse jokes, "Or if we did, we took care of them."

"This is not a conversation I wish to be having with either one of you," I say primly, or as primly as an unwed mother can. "I'm here to talk about your job offer, not to hear any proselytizing about my personal life."

"Who's preaching?" Uncle Jesse asks. "Jed here was just explaining that the people of Creek Water live by certain rules, is all. Sure, they're archaic and dried up, but being that we rely on this town for our income, we think it's best if we play along and don't stir the pot."

"About the job …" I prompt.

"Right, about the job," Uncle Jed helps change the topic. "We bought the old sewing machine factory down by the river a few months ago and we've got some big plans for it. We're going to turn the ground floor into a restaurant, coffee place, gourmet food shop, and the like."

Uncle Jesse says, "That's how we got the idea to hire you. We thought with your experience in New York City, you'd bring some real class to the operation."

"Are you planning to own all these businesses?" I ask, hoping the answer is no. If my uncles were to open a restaurant, they'd probably only serve fried pickles and jalapeno poppers.

"No, no, no," Uncle Jed says. "We're going to rent the space out to other businesses, but we thought we'd go ahead and own the gourmet shop, what with your expertise and all. What do you think?"

"Uncle Jed," I start to say, but he waves me off with, "Girl, I feel like Buddy Ebsen every time you say that. Can we just disperse with the uncle nonsense already?"

"Who's Buddy Ebsen?" I ask.

"Uncle Jed from *The Beverly Hillbillies*."

Uncle Jesse adds, "And I'm not that much older than you, so you best start calling me Jesse."

"I suppose if we're going to be business partners that would be okay."

Jed says, "Who said anything about partners? We just wanted to hire you on as our employee."

"No, sir," I say. "I've spent most of my life with this town thinking I was some kind of piglet sucking off the family tit. I'm not going to be anything less than your business partner on this venture."

"On the whole building?" Jesse wants to know.

"If I'm managing the whole building, then yes."

"But, girl," Jed says, "you didn't put up any of the capital."

"But *Jed*," I respond using his Christian name for the first time, "I'm the one with the know-how. Now do we have a deal or not?"

Jed looks at his brother and says, "This here girl's done grown into her britches in the Big City."

Jesse nods his head. "I'm okay with giving her ten percent." Then he looks at me and says, "But that means you don't get any money until we start making a profit on the project."

"Fine by me," I answer. "I'm going to live with Mama, and I

have enough savings to cover Faye's and my expenses for several months." And let's face it, living rent free, I might even be able to swing longer. I didn't want to be unemployed in New York or I would have blown through my savings in a fraction of the time.

We shake on it and Uncle Jed declares, "Your daddy would be right proud of you, Emmie. I'm pretty proud of you myself."

"Thank you," I say. "Now, I need to get out of here 'cause I'm starting to leak all over my dress."

Both of my uncles jump to their feet and don't so much as look at me. They're craning their heads upwards, pretending fascination with the tin ceiling. I think I'm going to enjoy being around them again. I just had to make sure I came home on equal footing. I'm not going to have any of the gossipy biddies in this town accusing me being a charity case, *again*. Heaven knows they'll find enough to say about me without giving them that, too.

Chapter Five

"Do you know what Auntie Lee told the ladies at the club about Faye's other parent?" I'm loath to call him her daddy because he's no such thing. He's merely an anonymous donor of genetic material. But that sounds so cold, and from my limited memory, that night was anything but cold.

"I know, Emmie, but I support her one hundred percent. There's no sense bringing this precious child home only to have certain folks make her feel unwelcome."

I roll my eyes so hard I think I just got a peek at the back of my skull. "By 'certain folks,' you mean Cootie Wilcox and her gang."

"Of course. Who else would I mean? That Cootie was a pistol in high school and she's still going strong. Only now she has more power than ever."

"Who gives her this power?" I demand. "Seems to me that if folks would just dethrone her already, they wouldn't have to walk around on eggshells. They'd be much happier."

"You know how it is in small towns, honey. Folks get bored and if there isn't any drama, they create it. It's human nature, I suppose."

I pick up Faye and inhale her fresh baby scent. It has an immediate soothing effect on my frayed nerves. "Mama, I don't know if you've heard, but they have this thing called Netflix now, and if you need drama, you can get as much as you want for a very reasonable monthly rate."

She comes over and wraps her arms around me and the baby. "If it was only that simple, sweetie." Then she sets us free and starts tidying up the baby toys in the living room. "I invited the family over for dinner to meet Faye, so why don't you get the table set for me?"

"Who's all coming?" I ask.

"Jed, Lee, Amelia, Beau, Davis, and Jesse, of course."

All three of my cousins settled right here in Creek Water. Amelia was two years ahead of me in school, Beau and I were in the same grade, and Davis was a year younger.

"Is Uncle Jesse dating anyone?"

Mama laughs. "You know him. He courts like it's his profession, but doesn't seem to be interested in settling down."

"Breaking hearts as he goes, I suppose."

"I believe that men have more wild oats to sew that we gals do. It's better he gets it all out of his system now," she says.

"I love your antiquated notions that men are somehow hornier than women. Who do you think they're sewing their wild oats with? Sheep?"

She shoots me a look that suggests I shouldn't be using such a word, before giggling, "Well, there's still Otis Gunther."

Otis is a sheep farmer on the outskirts of town. He's been a dedicated bachelor his whole sixty some years, but word is he always has a special animal friend. I can't even let my mind go there, so I don't. "How about the cousins? They have anyone serious?"

"Amelia was dating a nice lawyer who lives in St. Louis, but things have cooled off a bit lately." At my questioning look, she explains, "He wanted her to move up there and she wasn't having any of it. She's got her bead shop in town and says she has no intention of relocating."

Amelia has always been the artistic one. "You'd think she'd want to move it to the city. She'd get a lot more business that way."

"I don't think she cares so much about that. She's always loved Creek Water and she wants to stay put. Plus, she's made a darling home for herself above her store. It overlooks the river."

"What about the boys?" I ask.

"Beau was dating Shelby Wilcox, but she broke up with him on the grounds that he didn't take her seriously enough. Davis can't be bothered. He spends all his time carving and claims to be perfectly content." Davis makes the most beautiful furniture I've ever seen. He uses a variety of wood, but his aesthetic is always clean masculine lines. Folks come from all over the state to order from his showroom.

Faye lets out a little sigh in her sleep like a party balloon with a slow leak. I look down at my beautiful girl and I thank the good Lord for my indiscretion. Had I won that Demitasse Award I'd still be in the Big Apple instead of in the bosom of my family. It might just be time for Creek Water and me to make our peace.

Chapter Six

Auntie Lee is the first through the front door with her arms stretched out like she's welcoming a stadium full of fans. "Where's my baby?" she demands.

Handing over Faye, I know I probably won't lay hands on her again until she's hungry. Auntie Lee kisses her all over before ordering, "Davis, bring me a sweet tea and gin. I'll just be over here on the davenport where I'll be loving on my great-niece."

Davis stops to give me a hug on his way to the kitchen to assemble his mama's beverage of choice.

Beau is next to arrive. I say to him, "Shelby Wilcox, huh?"

He shrugs. "She's not so bad if she'd stop letting that mother of hers boss her around so much."

Jed and Jesse come in all smiles with their arms loaded down with pretty little packages wrapped in pink paper adorned with white grosgrain ribbons. Jed says, "Lee's been shopping for the baby." He hands his load over to me and asks Mama, "You got any beer in the house, Gracie?"

"I think there's some left from the last time you were here. Check the fridge in the garage." Unlike Cootie and her gang, who stopped giving her the time of day when Daddy died, my daddy's brothers have been very attentive to Mama over the years, treating her like she was their very own sister. When Mama was a Frothingham, with a live husband around, Cootie and company couldn't have sucked up more. But once she was widowed, she lost all value in their eyes.

Davis hands Auntie Lee her sweet tea and says, "Aunt Grace, I'm not going to be able to mow your lawn on Saturday, so I'm going to do it Friday afternoon, if that's okay."

"You're a good boy to keep helping me like you do, Davis."

"Well, shoot, you live right next door to my folks, so it's no trouble to just keep mowing a bit more once I get started." He doesn't even live with his parents, but he's their groundskeeper, too.

Amelia says, "Emmie, I want you to come down to the shop as soon as you get settled, so I can show you all the changes I've made. I've got the cutest little beading area where I give classes now."

"I can't wait," I assure her. "I might be able to come over tomorrow sometime after I meet your daddy and Jesse at the warehouse."

The next two hours are spent catching me up on the family business. The uncles have snatched up four other buildings in the warehouse district and have plans to renovate them: everything from a new grocery store to loft-style condominiums.

"The town's population is booming with kids in their twenties and thirties moving into the area. At least half who didn't even grow up here," Jed says.

"What in the world are they doing to pay the bills in a town like Creek Water?" I ask.

22

"Their bills aren't nearly so high here as they were in Kansas City and St. Louis, which is where they seem to be coming from. Plus, a bunch of them work remotely on the computer. There's even a cyber office downtown where people rent out workspace."

"What does the old guard think of all these changes?" I ask.

Auntie Lee, who hasn't stopped making silly faces at Faye since she came in, says, "Oh, honey, they're all for it. More bodies mean a thriving economy. Look at us, we wouldn't be revitalizing old downtown without all these kids moving in. They're bringing money."

Beau adds, "The median housing price has gone up five grand in the last year alone." He owns his own real-estate company downtown.

"I guess I'd better look into buying something before too much more time goes by then," I say. I haven't had a chance to think about my own place yet, but once I get settled, I'm going to need to regain my independence.

"No, ma'am, you're gonna stay right here with me," Mama says.

"I can't stay here forever, Mama." My God, talk about going backwards.

"I don't know why not. I don't need this much house and if you don't stay, I might just sell it and buy myself something smaller in town."

"We have time to talk about it," I tell her. "In the meantime, fill me in on what's going on at the club."

The Creek Water Country Club was a second home to me during my early childhood. My folks used to golf and play tennis there, and I learned how to swim and make armpit farts in the pool. All-in-all, I have nice memories of it. That is, until Daddy died. After that, Mama and I didn't go so often. A single mother doesn't hold the kind of clout that a married lady does, and some of the gals started to act like they didn't even know Mama. So, she gave up her membership and started to meet her friends in town for lunch instead of at the Players Grille.

Auntie Lee talked Mama into joining up again after I went to college, and now the two of them have their own clique. I smile at the thought of the Frothingham gang and Cootie's gang dancing it out in a *West Side Story* kind of rumble. It would be worth the price of the ticket, that's for sure.

Auntie Lee says to me, "We're having a tea for you there on Friday." My eyes bug out at the news. I would rather lick the pavement after a dog parade than be subjected to an afternoon with those women.

"Now before you go getting all hot under the collar," Auntie Lee adds, "your mama and I thought it'd be best to face everyone head-on. If you shrink away from them, they'll assume you're ashamed and they'll feed on that."

Mama adds, "You need to show up on their playing field with your head high. Stare them in the eye and don't back down."

This is the part of coming home I dreaded. How is it that well into the two-thousands grown women are still acting like it's nineteen fifty? It baffles the mind.

Chapter Seven

Mama takes Faye with her when she goes out for coffee with her friends while I meet the uncles at the old sewing machine factory. I'm wearing a sweet little Lily Pulitzer dress that buttons up the front, but I realize I need to pump before I can close it properly, which means I will have only two hours before I fill up again and bust out of the thing. I change into a skirt and twinset, so I won't be held hostage by my lactating bosom.

I briefly admire myself in the mirror and realize that with the exception of my gigantic boobs, I look just like I did before having Faye. Five feet, eight inches, and back into my size 8s. That pregnancy myth about your hair growing thicker and being shinier is true—I have to admit I've been fixated on my shoulder-length blonde bob and have kept taking the prenatal vitamins to maintain its luster. I look damn fine, if I do say so myself.

I happily climb into my daddy's old 1988 red Mustang convertible with the black racing stripes—Mama assures me it's all tuned up and ready to drive—and I throw my purse on the backseat. When I fire it up, Depeche Mode's "People are People" blares out of the speakers. Mama left all of Daddy's music in the car so whenever anyone drives it, they feel like they're spending a little time with him. "Hi, Daddy, you ready to hit it?" A big ol' smile is plastered on my face.

I don't have a lot of organic memories left of him, but I have pictures galore, and I have his brothers. The uncles talk about Daddy all the time, telling stories of how *Ol' Reed* used to play tricks on them by hiding their keys in the toilet tank, and filling the sugar canister with salt. They keep him alive for me as surely as if that stinkin' cancer never got him.

I pull out onto Pecan Grove Trail Road and observe the wide-open rolling green landscapes interspersed with watermelon and pea farms and feel great delight. I have a real fondness for this terrain, and even though I loved my years in New York City, it never fed my soul the way my home state does. Had it not been for Cootie Wilcox and her gossipy cronies, I might have stayed here like my cousins did. Instead, the club ladies' actions made such a negative impact on me that it tainted my perception and drove me away.

As I pull into town, I feel a wave of pure nostalgia rush over me. I adore the old brick buildings running the length of Main Street with their original store names still painted on the side—Whisper Willy's Chocolatier, Daisy May's Notions, and the Loyal Family Five and Dime. Of course, all of these buildings have changed hands at least a dozen times since then, but it's a constant reminder of the rich history of our town.

I've always loved the old warehouse district of Creek Water. Back at the turn of the last century, the area was humming with commerce. The boats would dock on the river and unload all their supplies right into the warehouses' cavernous depths. Now that everything comes in by truck or train or Amazon express, there's no need to store six months of grain and the like. So, they gradually became deserted.

I park next to Jed's giant truck. Seriously, I don't know how he gets into it without a stool. Auntie Lee tells him people are gonna think he's compensating for some deficiency or another, but he doesn't care.

I stop and look around and imagine this area as the heart of Creek Water before too much longer. The streets are still brick, and the streetlights have been replaced with those reminiscent of gas lanterns. The potential takes my breath away.

A smart-looking sports coupe pulls up next, and Zachary Grant gets out. He starts walking my way, but as soon as he spots me, he slows his pace.

"Hey, Zach!"

"Emmie." But he doesn't speed up, he stops moving altogether.

So, I go back and get him. He looks spooked. I always thought Zach was a bit shy which made me feel even worse about not explaining why I turned down his invitation to the dance at the club. I know it took a lot of courage for him to ask me out.

While we never knew each other well, Zach and I do have one thing in common, we both grew up without daddies. Mine died and his ran away with his secretary, as cliché as that sounds. His daddy moved to somewhere out west and started another family, plumb forgetting about the one he already had.

Zach's mama did okay though. She never remarried, but the money she had came from her family and not her husband. She didn't have to worry about where their next meal was coming from, so she threw herself into being both mama and daddy for her child.

27

I remember my mama telling me that Sarah Jane never went after her husband for child support. She'd said, "A real man will take care of what's his. If Richard won't do it on his own, then I don't want him role-modeling for my son."

Zach finally falls into step beside me, so I endeavor to make small talk. "So, you're my uncle's contractor, huh?"

"Yes, ma'am," he says looking down at his shoes with as much enthusiasm as if he was on his way to the gallows.

Oh, for Pete's sake, what does a girl have to do to have a conversation with this man? I figure, being that we're gonna be working together, we should at least be friendly. So, I try again, "Have you lived in town since high school?"

"Nope."

Crickets.

"Well, where've ya been?" I demand none too graciously.

He stops walking and stares at me like I'm a moron or something. Then he looks at his watch and says, "We'd best hurry, I've got plumbers coming right after we talk to Jed and Jesse."

I can't see how small-talking with me, while we walk across the street to the warehouse, is going to make him late, but whatever. Not everyone was born with manners.

I'm practically chasing him down the street now, and he doesn't even bother to hold the door for me when he walks into the building. What is wrong with this man?

Chapter Eight

I get chills when I see the inside of the factory. The ceiling must be at least thirty feet high, if not more. All the exposed piping is visible, which makes it scream industrial chic. "I love it!"

Uncle Jed hands us hard hats that we have to put on, so nothing comes crashing down on us. He explains, "Each of the three floors has fifteen-thousand square feet. We're looking at Filene's coming in over in that corner." He points in the opposite side of the factory.

"Filene's Steakhouse?" I interrupt. "How did you get them to move over here?" They currently have a prime location right on the riverfront with outdoor seating and everything.

Jesse says, "They're opening another restaurant here that will cater to a more modest crowd. With the second floor full of office space and the third-floor condominiums, they're bound to increase their monthly sales dramatically, being the only restaurant on-site and all."

They show me where they're going to put the coffee shop. They'll only serve muffins and cookies and the like, so they won't take business away from Filene's. "There's going to be a full-service spa, so the gals have a place to get their hair and nails done," Jed continues, while leading the way to a wall of windows overlooking the river. "Over here's where our gourmet market is going to go."

I'm beyond impressed by how cohesive their plan is. "Tell me about the second floor," I say to anyone who will answer.

Jed says, "We're sectioning it off into six separate spaces. Beau has already signed up to take one. He's going move his real-estate business over here. He'll get the listings for the condominiums and be responsible for leasing out the rest of the second floor."

My family is super into nepotism and seeing as though they're giving me a job, I'm perfectly okay with that. "And the condominiums?"

"Let's go up there and have a look-see, why don't we?" Jed says, leading us to the old freight elevator that looks so rickety it must be original to the building.

"How safe is this thing?" I ask. "I'd like to see Faye grow up and this looks like a pretty dicey operation."

"We've brought it up to code," Zach says. "We'll get to the cosmetics and make it look *respectable* after we're done hauling all the building materials." The ride up is very smooth, lending credence to its safety. Wait, why did he just put emphasis on the word "respectable"? If I didn't know better, I'd think Zachary Grant was making some kind of statement.

When we step out onto the third floor, Jed points up. "The ceilings are lower on the second floor, but we're back up to thirty feet here, so we can build sleeping lofts giving each unit a partial second floor. This'll increase the square footage, while keeping the two-story ceiling in the common living area. The corner units will be the largest at twenty-two-hundred square feet, and the others will vary between nine- and fourteen-hundred square feet."

I realize my mouth is hanging wide open when I gush, "This is quite an operation you have here."

Jesse nudges me, "And you own yourself ten percent of it, so you'd better be prepared to work, girl."

I totally am, too. As long as Mama can cover Faye, I'm prepared to do whatever it takes to get this place up and running.

Zach says, "I need to meet with the plumbers, so if you'll excuse me." Why did that man even come up here with us? Just so he could give me condescending looks and make judgmental comments? My blood is boiling at the thought.

"Take Emmie with you. She needs to know all the ins and outs of this operation. She might as well start with the plumbing," Jed says.

"I'm not opposed, but don't you think it's a better use of my time to talk with you about the gourmet shop?" I don't want the uncles to know how annoyed I am at their contractor, so I'm trying to appear like a team player. Even though I'm as amenable to their idea as Mama is to white shoes after Labor Day.

Jesse answers, "Jed and I have another meeting at the office. We'll be back in about an hour. Just hang with Zach and learn as much as you can." They walk away, giving me no choice, and leave me with a man that apparently doesn't want to be within ten feet of me.

Zach doesn't say, "Come on," or "Follow me." He just walks away and goes about his business while I trail after him like some pesky bug. I spend the next forty minutes listening to him talk to the plumber about urinals and floor drains. I couldn't be less interested.

When they finally get down to talking about fixtures, my eyes light up. "Have Jed and Jesse picked anything out yet?" I ask.

"They told me to put in whatever was the most economical, so that's what I'm getting," Zach says.

My eyes open in horror. Fixtures can make or break a space. "I worked in a top decor store in New York City. My job was to order door pulls, lighting features, and faucet handles for Silver Spoons. You've got to trust me, economical won't do at all."

"Let me get right on that," he mumbles sarcastically. Then louder, he says, "Look, Emmie, I've got my orders and I'm not going to get behind schedule because you want to change something that's already been decided on."

"You don't have to get behind schedule at all," I tell him. "Just do something else while I hammer out the particulars with my uncles. Seriously, Zach, bathrooms can be memorable. I remember all the great public restrooms I've used in my life."

He glares at me like I'm a wad of chewing gum he's stepped in on a hot day. I don't know what his problem is, but I'm gonna find out. I pull him by the arm to a less "plumber-filled" location and demand, "What's your problem?"

"You can't be serious?"

"I'm dead serious! You've barely acknowledged me and when you do, you're downright rude. Didn't your mama teach you better manners than that?"

"I don't think you should be questioning how my mama raised me. I think you ought to focus on where your mama went wrong with you."

"My mama didn't go wrong with me. What kind of thing is that to say?" I'm standing with my hands on my hips, my chest heaving like I'm trying to breathe fire or something, when I notice him staring at *my girls*. My top is quickly becoming soaked. Drat. I'm leaking again. Boobs ought to come with on and off handles. He gives me a look somewhere between fascination and disgust before he turns and walks off.

That's when it hits me. Of all the low down, rotten, holier than thou things. Zach Grant is judging me for having a baby out of wedlock! How dare he? Surely Mr. Hot Stuff has had a few worries in his past. There's no way he can walk around looking like that without having his choice of women ready to jump into the sack with him.

Chapter Nine

I'm so spittin' mad I want to punch Zach right in the eye. But more urgently, I need to find a private place where I can pump my breast milk. I figure I'll just button up my cardigan to cover the dampness of my camisole once I'm done. Then I can carry on with the morning without having to go home to change. Darn these boobs of mine. I'm making enough milk to feed a small third-world country.

I'm not particularly adept at expressing breast milk yet. For the most part, I've been able to nurse when the baby is hungry. But knowing that I'll be away from her during feeding times, I bought a hand pump I've been practicing on to keep the girls drained.

I check my extra-large purse to make sure it's still there— along with the cooler bags I use to keep the milk fresh—then make my way to the unfinished ladies' room. Luckily the stalls are in place, so I head for the biggest one.

I sit down on the commode and assume the position, fastening the suction cup thingy over my left boob before endeavoring to get the rhythm of the thing. Unfortunately, I've waited longer than I should and it plumb hurts when I start pumping. I let out a squeal that sounds borderline like I'm being stabbed. I eventually groan in sweet relief.

After that, the only sound that fills the air is the suck and release of the pump and my occasional murmurings of, "That's right, fill it up, baby," and "I'm on fire today!" I like to give myself little motivational talks as I go. Single motherhood, while rewarding, is not easy, so I cheer myself on where I can.

Once I'm done and get myself all situated, I remember my desire to give Zachary Grant a piece of my mind. But when I leave the stall, I run smack into Amelia instead. "What are you doing here?" I ask.

"I thought I'd stop by to see if I could lure you away for a coffee or something," she says. The look on her face is one of pure amusement.

"Are you laughing at me?" I demand.

She nods her head. "You could say that."

"Why?" I ask, wondering what I've done that's so funny.

"There were three construction workers standing outside the door when I arrived."

"What were they doing there?" *I mean, how creepy.*

"They were concerned about what was going on in here," my cousin says.

"I was pumpin' breast milk for Faye."

I'm totally confused until Amelia says, "Ah, well. I guess that's not exactly what it sounded like to them."

My face turns beet red as the fiery flames of embarrassment explode through to my epidermis. "Of all the perverted, privacy-infringing things!" I nearly yell. "I'm gonna go give those boys a tongue-lashin'."

Amelia shakes her head. "Let it go. You'll just be more embarrassed trying to explain why you were saying things like, 'We're pumpin' for glory, here!'"

Dear sweet, ever-lovin' Lord, I silently pray. *Be with me now at the hour of my need in the bosom of nosy, small-minded townsfolk.*

"I came by to see if you wanted to get a cup of tea with me," Amelia says.

"I'd love to, but it's my first day on the job. I'd best hang around. Plus, I need to talk to your daddy and Jesse as soon as they get back. They've gone and ordered the cheapest fixtures around for these bathrooms."

She nods. "Of all of Daddy's qualities, his frugality is not one of the better ones." As we walk out of the ladies' my cousin's eyes stray to the left. "What do you think of that Zach Grant? He sure is something to look at, isn't he?"

"No worse than any other man, I s'pose." I don't bother looking in his direction. I have his condescending face etched onto my brain like a canker sore.

"Why, Emmeline Frothingham, have you gone blind? That man is hotter than buttermilk biscuits straight out of the oven!"

"If you say so," I respond noncommittally. What I'm thinking is, no man who is that rude could ever be called good-looking. Mama taught me that beauty comes from actions, not looks. If that's the case, Zach is one of the ugliest men I've ever seen.

"He asked about you," Amelia says, giving me a conspiratorial look that we girls used to have while hiding behind our lockers whispering about boys.

"What are you talking about?"

I ran into him a few weeks ago and he said, "I hear Emmie's coming home. That'll be nice, won't it?"

"That's not asking about me," I declare. "That's called small talk, which in and of itself, I'm surprised he's capable of."

Amelia laughs. "Girl, are you on your period or something?"

I gasp out loud. "That question is a breach of the sisterhood!" It's understood that women are to never accuse one another of a hormonal imbalance. It's just not done. "I'll have you know, I haven't gotten my period back, yet. I'm still nursing. It's quite possible I won't get it until I'm done."

She rolls her eyes. "You're still pretty tetchy."

"I'm not interested in dating right now, Amelia. I have a job to do and a baby girl to raise. Men aren't even on my radar."

"I'm not saying you should marry him," she declares. "Just enjoy the view. I was in the same class with that boy for thirteen years and let me tell you, I never thought he'd turn out looking like that!"

I roll my eyes. "How 'bout you?" I ask. "Mama says there's a lawyer in St. Louis pining away for you and you won't give him the time of day."

"Aiden Quinn is not pining for me. Sure, we've dated, but he's more interested in having an ornament on his arm than he is in having a relationship. Last time we went out, we had dinner with one of the partners of his firm, and do you know what that man had the nerve to say to me?" she demands.

"I do not. Why don't you tell me?"

"He said, 'You look very pretty on my arm.' Can you believe that?"

"Amelia, that's called a compliment. Why in the world would you be insulted by it?"

"Because he didn't say I looked pretty on my own. He said I looked pretty hanging off him, like he was a Christmas tree and it was my job to make him look better."

"That's what you got out of that?" I ask. Then just to get even, I say, "Maybe you were on your period."

She smacks me on the arm and laughs. "Touché. Anyhoo, tell Daddy 'hi' for me and remind him that he's meeting me for lunch at the Broken Yolk."

"Sure will." When she walks away, I turn around to find Zach, but he's deep in conversation with one of the workers. As much as he needs his hide tanned, and as much as I'd like to do the tanning, I force myself to be professional. I'm going to comport myself in such a way that I don't give anyone anything to gossip about. No sense in painting a target on myself—bigger than the one that's already there.

Chapter Ten

"The gals at the market were cooing all over Faye like she's the prettiest baby they ever saw."

I stare down at my little girl and ask, "Mama, what in the world is she wearing?" She's got a bow on top of her head so big you can barely see any of the pretty brown hair she got from her sperm donor. It's so beautiful, it's like mahogany-grained wood in a sunset. Her hand-smocked romper is sweet too, but the monogram is so big it's nearly blinding.

"Isn't it darling?" Mama asks.

"Why's the monogram so big?"

"It's all the rage now. I went ahead and bought a machine so I can add her initials to all her clothes."

"Why?"

"Cause it's cute," she says.

"But no one else will ever be able to wear those clothes if you do that."

"So what? They're *her* clothes."

"Mama, I'm not going to keep all her things, and if I can't pass them down, then I'm being wasteful. There's enough need in this world that I'd like to do my part and donate some of

Faye's stuff to someone who could make more use of it."

Mama shrugs her shoulders. "I'm still doin' it."

"Could you at least make the monograms smaller and maybe put them in a less obvious place?"

She changes the subject entirely, which means she's going to do whatever she wants. "What are you going to wear to the tea at the club tomorrow?"

"I can't go," I tell her. "I have to work."

"No, ma'am, you're going. Auntie Lee already squared it with Jed. She explained how important it is to make your reentry into Creek Water's social scene as seamlessly as possible and he agrees."

I roll my eyes. "I don't care what I wear, then. I suppose I should dig out a baggy sweater or something, so I don't cause a stir with my pornographic-sized breasts."

Mama says, "I bought you the cutest dress this afternoon." She pulls it out of a cabbage rose-covered shopping bag. I actually take a step back when I see what's inside, it's that awful.

"No way! I'd look like some poor mail-order bride out of the Old West if I wore that." It's mid-calf length with a small navy calico pattern, but that's not the worst part. It's got a gigantic white lace collar that nearly hits the waist and a matching trim on the hemline.

"It's perfect," Mama says.

"Everyone will think this baby is the product of immaculate conception."

"That's the whole point, honey. We want to make Faye's start in this world look as asexual as possible. If you wear this, Cootie won't dwell on the reality of the situation."

"Mama, there was nothing dirty about Faye's conception. It was just good, old-fashioned sex." It was nothing of the kind. It was hot and sweaty and totally animalistic. There was an overstuffed leather couch, and I may have been bent over it … I stop to fan myself. *Lordy, that was a fun night.*

Mama says, "I bet old Harold had to pry Cootie's legs apart with a crowbar to get a baby in her, so anything less is going to be interpreted as raunchy."

"Fine, I'll wear it, but I'm letting you know right here and now, I am not going to spend my days in Creek Water kowtowing to that woman like the rest of you do. I've got more important things to do with my time."

Mama says, "We don't kowtow. It's more like a game of chess. We anticipate Cootie's every move so she doesn't get close enough to knock us off the board."

I shake my head. "I think you're all nuts, Mama."

"I only want the best for you and Faye, honey. You need to trust me. You don't want to make a powerful enemy your first week home."

"Why in the world would she even care enough about me to bother?" I demand.

Then Mama tells me something shocking, "'Cause Cootie had her eye on your daddy. She was determined to become a Frothingham, and she's never forgiven me for Reed falling in love with me instead of her."

"But daddy is gone, and her husband is still alive, so she must have forgiven you by now."

"Not hardly. I think she'd be just as happy if Harold wasn't around. She treats that man like dirt. Of course, to be honest, he's a bit of a lech. He's got a wandering eye."

"Mama, this has to be the worst soap opera ever written. Why do you even go to that club if you have to contend with all this drama?"

"'Cause my friends are there and I like to play tennis. It all works out fine as long as I stay out of Cootie's way."

I have no idea how I'm going to manage tomorrow's tea without telling that woman what I really think of her, but I suppose for Mama's and Faye's sakes, I'll have to do my best. I'm just not sure that'll be good enough.

Chapter Eleven

I look like I'm on my way to confession in Victorian times. Mama says I have to wear stockings because bare legs will be interpreted as loose. I'm seriously considering moving back to New York City so I can live a nice boring life where no one cares about the state of my legs or the father of my child. Maybe I could even lose out on another award and give Faye a sibling.

Mama takes one look at me and claps her hands together like I just pulled a rabbit out of my hat. "You look perfect." Then she hands me a little shopping bag.

I open it up and find a matching dress for the baby—full on with her initials emblazoned across the front like a neon sign. "My goodness, mama and daughter dresses!" I want to say I love it, but I don't. Although the style is much more suited to a baby than a grown woman.

Mama reads my mind and smacks my arm playfully. "Don't wear any perfume, okay?"

"Why? Because only harlots and French whores wear perfume?"

She gives me a look that says I should mind my tongue. "Because Cootie wears enough for all of us and I don't need a headache today, that's why."

I sigh mightily. "Fine. But just so you know, I'm going to have to feed the baby sometime while we're there and I'm going to have to practically strip naked for her to get to her lunch."

"You can use one of the changing stalls in the locker room." She hands me my purse, "Now, change the baby and let's go. I want to get there before everyone else so we can strategize the best place to sit."

I would rather have all four of my wisdom teeth carved out of my head with a grapefruit spoon than to go to this tea. I don't think I've dreaded anything so much since my first swim meet during my period. I used a tampon for the first time, and I didn't bother to read how to insert it properly. I wound up sticking the applicator up there along with the tampon and I think I lost my virginity to it. It was horrible.

To make matters worse, Faye is cranky. At five and a half months, she's teething and isn't at all pleased to have little bits of bone popping through her tender gums.

We get into Mama's SUV and she says, "Now remember, Tillie Smytheton is just as big a gossip as Cootie. She'll try to cuddle up to you and get you to trust her, but it's just so she can get your secrets. Don't fall for it."

"Mama, is there anyone that's going to be there that isn't out to get me?" I feel as vulnerable as George Washington walking into enemy camp in his underwear.

"Honey, Auntie Lee and I will be there, and you can rest assured that our friends will be your friends, so don't worry yourself none."

The club is just as I remember—big and imposing, but more than a little over the top. It's designed to look like a Southern plantation, with gigantic columns and a huge wraparound porch. The whole place is crawling with women in tennis whites and men wearing god-awful pastel plaid pants and polo shirts. All I can think of is, *These are the people who are judging me?* Queer Eye for the Straight Guy *would have a field day here.*

The valet takes Mama's keys and says, "The other Mrs. Frothingham is already here. She says to hurry on in and don't forget the ketchup."

Mama's eyes pop wide open as she pushes the button to open the back hatch. "Thank you, Christopher. I surely would have forgotten had you not mentioned it." She gets out of the driver's side and fetches something out of the back that she secrets away in her purse.

I collect Faye from her car seat and grab the diaper bag. I stop a moment to inhale her sweet baby smell—if ever I did need that antidote to calm my frazzled nerves, it's now—then I hurry to catch up with Mama. "What does, 'don't forget the ketchup' mean? Is that some kind of battle cry, like 'Remember the Alamo!'?"

"Nope. It's just a little something Lee and I have been working on. Don't you worry about it."

I can't do anything but worry, now. If Mama and Auntie Lee are plotting, there are bound to be casualties. It's not that they couldn't be very instrumental in winning a war, but they aren't the ones you'd want masterminding the battle plan.

As we ascend the stairway leading to the entry, I half expect Scarlet O'Hara to sweep past in a giant hoop skirt. Instead, we run into Harold Wilcox. He's probably sixty and appears to have a fake tan so dark his ethnicity could be challenged. He stops and takes my mama's hand and croons, "Why, Grace, don't you look lovely today." He leers at her like she's one of those cocktail wienies wrapped in biscuit dough.

Mama removes her hand, and with a tone so cold you'd think we were suddenly standing at the North Pole, says, "Thank you, Harold. I don't suppose Cootie came with you?"

"Yes, ma'am. She's in the dining room helping Lee set up for your tea."

Mama looks like she wants to punch something, or more accurately, someone. "Lovely, we'll just go catch up with her then." She pulls me along and says, "That does it, that woman is going down!"

Chapter Twelve

Compared to Mama and Auntie Lee, Cootie looks likes Sideshow Bob from that old *Simpsons* cartoon. The Frothingham women are lovely and slim. They look more like they're entering their forties than fifties. If you Googled feminine pulchritude, I'm pretty sure their pictures would pop up.

Cootie, on the other hand, has not aged well at all. The sands of time seem to have all settled in her bottom half, and her hair is teased so big it looks like she's trying to signal outer space. She has on more makeup than the entire cast of the musical *Cats*, has been Botoxed within an inch of her life, and her lips are three times the size of those of normal humans. She's plain hideous.

"Lookee who's heeeeeeere!" she says with a sinister sounding drawl that sends shivers crawling right up my spine into the fear center of my brain. "Warning, warning, incoming danger!" it seems to say.

Mama steps in front of me as though she's holding the garlic and we've just encountered Dracula himself. "Cootie, what are you doing here so soon? Tea doesn't start for another hour."

"I was just sure you and Lee would want my help," she says. "After all, your hands *are* pretty full lately." She tries to pointedly look behind Mama at Faye and me. But Mama stays between us like a mother bear protecting her young from a rabid cougar. Do cougars even get rabid? I'm not sure, but you get my point.

My earlier annoyance has moved straight into dread. This woman is downright terrifying.

Mama says, "You don't need to worry yourself, Cootie. Lee and I are just fine. So, you run along and come back later."

"I wouldn't hear of it," Cootie declares. Then she says, "I could hold the baby, while y'all get everything set up." Glancing over at the table, she adds, "Which looks like it'll take you awhile."

I would no sooner let this woman hold Faye than I'd let a shark give her swimming lessons. My motherly instincts kick in and I say, "Why, aren't you the sweetest, Mrs. Wilcox, but I was just going to take Faye off to the locker room to feed her."

"I'll show you the way." She's at my side before I have a chance to make the sign of the cross. I briefly try to remember the best way to protect myself from a vampire attack. I'm almost certain it requires a stake to the heart. Either that or a silver bullet, but I'm currently not packing any heat, more's the pity.

Mama says, "What a wonderful idea, Cootie." I cannot believe she's leaving me in the hands of this woman. I take a deep breath for courage and follow along.

Cootie says, "We were just sick to hear about your *fiancé.*"

"It was a terrible tragedy," I concur. "But at least we had Faye. It's such a comfort."

She looks down at the baby. "It's too bad she didn't get his last name, though. That would have been such a nice tribute to him, don't you think?"

My god, this woman is relentless. I smile as though it's

painful to do so—which, really, it kind of is—and say, "Armie made me promise that if anything ever happened to him I'd give Faye my name. He didn't want to hold me back from marrying again someday and thought the baby should have my husband's name."

"So, he knew you were knocked up?" she asks none too kindly. I mean, who says "knocked up" anymore? What an insulting term.

"Of course. We were going to be married during his next leave, but well …" I try to force tears to my eyes—I'm afraid it looks more like I'm constipated though—and say, "I truly can't talk about it. I'm sure you understand, Mrs. Wilcox."

"What *was* his last name?" she asks.

I blurt out "Hammer," before I can stop myself.

"Armie *Hammer*, like that actor?"

"What are the odds, huh?" Why did I say Hammer? This woman has totally knocked me off my game. In fact, I've got no game. I'm straight improv right now, and fear crackles in my nervous system like water on hot bacon grease.

"Where are his people from?" she asks relentlessly.

"Toledo." OMG, Toledo? Why didn't I say Beverly Hills or Chicago or something impressive sounding?

"Toledo? Where's that, Indiana or something?"

"Ohio," I answer.

"Never been there," she says. "How 'bout his folks? They must be thrilled to have a granddaughter."

"They've both passed," I say, wishing the ground would open up and swallow me. But with my luck it would just spit me back out.

"Hmmmmmm. That's too bad," she says, clearly trying to

figure out what question in her arsenal she should ask next. She settles on, "I guess you done got yourself a nice chunk of money from the government for the baby, though."

She must have spent days concocting this interrogation. "Mrs. Wilcox, I'd love to chat, but I really need to see to Faye. If you'll excuse me." I try to walk away slowly, as though I'm not being pursued by a Cerberus, but I'm not very successful.

How in the world am I going to get through this afternoon?

Chapter Thirteen

Alone in the locker room, my dress, which buttons up the back, proves even more challenging than I expected. After serious contorting and a few unintentional yoga poses, I manage to get enough buttons undone to shimmy out of the top half of this archaic excuse for fashion. After all that, Faye isn't even hungry. She still latches on but only to use my nipple as a chew toy to help her cut her teeth.

Contact of a sharp edge of a tooth to tender flesh causes me to flinch and pull away. I admonish, "No, baby!"

She reacts to my stern tone by bursting into tears. *Dear Lord, if you're gonna send me into a nest of vipers, please, the least you can do is keep my baby happy, so I can have my wits about me.* Faye settles down after a few moments of my reassuring her.

Once I compose myself, I try to formulate a plan to get back into my clothes. I look around the locker room, but darn it, I'm all alone. Irritated at my mother and her need to throw me this party, I want to cry. But that's not going to change the fact that I need help.

I peek out the door in time to see Harold Wilcox exit the men's locker room. There's no way on earth I'd ever ask his assistance, so I go back into the fluffing room with all the mirrors and hairdryers and wait. Every two minutes I look out to see if anyone walks by that can be prevailed upon to rescue me. Nobody.

Twenty-eight minutes, and fourteen checks later, I realize I'm in jeopardy of being late for my own tea party. That's when I spy Zachary Grant coming down the hall. I have no choice but to try to flag him down. "Zach!" I whisper/yell. "Can you help me?"

He appears shocked to see me, and then looks around to make sure I'm really talking to him. "Are you calling me?"

Unfortunately, yes. But I don't say that. "Could you please help me for a sec?"

He walks over and spies Faye. Then asks, "Whose baby?"

"Mine," I answer protectively, holding her closer to my bosom. "This is Faye."

He looks spooked again, which is apparently one of the two looks he's capable of in my company. The other is anger. "How old is she?" he demands.

"Just over five months."

He looks like he's trying to solve a calculus equation in his head, but I don't have any time to figure out what his problem is now. "Listen," I say, "I'm in a bit of a pickle. I can't button my dress back up by myself and my mama's waiting for me in the dining room." I forge ahead and ask, "I don't suppose you could lend a hand?"

"Why are your buttons undone?" he asks cluelessly.

"I was feeding the baby." Duh.

"Why did you wear a dress that you can't button up by yourself?" he demands as though he can't believe I'd be so stupid to be caught in the position I'm currently in.

I lose all use of my manners and instead of explaining, demand, "Are you gonna help me or not?" I belatedly worry that if he doesn't, I could be stuck here for another hour waiting for someone to come to my rescue.

"Turn around," he grumbles.

"Not out here! What if someone comes by and sees you?"

"Emmie, I'm not allowed in the ladies' locker room, so this is pretty much your only option," he says.

I put Faye on my hip and grab his arm with my free hand. "No one's been in here in eons. Please?" I beg.

He hesitantly follows me in, and I point the way to a changing stall. "Over there, so if someone does come in, they won't see you."

Once we're secreted away, I turn around and present my back. "You can see how tiny the buttons are. I couldn't manage them on my own."

But Zach doesn't say anything. Instead, he very lightly traces the tip of his finger from the base of my skull down to the first fastened button, which is nearly at my waist. Shivers of delight erupt all over my body. What in the world is he doing? I want to say something, but my mouth has suddenly gone bone dry.

Heaven knows how long we stand there not talking when he leans in and runs the tip of his nose along the side of my neck. I know what you're thinking, and I one hundred percent agree with you. No single mother should be standing half-dressed in a locker room—holding her baby even!—while a near stranger sniffs her neck. What are we, animals?

But lordy, I cannot seem to put an end to it. Not only am I at this man's mercy, but I seem to have forgotten the English language. His hot breath moves to the back of my neck and my innards drop like I've just done a triple sow cow off the Empire State Building. I have not felt anything remotely this titillating since the night Faye was conceived.

I'm about to turn around and throw myself into his arms, when the door opens. We both freeze and hold our breath.

"Emmeline, are you still in here, girl?" It's Cootie!

I urgently point to the bench next to us and indicate that Zach step up on it lickety-split before Cootie sees his feet under the curtain. He hurries to follow my silent directive. "I'm in here, Mrs. Wilcox. I'll be out in just a sec."

"I'll wait for you," she announces. *Of course, she will.*

Crap and croutons, what do I do now? I turn to look at Zach, but with him on that bench, my eyes are in direct alignment with the fly on his trousers, not his eyes. Oh, my! He seems to be as affected by whatever just went on here as I am. I feel a delicious heat nearly overcome me. I'd probably swoon if Cootie wasn't out there waiting for me.

I inhale deeply, turn around, and force myself to scurry out from behind the curtain, carefully closing it behind me. I head toward the fluffing room where I heard Cootie's call originate. "I don't suppose you'd mind giving me a hand with my buttons?" I ask sweetly.

She says, "Is that why you were in here for so long?" Then she eyes me closely, "Why are you so flushed?"

"I seem to have underestimated my ability to redress myself after feeding the baby. I struggled a bit."

She doesn't look convinced, but says, "You really ought to stop that nonsense now that she's old enough for solid food." She points at my boobs.

"Actually, my pediatrician says it's best to nurse her exclusively for six months before introducing anything else."

"That's ridiculous," she says. "Why, Shelby only fed for three months. Then *that* was enough of *that*." I'm surprised Cootie let her nurse at all. Actually, I'm more surprised Shelby didn't turn to a block of ice or starve to death while suckling Cruella de Vil, here.

I try to regain control of the conversation and ask again, "Could you help me with my buttons?" As she comes closer, I'm engulfed in a cloud of heavy floral perfume. Mama's right, she must bathe in the stuff.

Once I'm all fastened, I readjust Faye and say, "We'd best get back to the dining room. Mama's going to wonder what happened to me." Just as we're walking out the door, we hear a very masculine sounding sneeze come from the changing area.

Cootie demands, "What was that?"

"I didn't hear anything," I say. Playing dumb is my only option. I cringe at the thought of what would happen if Cootie finds a man in the ladies' room with me. My reputation is already questionable, but it will be in shreds if that happens.

"I heard a man sneeze," she declares.

I point to the men's locker room right in front of us. "It must have come from in there."

She looks back in the ladies, and I see her checking the stalls for feet. When she doesn't find any, she turns back to me and says, "I guess so." But she doesn't look convinced.

As we head to the tea party, I wonder what just transpired between me and Zach. I take a moment to thank my lucky stars that whatever it was, Cootie doesn't know about it.

Chapter Fourteen

Our little corner of the dining room is chock-a-block full of ladies in chiffon dresses and pearls. They look like they just sashayed out of 1960. I wonder how it's possible these gals haven't progressed with the times. Most of them have never had a career, they just come to the club every day and concoct enough drama to keep themselves entertained. At least Mama and Auntie Lee work with the uncles.

Sarah Jane Grant is the first to greet me. "Emmie, welcome home! Zach told us you were back in town. I'm just tickled for your whole family."

Just the mention of his name makes me feel all tingly again. "Thank you, ma'am. I'm happy to be here, as well."

"Can I take that adorable baby off your hands? I would just love to have one of these of my own, but my son is determined not to give me a grandchild."

I happily hand Faye over. Sarah Jane has always been a friend to our family, especially after Daddy died. She steadfastly stood by Mama's side when a good number of her other *friends* lost interest. Sarah Jane knew firsthand how cruel the club ladies could be to a single gal in their midst, although her situation had to be a world harder as her husband ran out on her.

I turn to greet the rest of the guests and immediately discern the two camps in attendance. Mama and Auntie Lee's group are all smiles and truly look delighted to be here. Cootie's gang looks like they've been sucking on a bucket of lemons—sour doesn't begin to cover it.

Cootie announces, "Emmaline was stuck in the ladies' unable to get her dress back on."

Tillie Smytheton demands, "What was she doing with her dress off?" She glares at me as if to suggest something untoward was going on. Which of course, it nearly was. Thank goodness it didn't get that far.

"She says she was feeding the baby." Cootie lets innuendo hang in the air like a cloud of mustard gas.

I point to Faye and explain, "She was hungry." Driving the point home, I twirl around, "Silly me, my dress buttons up the back," and then I give Mama a pointed look.

She quickly changes the focus, "Ladies, may I please have your attention?" The gathering of twenty or so turn to look at her. "I'm so pleased you could join us today in welcoming Emmie and Faye home. The Frothingham family is finally all together." I love how she throws in the family name to reinforce who they're dealing with.

My great-grandparents four times over were the founders of Creek Water. There's a Frothingham Lane, a Frothingham Court, and even a Frothingham Park. Mama's making sure her assemblage doesn't lose sight of the fact that we are, in fact, central to this town's existence.

She continues, "If you'll all just find a place to sit, we can start." She points for me to take the place at her right and then says, "Cootie, dear, why don't you sit on my other side?" Best to keep your enemies close.

The table is beautifully laid out with blush-colored peonies in silver Revere bowls running down the center, and pink baby confetti sprinkled on the white linens, and of course, the napkins have been folded into swans. It looks picture-perfect, like a spread in a magazine. Mama's friends all sit on the same side of the table as me, facing Cootie and her cohorts, who've chosen to sit on her side of the table. It's the Hatfields and the McCoys country club-style. Mama stands at the head of the table and signals the waiters to begin.

They bring out three-tiered trays of watercress and cucumber sandwiches along with egg salad, and smoked salmon with fresh dill. They're all very delicate with the crusts off. I didn't have breakfast, due to a nervous stomach, so right now I'm hungry enough I could eat ten or twenty of these tiny bites. I start with four to keep the tongues from wagging.

Auntie Lee proudly brags, "Emmie was the head buyer up at Silver Spoons in Manhattan."

Bitsy Buford, from the other side of the table says, "Too bad she doesn't have a man to take care of her. I think it's a shame when a mother has to go to work."

I nearly spit my egg salad out. "Mrs. Buford, I went to Duke University and got a business degree. I assure you I did that so I could have a career of my own."

Mama raises her left eyebrow to caution me, *don't step into their trap, Emmie.* But I just can't help myself.

Bitsy says, "I know you went to Duke, dear. My sweet Ashley

went to Duke, also, but she found herself a nice medical student to marry."

I want to ask what kind of degree you get when your major is husband-hunting, but Auntie Lee shoots me a warning look. I fill my mouth with sandwiches instead.

Mama drops something on the floor. I lean over to pick it up, but she's beat me to it. I watch in shock as she grabs something from her purse and nearly dives under the table. When she emerges, she laughs and says, "That little sandwich got away from me." No one pays her any mind.

After I consume my fill of sandwiches, an assortment of sweets is served. Shortbread, chocolate-dipped strawberries, and tiny tartlets abound. I eat until I'm about to pop. Not only is the food divine, but eating helps keeps my mouth full, so there's no room for my foot—which is a godsend. As I listen to the catty comments, I want nothing more than to speak up for the poor folks some of these ladies are lambasting.

One of them declares that her gardener is walking a thin line because he's been pruning her bushes with a diagonal cut instead of a straight cut. "Everybody knows that's just asking for trouble." Kill me now.

After Cootie's crew seemingly empties their store of nastiness, one of the *ladies* announces that her son is recently engaged to one of the Hamelstocks of St. Louis. When no seems to understand the significance of the name until she explains, "The non-dairy creamer folks?"

At that, there are smiles and congratulations. Non-dairy creamer isn't exactly banking or oil wells, but money is money to these gals.

Once the dishes are cleared and the pink champagne poured, Mama says, "Emmie, why don't you open up your gifts?"

I hadn't expected this to be a baby shower, but apparently, I was the only one, because the gift table is loaded down. After settling in on a chair with Faye happily cooing beside me in her carrier, I open a small bag first. Inside is a Tiffany-blue box with a sterling silver rattle in it. It weighs so much Faye might give herself a concussion if she accidentally hits herself on the head with it.

There are more darling dresses than I can bother counting. Each has the baby's giant initials embroidered across the front. The whole club must have gotten the memo about monograms being back in style. There's a diaper bag, a silver baby cup, and even a clothes hamper in the shape of an elephant. I wind up opening Cootie's gift last. It's a rather large oblong box that weighs too much to be a baby blanket.

Once I unwrap it and take the lid off, I'm positively speechless. Cootie Wilcox bought me a wooden shelf with three little canvas drawers. They say "Coupons, More Coupons, and Bills." What in the actual hell?

When I look at her for clarification, she explains, "Being that you're the head of your own household, I figured this would come in handy."

Before I can throw the thing at her, Faye squawks, and Mama stands to signal that the party is over. "Why, ladies, thank you so much for helping us celebrate today. I'm sure you'll understand that we need to head home to get Faye down for her nap."

As the other guests stand to leave, I notice Cootie's dress. It has bright red zig-zagging streak running down the bottom half.

Mama looks too, and declares loud enough for everyone to hear, "Good heavens, Cootie, I think your time of month has arrived!" Now I know what Mama was doing under the table.

The Ketchup War has begun.

Chapter Fifteen

Mama and Auntie Lee nearly bust a gut laughing after Cootie runs out of the room followed by her posse. Mama says, "You know she's gonna try to get even now."

"I think she already did," Auntie Lee says. "Did you see that horrible gift she gave Emmie? Of all the nerve!"

"At least the other ladies brought nice things," I say, trying not to add fuel to their fire.

"Good thing, too," Auntie Lee says. "Otherwise we'd have had to declare war on them, too."

I look between my two relatives and accuse, "You two are enjoying this, aren't you?"

Mama answers, "Damn straight. I've been waiting for the right opportunity to bring that woman down a peg or two. And just so you know, I'm ready for whatever she does to retaliate."

"You and me both, sister," Auntie Lee says, and gives Mama a high five followed by a little shimmy and a fist bump. It's a move they've definitely executed before. One that required rehearsal.

I look around and ask, "How in the world are we going to get all this stuff out to the car? I guess if you'll sit in here with Faye, I can start running it out."

They're more than happy to let me as they're already hard at work hatching their next plot. I fold up all the dresses and put them in the elephant hamper. Then I tuck a few picture frames and other knickknacks around the sides, before hoisting my load.

It was a nice tea for the most part, and Faye made out like a bandit. The hamper is so cumbersome, I stagger out of the dining room into the foyer. I shift my load a bit, so it doesn't slip out of my arms. As I do so, I lose sight of where I'm walking and wind up veering into the path of oncoming traffic. I run smack into Zach Grant and lose control of the hamper.

He reaches out to help me catch it before everything flies out willy-nilly. He's not quite fast enough. Instead of catching it, he rescues me. I fall into his arms instead of on the ground where gravity was sending me, and my-oh-my does it feel nice. I get a whiff of his spicy scent and I suddenly feel like a badger in heat.

I'm about to lean into him, and maybe even climb him like a tree, when I hear someone clearing their throat next to us. A decidedly female voice says, "I'm pretty sure you can stand on your own now, Emmeline."

I look up straight into the eyes of Shelby Wilcox. She's a pretty version of her mother, but she still has Cootie's nasty look about her. I push myself away from Zach and say, "Why, Shelby, look at you." Which is about the most non-confrontational thing you can say to a person.

"Yes, look at me," she says. "Would you please remove yourself from Zach's arms?"

I'm actually trying to, but he doesn't seem to be interested in letting me go. Finally, I look up at him and say, "Thank you, but I think I can stand now."

He reluctantly releases me. Shelby grabs his arm and winds herself around it like she's making one of those hot pads we loomed as kids. It's a sign of pure ownership. "He's with me." Then she looks up at him and bats her eyes, "Didn't he turn out to be something else?"

Zach stares at his feet and refuses to meet my eye.

"He's sure somethin'," I say. Then I add, "Thank you for rescuing me, Zach." I bend over to collect Faye's new loot.

"That's right, you have a baby!" Shelby says like I've just adopted a puppy from the pound. "That must be so hard all by yourself." Her lack of sincerity is as thick as fresh tar.

Zach comes to my defense and says, "Her fiancé. died, Shelby." But he glares at me when he says it. What did I do now?

"Yes," I say. "Poor Armand died while serving our country."

"I heard it was friendly fire," Shelby says. "It's not like he was actually protecting anyone."

"You bitch!" It's out of my mouth before I can stop it. "All that matters is that he gave his life in the pursuit of our freedom. He was training for battle and now he's gone. How dare you make light of his sacrifice?" I'm about to lunge at her when I remind myself he's not even real.

Zach kindly says, "You must have loved him very much."

"Of course, I did. He was going to be my husband. We have a baby." I actually feel myself tear up. Obviously not because of the loss of the fictitious Armand, but because I don't even know who Faye's daddy is. I wonder how many years will go by before I convince myself he really was my knight in shining armor, tragically taken from me in his prime, not some stranger I picked up in a bar.

Shelby pulls Zach away and I hear her say, "She shouldn't have let herself get into trouble like that."

Zach says, "I don't think she had a say in it, Shelby."

What in the world is he talking about? Of course, I had a say in it. As far as my foggy memory goes, I said something along the lines of, "Oh, my God, yes! Right there! More!" I need to stop thinking about that night. Clearly, this town has made its decision about me and I'm going to have to be on my best behavior. I'm probably only saying that because Zach seems to already be spoken for. Although, if that's so, why in the world was he toying with me in the locker room? I shudder at the thought that he thinks I'm a woman of loose morals and thinks he can take advantage of that for his own pleasure.

Chapter Sixteen

I take extra pains with my appearance this morning. It's not like I'm consciously dressing for Zach, but if I am being honest, I'm sure there's an element of that. Whatever almost happened between us at the club has played over and over in my mind, like that movie *Ground Hog Day*. I'm starting to wonder if maybe I imagined his interest. Is that possible? Could I be that desperate for male attention? Quite honestly, with the baby and all, I didn't realize I was even missing it.

When I walk into the kitchen, Mama says, "You look nice."

"I'm gonna burn the dress you bought me for the shower," I tell her.

"That's fine. We just had to make the right first impression. You can dress like yourself again."

"Thank you," I tell her. I sweep a hand over the clothes I'm wearing, "I'd planned to. Can you imagine me wearing that to work?" Then I ask, "So what's going on with Shelby Wilcox and Zach Grant? I ran into them at the club yesterday."

Mama rolls her eyes. "That Shelby is busy trying to make your cousin Beau jealous. I'm afraid Zach doesn't mean a thing to her."

"That's not how she was acting yesterday," I say. "She acted like I was trying to steal him away from her just by breathing the same air."

Mama looks up from measuring her coffee grounds and suspiciously asks, "Are you interested in Zachary Grant?"

"What? No! Good lord, Mama. I have enough going on without complicating my already messed-up life. For Pete's sake, as if!" I feel like I'm protesting too much and decide I'd better simmer down before she suspects differently.

She lets it drop and says, "Cootie thinks your cousin should have asked Shelby to be exclusive and advised her to dump him."

"Who else has Beau been seeing? I ask.

"No one that I know of," Mama says. "He just isn't ready to commit himself to one gal."

"Well, if he's not seeing anyone else, then wasn't he already exclusive with Shelby?"

Mama says, "She wanted some sort of declaration of the fact and she pushed it. She figured that being they'd already been out on three dates, that he should take himself off the market."

I can kind of see where she's coming from. I mean if Beau didn't know that he liked her enough to date her exclusively after three dates, then it's clear he's not that into her. I don't tell Mama that, though. She's from the school of thought that a person needs to know what their options are before fully committing themselves. I don't disagree with her; we just have different timetables.

"What about you, Mama? Are you seeing anybody?"

"My word, no. Who would I date in a town like Creek Water?"

"I don't know. There has to be somebody. Maybe a nice divorced man or widower or something."

She shakes her head. "I'm not interested. I've got a nice house, a job I enjoy, and my baby and grandbaby are home. I'm full up, honey."

I almost say that she'd have more room if she'd get rid of some of Daddy's things. It's been twenty years since he died and she has not once, that I know of, given her romantic life a second thought. Yet her closet is still half-filled with his clothes. I'm gonna have to keep my eye open for her.

I grab a muffin off the counter and give Faye a big smooch on top of the head. "I'm off. Can you bring the baby down to the warehouse at eleven when she's ready to eat again?"

I could pump, but I hate to go that long without holding her. Babies are full-blown addictive to their mamas. It's a mystical bond that goes beyond mere hormones. The kind of love where you'd lay down your life for the other person is nothing short of a gift from God. And I want to spend as much time with my gift as humanly possible. Also, I'm kind of afraid to pump at work now.

"Sure thing, honey. We'll bring you lunch, too. Shall we?"

"Sounds good, Mama, thanks." I give her a hug and then walk out to the garage. A year and a half ago my life was very different. I was a single, career girl living her dream in New York City. Now, I can barely remember who that person was. Quite honestly, now that I'm back, I'm not sure I'll ever leave Creek Water again, even if it means battling it out with Cootie Wilcox. Having a baby changes everything.

Chapter Seventeen

I worked Mondays through Fridays at Silver Spoons. But the construction crew at the warehouse works on Saturdays, too, so I plan on being there. I don't know what Zach's hours are, but seeing as he was at the club with Shelby yesterday, which was Friday, I wonder if he's a hands-off kind of boss. You know, telling his employees what to do while he goes off and plays. I do believe I will lose a good deal of respect for him if that is the case. Not that I currently have that much respect for him. He's not treated me at all well, and even though my body seems to be attracted to him, my brain is screaming, "Girl, you can do so much better than a rude person who manhandles you in the locker room at the country club."

Both of my uncles are already on site, wearing hardhats and reflective vests, when I show up. I thought I'd beat them to the punch as it's only eight o'clock, but I guess I underestimated their excitement. I hurry to put on my own hat and run over to meet them.

"Morning, Emmie," Jed says. "We were just trying to figure out how much space we're gonna need for the gourmet shop. The architect is meeting us here in a couple hours so he can finalize the plans for the glass walls."

"Glass walls?" I ask.

"We got to thinking that part of the charm of this space is its size. So, if we only use glass to separate the stores from each other, it'll keep that charm intact. What do you think?"

I think it's a great idea. Normally, storefronts have some kind of display window, but if the whole wall is a window then the store itself becomes the display. It'll increase their usable square footage."

"Exactly," Uncle Jed says. "Now how big do you think Emmeline's needs to be?"

"Emmeline's?" I ask. "You're naming the store after me?"

"Of course, darlin'. But before you get a big head over it, we're only doing it because your name sounds classy. If Gracie and Reed had named you something like Sissy Poo or Bobbie Jean, we couldn't have done it."

"Bobbie Jean Minkler's name is Bobbie Jean and she's a lovely lady."

Jesse replies, "Yes, she is. And her name is perfectly suited for the diner she owns. It sounds like a place where you can get some good pie. It just doesn't sound like a place where you'd drop a hundred bucks on a trinket."

Jed smacks his lips. "Let's go over to Bobbie Jean's for some pie when we're done here."

"Excellent idea," Jesse replies. "Now, what kind of stuff should we sell at Emmeline's?"

I say, "It depends on who your target market is."

"Our customers will be anyone who's got enough money to drop a C-note on a saucepan. So, I'm guessing club ladies?"

"The club ladies Mama's age and older like to go shopping in

St. Louis. They didn't spend enough in town to support the stores that closed down. Remember how they used to love that dress shop, Draper's? They could get their Estée Lauder without having to drive three towns away for it. But they still didn't spend enough to keep the place in business."

"So, who do you suggest we cater to?" Jed wants to know.

"You gotta go after the people who moved here to get away from the city. Target the younger folks who choose to be here and aren't just here 'cause it's all they know."

"But how much could they afford to spend? It seems to me they don't have the kind of money needed to keep us afloat," Jesse says.

"You already told me that a bunch of them make their money working remotely. Didn't you say they opened a special cyber office where they could rent space?"

Jed nods his head. "That's right, we did. But just 'cause they can afford their rent doesn't mean they can afford the extras."

"Then give them enough small ticket items to draw them in. That way they can see we also carry big-ticket items if they can afford them," I explain.

"Like what?" Jesse wants to know.

"Like little beard-grooming kits. That's a great gift idea as well as something a person would buy for themselves. Or henna pens and tattoo stencils. That kind of thing."

Jed nods his head. "There's more facial hair in town now than there was in the seventies when I was a boy. And the tattoos would have your Grandma Frothingham fanning herself to keep from falling over in a dead faint. Okay, girl, what else you got?"

"Kitschy oven mitts and clever magnets for their refrigerators—

fun little odds and ends that won't cost a fortune." At their expectant looks, I add, "We'll need an area for gourmet jams, and chocolates and things they've never been able to buy in town before. Plus, those are great for impulse buys. We could have a few select cookbooks and party invitations, wine glasses and beer mugs are a must." I go on and on while the uncles stare at me with something akin to awe. "These are just the items to draw them in. Once they're here, they'll see the cookware, chef quality knives, and expensive dinnerware."

"How much money are you going to need to stock the place before opening?" Jed asks.

"I'd say if you factor in everything from display cases to inventory, we could do it for about a hundred grand."

"One hundred thousand dollars?" Jed demands.

"How much were you thinking?" I ask.

"We were thinking about twenty-five," Jesse says.

"You could certainly open a shop for that, but you'll have to rethink the kind you'd have," I tell them.

Jed wants to know, "What kind of store could you open for twenty-five?"

"Maybe a card shop that sells a few knickknacks," I say. Of course, my talents would be wasted on something so piddly.

"Would there be a market for that?" they want to know.

I shrug my shoulders. "Maybe." *I'd be bored to tears if that's all it was.* "Let me put together a few different ideas for you and we can revisit the kind of store after that."

"I guess we can't decide on how big it's gonna be until we know that, right?" Jesse asks.

I tell him, "Just remember, the bigger the place, the more

inventory you'll need to fill it, and the more money you'll make in the long term. A card shop isn't going to rake in the bucks you're hoping for."

They look disheartened, but that's life in the fast lane for you. I'm about to assure them we'll work something out when I spy Zach coming our way. He looks like a man on a mission, and that mission appears to be me. What in the world have I done now?

Chapter Eighteen

Zach is moving so fast you'd think his britches were full of fire ants. He looks like he's a cross between mad and determined. When he reaches us, he says, "Emmie, I'd like a word."

"I'm right here," I say.

He looks at the uncles before adding, "In private."

I immediately flashback to what happened the last time we were private, and a delicious wave of heat rolls over me. Of course, I'm pretty sure that's not what he has in mind.

The uncles get all jumpy and Jesse says, "We were just heading to Bobbie Jean's for some pie." They're off like ticks on a hot griddle.

"What can I do for you?" I ask Zach. I know what I'd like him to do for me, but there's no way I'm going there. Plus, I'm mad at him for treating me like I'm not respectable.

"I'd like to take you out for dinner tonight," he declares while staring me dead in the eye. Where did that come from?

"You would? Why?" I demand more than a little astonished. What about Shelby, I wonder?

"We have a few things we need to discuss," he says all matter-of-factly.

"We do? What in the world do we need to talk about?"

"Are you available or not?" he asks.

"Well, I s'pose, but I'd have to bring Faye along. Mama and Auntie Lee are manning the ticket booth at the Ladies of the Creek fundraiser tonight." It's a group in town that raises money for the extras, like hosting the ice-cream socials at the pavilion in Frothingham park during the summer band concerts, buying those giant blue ribbons for the winners of the Creek Water Summer Carnival and Games, and supplying backpacks and shoes for local kids in need.

"That's fine by me," he says. "Mama says she's a good baby."

"Where should we meet you?" I ask. I'm more than a tiny bit uncertain if this is a business meeting or a personal thing. The only reason I'm saying yes is because it sounds like it's probably business.

"I'll pick you up. I'll be at your mama's at five thirty." Then he walks off.

Before I can process what just happened, he turns around and comes back. "And just so you know, Shelby and I are not an item. She's just trying to make Beau jealous."

"You know that?" I ask.

"Of course, I know that."

"Why in the world would you bother spending time with her if you know she's just using you?" I ask.

He shifts nervously from side-to-side. "I'm just trying to help out a friend, is all."

I know I've been hot and cold on Zach, but mostly because I feel like he's been judging me about having a baby without a husband. On the surface, he appears to be a prize, if you don't take his odd behavior around me into consideration. I wonder if it's a chronic condition or if I just bring out the worst in him.

"And?" I demand. It's none of my business, but I feel like there's more to it than that.

"I know what it's like to want someone who doesn't want you back, and I thought it would be nice to stand up for the underdog."

With a sigh, he clarifies, "I fell for someone pretty hard recently. I thought we had a really deep connection, but it turns out I was the only one to think so." Thank goodness he isn't talking about me and my rudely turning down his dance invitation all those years ago. I really do feel bad about that and wish I'd have been more upfront with him about why I said no. But let's face it, at sixteen years old, I simply was not that eloquent.

I still don't know if that makes our dinner a date or not, but it's definitely ratcheting up my curiosity. "I'm sorry about your recent experience," I say, unsure of the proper response to this information.

"You've had a big loss, too. You know heartache."

The look on my face must be asking "what loss?" because he says, "Armand?"

"Oh, yes, Armand!" I shake my head and try valiantly to look like I'm still in deep mourning for the fabricated love of my life. "Yes, I'm just not sure I'll ever be the same."

"I can't imagine a sadness of that magnitude. I'm truly sorry."

"Thank you." I'm the world's worst actress. I understand why Auntie Lee perpetrated this myth; I really do. I know she only had my best interests at heart. And while I'm sure the club ladies would have raked me over hot coals of judgment, I'm not sure it's worth having to live a lie of this magnitude. 'Cause let's face it—they're still judging me.

Zach says, "Well then, I guess I'll see you tonight."

"We'll be waiting," I say, possibly starting to wish this was a real date. Even though Zach gives me occasional disapproving looks, I know he could make some lucky gal a fine boyfriend. I say a brief prayer that Shelby won't come to her senses and go after Zach instead of Beau. I don't know what girl was stupid enough not to return Zach's interest, but I do know he deserves better than someone from Cootie's line.

When he gets about halfway to the door, Zach comes back again. "One more thing …" he says.

"Yes?" I stare at him expectantly.

"I'm sorry if I disrespected you in any way at the club yesterday. You know, in the locker room?"

Oh, my god, we're going to talk about it? I thought I'd either imagined it or we'd decided by some unspoken agreement to pretend it never happened. "You mean when you helped me with my buttons?" I try to steer the conversation into safe territory.

"I never helped you with your buttons," he says, taking another step closer to me.

"Well, you were going to before Cootie came in." I unsuccessfully try to swallow down a basketball-sized lump forming in my throat.

He leans in and whispers, "I was going to do *something* before Cootie came in …" Then he sniffs the side of my hair and I have to reach out and hold onto his arms to keep my knees from giving out on me.

Spontaneous combustion is a thing, right? 'Cause right now

my body is so hot, I'm pretty sure I could light a match. We're standing there, in what can only be construed as some kind of lovers' embrace, when Zach says, "I'll see you tonight." And he turns and walks away for good this time.

Chapter Nineteen

I'm useless the rest of the morning. I try to work out a proposal for the uncles, but my mind can't seem to stray from the image I've created of Zach and me standing with our arms nearly wrapped around each another, and him saying, "I was going to do *something* before Cootie came in ..."

I don't know what he thought was going to happen, but I let myself imagine a whole slew of exciting possibilities. Hence, my inability to focus on my work. When Mama pushes the stroller in so I can nurse the baby, I tell her, "I'll keep her. You take Daddy's car and I'll take yours, so I have her car seat."

"Are you sure?" she asks.

"Yeah. I'm gonna spend the day getting to know Creek Water again. I need to walk around the shops and see what kind of merchandise is already here, so I can advise the uncles on what our store should sell."

"Good thinking, honey. You should hit the new shops on Main Street. They've mostly sprung up in the last couple of years."

"Thanks, Mama." Before she walks away, I add, "I have a meeting tonight, so if Faye and I aren't home when you get back, don't worry."

"Okay, baby. I might be late, myself. I'm going to meet Jesse for supper after the fundraiser. I think he's having lady problems he wants to discuss."

"Love you, Mama."

"Love you, too." She gives Faye a kiss on the head and walks off. Mama looks like a ray of sunshine in her sleeveless summer dress. Her hair doesn't have a spot of gray in it yet, and her figure speaks to the amount of tennis she plays. It breaks my heart that she doesn't have a man in her life.

Don't get me wrong, I don't think men are the end-all to-die-for, but Mama loved being married to Daddy. She's one of those women who's destined for romantic partnership, and it would be a real tragedy if that part of her life had ended when she entered her thirties. Being that she's only fifty, she has plenty of good years left.

After feeding Faye, I put her back in her stroller and head out into the beautiful June day. It's already hot and muggy, which means it's going to be a real scorcher of a summer. I point the baby carriage toward Amelia's bead shop and leisurely amble up and down the streets of the Creek Water. It's so different from how it was during my formative years. I find myself utterly charmed.

Bead It is on the corner of Main and Magnolia streets, just a few blocks from the old sewing machine factory. The store has a bohemian-chic vibe, like Amelia. There are brightly colored apothecary chests with tiny drawers full of colorful beads, Turkish rugs adorn the dark wood floors, and chandeliers with multi-colored crystals hang from the ceiling. This place would be an instant hit in the Village in New York City. I can't imagine why my cousin doesn't want to try her hand at an urban shop.

"Amelia!" I call when we walk in.

"I'll be right out!" she replies from the back of the store.

I look at the display cases full of her jewelry and wonder where she gets it. It's totally unique with large chunky stones you wouldn't necessarily think would pair well. Amber and turquoise on their own are quite popular, but you rarely see them strung together, and it really works. She's also got a line of black pearl and leather bracelets, and carnelians strung with hand painted beads on colorful silk cords.

Amelia walks through a beaded curtain. She's wearing an embroidered peasant blouse with a long flowy skirt. Her sandy hair hangs straight down her back and she has a beaded headband wrapped across her forehead. "You look gorgeous, as always," I declare.

She kisses my cheek. "Back at you, Em, even though you look like a Junior Club Lady. What's going on with your prematurely middle-aged look?"

"Bite your tongue," I admonish.

But she just looks me up and down as if to say, "really?" What she says is, "You're just so conservative and prim-looking."

"Amelia, I have giant boobs, thanks to nursing, and I've just come home with a baby and no husband. Believe me, I'm going to look like a wanna-be club lady for a while yet. Mama figures the less I give them to judge me on, the better. I'm inclined to think she might be on to something."

"I say screw 'em. You don't need to be anything other than who you are."

"I agree with you wholeheartedly, in theory. In practice, it's another matter. Now, enough about me, show me your store."

She shows me everything. And when I ask who makes the beautiful jewelry in the front case, she says, "I do."

I ask, "Would you be willing to put together a line for us to sell at the new store?"

"For your gourmet shop?" she asks.

"I'm not convinced it's going to be a gourmet shop, yet. I'm thinking it's going to be more of a gift/gourmet shop. I need to look around Creek Water to see if there's a need that's not being filled."

"I'd be happy to have you sell my stuff there. I don't get a lot of people in here who buy jewelry. They're mostly here to learn how to make their own. Branching out into your place might be a way to draw them over to my shop."

"Exactly," I say. "Now, I'm going to go grab a coffee. Can I bring anything back for you?"

"No, ma'am, I only drink tea and I have plenty of that here. But if it's coffee you're after, you might want to try She Brews down the street. They've become quite popular."

After leaving her store, as I'm about to cross the street, I catch sight of something that stops me dead in my tracks as tingles of annoyance dance down my scalp. Zachary Grant is sitting outside the frozen yogurt shop and he's not alone.

Chapter Twenty

Why in the world is Zach having yogurt with Shelby Wilcox right after flirting up a storm with me? Is this a friendly thing or was he lying to me about not being interested in her? I'm torn between going over there to confront him and fleeing down the street in the opposite direction.

I don't have a chance to make up my mind because Shelby catches sight of me and starts waving like she's trying to signal a rescue ship from a deserted island. She's making sure that I know she's staked her claim. Meanwhile, Zach's trying to duck off to the side, like I might not see him. Well, that does it, I have to go over there now.

I cross the street with my eyes trained on them the whole way to make sure Zach doesn't try to leave. When I get to their table, I say, "Shelby, Zach, fancy meeting you here." I let my eyes bore into Zach's like I'm demanding answers.

Shelby looks at the baby, and completely out of character, and somewhat longingly, says, "My word, she's simply beautiful, isn't she?" She looks up like she's surprised herself by saying that out loud. But she unexpectedly nods her head sharply like she's decided to own it.

"Thank you, Shelby."

She can't seem to help herself and adds, "She must look like her daddy."

"Yes, she does. She has his hair and his eyes." I'm just guessing she does, as she doesn't have mine.

"We were just discussing our weekend plans," Shelby says. "I think we should go boating on the river and Zach thinks we should scurry away to St. Louis. What do you think we should do?"

Before anything untoward can come out of my mouth, 'cause believe me, I can think of a couple choice suggestions, I turn to Zach. He looks like he wants to crawl under the table to hide. He quickly explains, "I told Shelby I might need to go to St. Louis this weekend to pick up some supplies for the warehouse and she said she wanted to go along." Then he turns to Shelby and says, "But I told her I didn't think that was a good idea, so she suggested boating."

The expression on Shelby's face is priceless. She's obviously shocked Zach would rat her out like that. She reaches across the table to hold his unresponsive hand, and says, "We'll just figure it out later, when we're *private*." Then she eyes me like that time is now, and I'd best move along.

But I don't want to move along. I'm thoroughly enjoying making them both uncomfortable. "Would y'all mind if I leave the baby here while I go order myself a yogurt?"

You'd think I'd just asked her to babysit my pet barracuda or something. The counter is only a few feet away and I can see them the whole time, I'm not actually counting on them to keep Faye alive. Also, she's sleeping, so she won't need anything for the next few minutes.

Zach smiles down at Faye almost wistfully, and says, "We'd be happy to." That look and those words stir up some powerful longings inside me.

To cool myself down, I go and order a unicorn swirl, full of enough food coloring to tie dye an entire bolt of fabric. But it's so pretty I can't resist. Plus, maybe a little unicorn magic will rub off on me. Either that or I'll grow a horn and discover I can fly. My life is an ever-changing array of surprises.

When I get back to the table, Shelby is in a near huff as I pull out a chair to join them.

"You're sitting here?" she demands.

"I thought you waved me down so we could eat together," I say innocently.

Zach unsuccessfully tries to stifle a laugh and Shelby shoots him a glare that says she'll cut out his tongue if he dares. She forces a smile in my direction. "Seeing that you don't have anyone else to eat with, you might as well join us."

"Aren't you sweet?" I say. *Sweet like a boa constrictor.*

"Yes, well, we all feel so sorry for you, Emmie. I mean getting yourself in such a state and all." She shakes her head.

"You don't need to feel sorry for me, Shelby. I've got a beautiful little girl and a wonderful family. If anything, I feel sorry for you."

"Me?" she demands. "Why in the world would *you* pity *me*?"

"I heard how much you like my cousin Beau and that he just doesn't feel the same way. It must be tough to have such deep feelings spurned."

Zach looks like he's about to shoot yogurt out of his nose. He tries to mask his reaction by coughing, but you can tell Shelby isn't buying it.

She stands up with her hands on her hips and says, "I'll have you know, Emmeline Frothingham, that your cousin is not good enough for me. Do you hear me? And furthermore, how dare you? You're nothing but trash!"

She turns to Zach and says, "I'm ready to go."

He points to his yogurt. "I'm still eating. I guess I'll catch you later."

"Well, I never." She shoots daggers between the two of us.

I smile sweetly and say, "Girl, you don't know what you're missing."

Then it's just me and Zach.

Chapter Twenty-One

"You really put Shelby in her place, didn't you?" Zach lets loose the mirth he's been trying to contain.

"I swear, that girl just doesn't know how to keep a civil tongue in her head."

"Before you arrived, I was telling her that I didn't think we should pretend to see each other anymore."

"Really?" My eyes go all buggy. "Why?"

"I thought you knew," he says. "I've met someone I'd like to get to know better, and I don't think it would be respectful to her to be parading around town posing as Shelby's boyfriend."

My insides go all gooey like a freshly toasted marshmallow on a s'more. Until I wonder, *he means me, right?*

My heart races in triple time and my palms go all sweaty as I bravely ask, "Anyone I know?"

"I'm pretty sure." His smile is devastating, but he doesn't say anything else.

We finish our yogurt quietly, but not uncomfortably. We're at ease sitting together without filling the space with sound. Until Faye wakes up, that is. That girl lets out a scream that could win her the starring role in a horror movie.

I immediately pick her up and bounce her on my knee, but that's not what she wants. She wants to eat. I say, "I best take her to the bathroom and feed her. If you'll excuse me."

"Why do you have to take her to the bathroom?"

I look around at the other tables. "I don't want to offend anyone."

"Are you offended when people eat?" he asks.

"You misunderstand. I need to nurse her," I explain.

"And?" he says. "What's the problem?"

"Some folks don't like to see women nursing in a restaurant. It makes them uncomfortable."

"Then they should eat at home," he scoffs.

I know he's right. It's just this small town is full of small-town people I've known my whole life, and I don't want to give them anything else to judge me on. But Zach's right, they shouldn't judge me for giving my child lunch. I drape a blanket across my chest before unbuttoning my dress and adjusting Faye.

God bless my little girl, she is not a quiet eater, she slurps and grunts and enjoys every moment of her meal. Her noises are making conversation more than a bit awkward.

Zach stares at the blanket like there's a herd of wildebeests tearing apart a fresh kill. "She's pretty hungry, huh?"

"She's an enthusiastic diner," I manage.

I can't be sure, but I think he mumbles something along the lines of, "Lucky girl."

When she's finally done, I ask, "Would you mind holding her while I get myself buttoned up?"

"Do you need help with your buttons?" he teases.

"These buttons are in the front. I think I can manage them

on my own." I smile, trying not to let his flirtations undo me. But truth be told, I'm feeling a little undone.

As soon as he takes Faye from me, she lets out the biggest belch you've ever heard, right before spitting up all over him. "Oh, my goodness!" I declare. "I'm so sorry. Here, let me take her back." Which I do, before buttoning myself up. Thankfully, I'd already put my boob back in my bra.

Zach stares at the edge of my industrial-strength foundational garment with an expression that looks an awful lot like lust—which I do not believe this particular item of clothing was designed to elicit—especially while one is covered in baby puke. I wonder if he's going through a dry spell or if he's still hung up on that other woman.

Once I put the baby back in her stroller, I reach out to help Zach clean up the mess. "Tell me about your gal, the one who got away." I'm trying to distract him long enough to get my girls situated.

"I don't think I'm ready to do that, yet. It's pretty personal, you know?" Then he asks, "Do you want to talk about Armand?"

"No!" I nearly shout. "I mean … no. I guess what I'm trying to say is … no."

"So no, then?" he asks with a glint of humor in his eyes.

"Right. No. I'm trying to heal from all that. There doesn't seem to be any reason to talk about it." This topic needs to end, like, yesterday.

"You ready to get going? I'll walk you back to the warehouse."

"That's sounds nice. Point out all the local hotspots to me as we go. I'm trying to get a bead on the new demographic of Creek Water so I can figure out how to best appeal to them when we open up our shop."

For some reason he pushes the stroller while I walk beside him. To be honest, he looks adorable, but I guess any good-looking guy with a rockin' body like his, pushing a baby in a stroller, is chum for the ladies. I don't think I ovulate while nursing, but darn if I don't think I just felt an egg drop.

He points out a tattoo parlor, of all things, called the Ink Spot.

"That's quite a change, huh? Used to be if you wanted a tattoo you had to go to Henderson."

"It's just a sign that our population is getting younger."

"You mean Cootie Wilcox hasn't been seen darkening their doorstep yet?" I tease.

"No, ma'am, and thank the good Lord, I might add. Can you imagine the kind of thing she'd get tattooed on that butt of hers?"

"Maybe a turkey vulture or Godzilla or something," I joke.

Across the street is a new vintage clothing shop called Lucille's. The mannequins in the window are wearing dresses that look like they're from the fifties. But they all have some modern-day accessory, like biker boots or a backpack—something that shows the old and the new colliding. It's very clever.

During the rest of the walk, we pass a beauty parlor, a movie theater, an arcade, a coffee shop, a couple of restaurants, and an antique mall. As near as I can figure, Creek Water could use a slew of different stores, including some trendy ones. I feel like we're right on base with a gourmet/gift shop that specializes in kitchen gadgetry. I just have to pry open the uncles' wallets long enough to make that a reality.

When we finally get to the factory, Zach says, "I'm going to head in and talk to the architect. You got any work to do inside?"

"No," I say. "I'm going to go home and start doing some research online. I feel like I've got a good idea who our target market is going to be, and I want to start hammering out the kind of money I'll need to open the place I want."

"I'll see you tonight, then," he says. He leans in as though he's going to give me a kiss on the cheek but has second thoughts and reaches out and touches my arm instead. My body reacts as though I've been touched by the live end of an electrical wire.

"Bye," I tell him, wishing that he'd gone in for the kiss instead. Ah well, maybe tonight after dinner, if I'm lucky. I seem to have completely forgiven him for his earlier judgmental behavior toward me. It's amazing how hormones can short circuit your thinking.

Chapter Twenty-Two

Mama isn't home when I get there, so I put Faye in her baby swing and give her a collection of chew toys to help her gnaw her teeth in. Then I sit in front of the computer to get busy, but my brain isn't interested. My thoughts keep drifting elsewhere.

Faye interrupts by squalling to let me know she's ready for a snack and a nap. After we've completed her feeding/diapering routine and she's settled down in her crib, I decide to go to my closet and figure out what I'm going to wear to dinner tonight. I should have asked where we were going, but I didn't want to appear too excited. A girl must keep her cool, right?

I stand in front of the open closet and stare at my options. What says, "I'm gorgeous, but there's more to me than just my boobs?" I pick up a variety of things that I think might be a tad too risqué if this turns out to be a business meeting and not a date. According to Mama and Auntie Lee, boob cracks aren't appropriate for the office, but may make a limited appearance at corporate events held after five. Having said that, my current cleavage is a tad extreme, so I decide to air on the side of caution.

I go with a longish, pink linen skirt with some ballet flats and a sweet little white cotton blouse with eyelet details. It's a very feminine outfit that even Cootie Wilcox couldn't consider inappropriate. By the time I'm done sorting all that out, Faye is awake from her catnap and ready to be dressed in one of her new outfits. It's a matching shade of pink with tiny roses and of course, a ginormous monogram.

At five twenty, I'm pacing around the living room like Zach is an hour late. When he rings the doorbell at five twenty-five, I nearly jump out of my skin in excitement. He's here! I fluff my hair in the mirror real quick and put on a fresh layer of lip gloss. Then I let him in.

Boy howdy, does he look good. He's wearing a pair of khaki pants with freshly pressed creases and an aqua-blue linen shirt rolled up at the sleeves. The color really sets off the green in his eyes. He's carrying a bouquet of sun flowers.

"Come on in!" I say a bit too brightly like I'm welcoming Armie Hammer himself. I've clearly got no game. Not that I was ever that smooth with men, but I fear motherhood has made me even less so.

I take a quick peek at his backside when he walks by and let me just say—wow. That boy sure knows how to wear pants.

He hands me the flowers and says, "They look like you, all happy and sunny and beautiful."

"Thank you," I say as a tsunami wave of lust slams into me, making my knees tremble. "Let me just put them in a vase." When I come back, I ask, "Would you like to sit down and have a refreshment? I just made some tea." One thing I missed dreadfully about living in New York City was the sorry lack of sweet tea.

"No, ma'am. I think we'd best get going. We have a six

o'clock reservation at Filene's. I got us a table on the river."

"Filenes? That's pretty fancy." I'm about to add "for a first date," but I change my mind at the last second. While I now believe this *is* a date, I still want to make sure before I say anything. I mean, yes, he broke it off with Shelby, and yes, the chemistry between us is explosive, but who knows, maybe I'm just a well of wishful thinking. I'll wait it out and see if there's a goodnight kiss before I start counting my chickens.

I offer, "Why don't I drive? Faye's car seat is already in Mama's car."

"That's fine by me," he says. He hands me the diaper bag and takes the baby, who's strapped in her carrier. It's seriously arousing how he takes control of the situation. It's hard to admit, but I find I like sharing the load. I want to be one of those tough-as-nails women who can do it all with no help. But let's face it, having someone to look after you is an aphrodisiac of the highest order, especially as I've been mostly doing this parenting thing all on my own. Mama helps now that I'm home, but even she can't compete with a handsome man.

Once we're all situated, I turn on the radio. Mama's got it set to one of her oldie's stations and The Wallflowers "One Headlight" comes on. I look at Zach in the passenger seat and notice he's singing along in such a way that you'd think Jakob Dylan himself was sitting next to me. Mama used to play this song when I was little and I'd tell her, "I'm gonna marry that voice someday." Chills shoot up my spine at the memory.

I'm parking the car by the time the song ends, and Zach offers, "Let me carry the baby."

"That's very sweet of you." Once again, I admire how pretty

they look together. Walking into a nice restaurant in my hometown, with a gorgeous man and my little girl, feels right. This is how life is supposed to be.

Zach gives the hostess our name, and she bats her eyes all flirtatious-like. He notices and lifts the baby's car seat up onto the host stand. She immediately interprets that, "Grant, party of three," might not just be Zach alone, and belatedly acts like this is her job and not a pickup joint. "Follow me."

The deck behind the restaurant extends out onto a dock over the water. It's beautiful out here. We're one of the first tables to arrive, so it feels like we're having a private little party.

I show Zach how Faye's car seat is designed to snap right in the highchair. He's quite impressed by that little feature. I sit in the chair he gallantly pulls out for me.

He says, "They make fantastic margaritas here, if you're game."

I shake my head vigorously. "No, thank you. Tequila and I are a dangerous duo."

His eyebrows shoot up in question. "How so?"

"I get this little thing called tequila amnesia whenever I drink it." I add, "I apparently do things I'd never do under the influence of chardonnay."

"Like what?" he asks with a layer of concern in his tone.

"Like I don't even want to talk about because it's too horrifying."

Zach scoots his chair farther away from me like I've just admitted to having leprosy. A chill washes over me and encompasses the table as surely as if it was late autumn instead of summer. I feel the need to defend myself from his concerns. "I haven't murdered anyone if that's what you're worried about."

He clearly fakes a smile. "If you say so."

I have exactly zero idea what's going on here. Two seconds ago, I was on a nice romantic date or business dinner, and now I'm even more confused about what it is. All I know is the air is very different. It's thick and suspicious and not at all date-like. It's like I've confessed to being an alcoholic in addition to being a single mother. Like suddenly, there are one too many things wrong with me and he can't look past them anymore.

The waitress comes over and takes our drink order. I ask for a glass of wine and Zach orders an iced tea. When she leaves, I say, "I thought you might get a margarita."

He shakes his head. "No, ma'am. I need to hurry up and eat. I've got some more work to do tonight."

"Oh," I say. I've got nothing else. I guess this really is a business dinner and I'm not the girl Zach talked about having his eye on, after all. At this moment I seriously start questioning my ability to read people.

After several minutes of uncomfortable silence, Zach says, "I thought we'd check out Filene's and get an idea of their needs so we can make sure their new space in the factory is as ideal as possible."

"Oh," I say again. My goodness I'm just a witty conversationalist, aren't I? I try to flag down the waitress to change my drink to straight water but I'm too late. Tonight is going to last a thousand years, I just know it.

Chapter Twenty-Three

My salad is delicious, very trendy and tasty, bib lettuce, mandarin oranges, bacon, blue cheese, and toasted almonds. Yum. I pull a receipt out of my purse and jot down the ingredients on the back, so I can remember to duplicate it at home for Mama. I'm probably enjoying it so much because I have absolutely nothing else to focus on. The baby is busy playing with her toes, and Zach has said exactly five words to me in the last ten minutes. There was, "no, thank you," when I asked if he'd like to try my salad, and "you're welcome," when I thanked him for handing me the pepper.

Finally, when I've finished my salad and there's nothing else to focus on until the steaks finally come, I can't take it anymore and I ask, "Have I done something to offend you?"

He looks up at me all cool and distant. "No, ma'am." Then crickets.

I'm busy thinking, *What in the fresh hollandaise hell is going on here?* Either this man has a multiple personality disorder or I'm going nuts. He was so attentive and lovely until we sat down and talked about my inability to metabolize tequila like a lady. Then, he's Jack Frost. What did I miss? It's like he's back to judging me, but this time for being a boozy lush. I wonder if he's some kind of born-again Puritan or his ex was a lush or something

When the hostess comes over to ask if we're enjoying our steaks, he smiles up at her like he's trying to melt her butter. "It's delicious, thank you." He gushes like she personally killed the cow and cooked it for him. So much for being a Puritan. Clearly, he's interested in pursuing a relationship with someone, just not me. The poor girl is a bit unsure of how to respond given his earlier lack of interest at her attempt at flirtation. She manages a weird sort of smile before I scowl at her and send her scurrying away.

I can't take the silence another second and say, "So, you haven't always lived in Creek Water, huh?"

He looks up and mumbles, "Nope."

"Where were you before?" I ask, desperately trying to force words out of him.

"Chicago."

I want to bang my head on the table in frustration. "How long have you been back?"

"I came back a year ago last winter."

"That's recent," I say. I'd thought he'd been back a lot longer than that. He just seems to fit here so well. "Why'd you come home?"

"I'd been thinking about it for a long time. There's a comfort to living in a place where people have known you your whole life."

I wonder if he was running from the girl he told me about and decided home would be a safe place to land. I'd get that. I was running too, although, I'm not exactly sure from what. I never did recover my career mojo after *The Event* and Faye's appearance made it sort of necessary to have a bigger support system. My friends in New York were intrigued that I was going to have a baby, but they were nowhere near that place in their own lives. I don't think I could have counted on them for much more than a random Saturday afternoon babysitting.

"You living with your folks?" I ask.

"No, I've got my own place." He doesn't offer anything else. So, I finally just give up and eat my dinner. I occasionally wave a new toy in front of the baby to keep her occupied, but when she falls asleep, I just chew.

When our plates are cleared and the waitress asks if we want dessert, I reply, "Dear god, no." At her shocked expression, I add, "I couldn't eat another bite."

She brings the check and I reach into my purse for my wallet. Zach says, "I got this."

I shake my head. "It's not like we're on a date or anything. I'm happy to pay my own way."

"No, really, I'll use my corporate card and write it off as a business expense."

Be still my beating heart. I zip my purse back up and let him. In truth, I feel like he owes me after wasting my day by encouraging my feelings.

The car ride home is the complete opposite from the one to the restaurant. There is no easy camaraderie or singing along to old songs on the radio. I have an overwhelming urge to scream in order to break the silence.

When we get back to Mama's, I retrieve the baby and head to the front door. Zach doesn't say a word to me, and makes no effort to walk me in. Instead, he just stands there and glowers at me.

I want to turn around and scream, "Don't let the door hitcha' where the good Lord splitcha!" but he's nowhere near a door so that wouldn't make much sense. My emotions are reeling, and I need to not be in his company right now.

How in the Jolly Green Giant am I ever going to be able to work with this man?

Chapter Twenty-Four

I decided to wait up for Mama. I felt like I could use her expert opinion, but I fell asleep somewhere around midnight and she still wasn't home. She's definitely living a wilder life than I am.

Being that it's Sunday, I let myself sleep in. I put Faye in bed next to me last night, so she can eat on-demand, and I wouldn't have to get up for anything. I dreamed about the night of *The Event* and I'm not talking about the dinner at the Met. I dreamed about Faye's daddy, but in my fantasy, we were in love and he'd just popped the question. I can't see his face, but I vaguely remember an intriguing tattoo on his arm. In my vision, I know that he's the one I want to spend my life with.

I wake up totally disoriented and more than a little disappointed. For as nice as the dream was, I wish I hadn't had it. I feel more alone than ever, especially in light of my atrocious dinner date last night.

The baby is busy gnawing on her fist like it's a meaty bone. I stare at her and marvel at her existence. It must be an amazing experience to share this kind of love with the other parent. I take a moment to feel both grateful and sorry for myself.

As Faye hasn't started to roll, I barricade her in the bed with pillows before taking myself off to the bathroom. I look as pretty as a monkey's butt this morning. I have dark circles under my eyes and my skin is all blotchy and red. After seeing to a call from nature, I rinse my face with cool water to try to perk it up. Then I head to the kitchen.

Mama's already gone. She's left a note on the counter saying that she's at church and then she's going to brunch with the family right after. The reservation is at the Steamboat Inn at noon if we want to join them. I look at the clock and see it's only ten. Suddenly, I'm desperate to get out of here and blow off the stink of last night's encounter with Zach.

Upstairs, I feed the baby and take a quick shower. Then I take pains to look nice for my family. I put on a pretty floral sundress and dress Faye in one of her new outfits. We're in Mama's car and heading toward the Steamboat by eleven thirty.

On the way to the restaurant I resolve to forget about Zachary Grant. It's not like I've invested that much energy into him, and the one good thing about this whole debacle is that I now realize how much I'd like to date again—maybe even get married one day and have more babies. Of course, that would require me meeting a non-judgmental Puritan without a personality disorder—split, borderline ... I don't know what the diagnosis is, but it's certainly something. I can only hope some nice sane men become citizens of Creek Water with the influx of new residents.

I'm the first one to arrive at the restaurant, a real live boat, and decide to wait on deck for the rest of the Frothinghams. The river is beautiful, and I sit and marvel at its gorgeousness, so mighty and full of purpose. I think of old Samuel Langhorne Clemens is working on a similar vessel, on this very water, hearing his future name called out time and again. Whether you're from the northern end of the state or the southern, we all have enormous pride in our native son, Mark Twain. His poetry of the great Mississippi is the closest version to the truth I've ever read.

I'm so lost in my reverie that I don't even hear Mama show up. When I finally notice her, I ask, "When did you get here?"

"A few minutes ago. This is one of my favorite views. I think the Mississippi should be one of the wonders of the world, don't you?"

I laugh. "Well, it is for us, but I'm not sure the people of Egypt would agree. They're kind of sold on those pyramids of theirs and I'm thinking they're pretty proud of the Nile."

"What do they know?" Mama teases. "Come on, the family's already been seated." I must have been staring off into space for ages for the family to have come aboard without me even noticing. Of course, I was facing the other direction, but still.

The whole Frothingham crew is situated in the center of the dining room seated in big wing-backed chairs. Auntie Lee stands up first and comes for Faye. "I saved her seat right by me," she says. I hand over my baby. I'm thrilled my daughter's growing up surrounded by so many people who fell in love with her so immediately and so deeply.

Amelia calls out, "Come sit by me, Emmie."

Everyone's dressed in their Sunday finest. The men all have on suits, and the ladies are decked out in pretty dresses with stockings. I swear, if I never leave this town again, I will not be persuaded to wear panty hose. I don't care what Cootie Wilcox thinks of me.

Then, as if conjuring evil spirits, in she comes. Cootie, her husband Harold, Shelby, and wouldn't you know it, Zach. Has that dirty rotten son of the devil has gone back to pretending to be her boyfriend? I guess he has good and truly written me off.

Shelby startles when she sees my family, and you can tell she doesn't know whether to go on the offensive or ignore us entirely. Cootie witnesses her daughter's quandary, and like the queen battle-ax she is, makes the decision for her. The matriarch of the Wilcox gang veers her troops off the hostess's trajectory and heads our way.

She drawls, "Well, if it isn't the illustrious Frothinghams. Don't you all look nice today?"

Don't fool yourself into thinking she's changed her ways. Far from it, I'm one hundred percent sure the very next thing that comes out of her mouth is going to more than make up for any niceties she'll accidentally utter.

She marches herself right in front of Beau and stops dead in her tracks. "Beauregard, I want to thank you for not wasting anymore of Shelby's time." She turns around and smiles at her daughter. "If you hadn't come to your senses, my little girl wouldn't have realized her true feelings for Zach, here. And truth be told, he's a far better catch."

Shelby and Zach both look like they wish they were anywhere but standing on center stage of a Cootie Wilcox production. God love Beau though, he stands up and raises his champagne glass to them and grandly announces, "Thank goodness indeed, Mrs. Wilcox." Then he bows slightly at the waist and proceeds to toast, "To the happy couple."

I don't know what gets into me, but I stand up too, and with my water glass raised high, I add, "You sure do deserve each other."

Then my whole family joins in. It's clearly not the reaction Cootie was hoping for. She tears off like a bee is trying to sting her where the sun don't shine, rushing her crew away as quickly as possible. As they continue on to their own table, Zach turns around and gives me a look that suggests we have some unfinished business. I couldn't disagree more. As far as I'm concerned, we are one hundred percent through. I do not have any intention of putting myself in the path of his judgment again. I don't have to explain myself to him or anyone else.

Chapter Twenty-Five

My family appears to be completely unaware of the scathing looks shooting across the dining room between me and Zach. They just chat aimlessly about their week and enjoy their meal. I'm barely able to pick at my quiche.

Beau catches my eye and says, "Emmie, would you mind switching spots with me? I'd like to talk to my sister for a few minutes."

I wouldn't mind at all. In fact, I'm so relieved at the thought of having my back to the Wilcox table, that I'm standing next to him with my plate in hand before he even gets up. Finally, I'll be able to enjoy my meal.

Once I have a mouthful of quiche, I look up and discover that Beau isn't talking to Amelia at all. He's staring intently at Shelby. There's no way she can miss his laser-like death stare. I only wish I could turn around and see how she's handling it. More importantly, I'd like to see what Cootie's making of it.

Auntie Lee announces, "We made twenty-six hundred dollars at the benefit last night. Isn't that amazing?"

Everyone murmurs their congratulations and I lean over to Uncle Jed and whisper, "How much did you donate?"

"One thousand," he answers with a twinkle in his eye. Then he adds, "It's not so much where the money comes from for your aunt, it's the pursuit that she loves."

"How much did Jesse donate?"

He laughs, "Six hundred."

I shake my head, "So all those weeks of work they put into this thing and most of the money came from their own family?"

He answers, "They pulled in a thousand that we weren't responsible for. That'll buy a lot of ice cream."

"You still playing the trombone in the community band?" I ask. My family loves music but historically is not the most talented in that arena. They don't let it stop them, though.

"Yes, ma'am. I was the whole trombone section last summer. I couldn't let the town down by not doing my bit."

"What about Jesse, is he playing the sax?"

"If you call what he does playing, then yeah, he's still doin' it."

Uncle Jesse likes to go above and beyond what's printed on the music. He says he wants to give the people their money's worth. It's been pointed out to him on more than one occasion that it's a free concert.

Jesse is sitting next to Mama and the two of them are cutting up about something. Auntie Lee is solely engaging with Faye. Amelia keeps looking at her brother, taking note of his obsession with Shelby. So, I say, "Davis, catch me up on your life. How's the furniture biz treating you?"

"It's booming. You should stop by and see my workshop sometime."

"You still in that building behind the Easy Pump?"

"No, ma'am. I moved over to one of the warehouses Daddy and Jesse bought by the river. They don't have immediate plans for it, so I'm gonna let myself spread out for a while."

"You got anyone special in your life?" I already know the answer to that question, but I'm hoping to find out a bit more.

"Sure don't," is all he offers. Davis is the strong, silent type. He keeps details about his life pretty close to the vest. At one point, Auntie Lee thought he might be gay, but that proved to be an inaccurate speculation when he was discovered in a somewhat compromising position with one of the recently divorced club ladies.

"You looking?" I ask.

He shrugs. "Not too hard, that's for sure."

"Why not?" I demand. Davis is every bit as good-looking as his brother, just in a less buttoned-up kind of way. He's more comfortable in holey jeans and t-shirts than dress slacks and buttoned-down shirts.

He points at Shelby. "'Cause of girls like that. I figure until there's a mama I want to date, there's no point asking her daughter out. It's a twofer in this town. All the gals drag their mamas in on everything and before you know it, they're coming out to dinner with you." I think back to the club lady he was involved with and wonder if maybe Davis doesn't actually want to date the mamas instead of the daughters.

"What about some of the new gals in town? Surely their mamas didn't move here with them."

"Emmie," he says, "do me a favor and stay out of my social life. I'll reward you by not asking why you couldn't seem to eat your eggs because you were too busy staring at Zach Grant. Sound like a deal?"

"It surely does," I answer. My word, if Davis noticed how preoccupied I was with Zach, everyone else must have, too. Including Zach. I'm going to have to beef up my acting skills. Either that or find a way to never be in the same room with him. I'm not sure how I'll manage that though, being that we work together.

Chapter Twenty-Six

Auntie Lee announces, "I've had so much sweet tea my eyeballs are floatin'. If you'll all excuse me." She stands up to use the ladies' and says, "Emmie, Amelia, would you like to join me?"

Uh-oh, when a Frothingham woman needs reinforcements in the bathroom, you'd better believe it has nothing to do with having to use the facilities. I pick up Faye, who's just started to fuss, and say, "I'll bring the baby and feed her."

Amelia is on her feet right away, as well. Then the three of us proceed to a lovely little parlor below deck. When we walk in, Auntie Lee checks to make sure we're all alone. Once she's established our privacy, she locks the door and demands, "What in the name of Bojangles is going on with Beau and Shelby Wilcox?"

"What do you mean, Mama?" Amelia asks.

"What I mean is, why did he have to exchange places with Emmie just so he can keep his eyeballs on Shelby? I thought they were through."

Amelia shrugs. "Got me. Maybe you should ask Beau."

"Young lady, if I asked your brother directly, he wouldn't tell me squat. He's slicker than snot on a doorknob when it comes to his social life." Then she turns to me and asks, "What do you know?"

I answer, "All I know is what Mama told me, and that's that Shelby is using Zach to make Beau jealous."

Auntie Lee says, "Didn't you have dinner with Zach last night?"

"How in the world do you know that?" I demand.

"Cloris Absher heard it from Adelaide Bohnefeld. Cloris told me at church."

I shake my head in awe. This town's grapevine is the stuff of legends. "How did Mrs. Bohnefeld hear?"

"Her granddaughter works at Filene's. She said your date didn't look to be going so well. Don't worry, honey, you'll regain the use of your skills soon enough. A baby can knock you off your game for a bit."

"Auntie Lee, Zach and I were having a business dinner, but I thank you for your reassurance."

"Was that business at the yogurt shop, too?" Amelia asks. She wiggles her eyebrows like she's some world-class detective.

"What is this, The Inquisition?" I forget how very interested my family can be in the private affairs of their own kind. "For your information," I look between them, "Zach and I work together. We are friendly, we are not dating." More's the pity. Although now that I know there's something wrong with him, I'm clearly not going to be barking up that tree again.

"Did he say anything about Shelby and Beau?" Auntie Lee asks.

"He seems to agree that Shelby is just using him," I tell her.

"Why is he putting up with that?" she demands.

I sigh. "He says he's trying to be a friend, but I think he's trying to forget another woman."

"What other woman?" Amelia asks.

"Some gal from Chicago that didn't like him as much as he liked her."

Auntie Lee crosses her arms and squints her eyes up in deep concentration. "I do not want that Shelby Wilcox anywhere near Beau, do you understand me?"

"Mama," Amelia says, "how are we supposed to keep them apart? Beau is grown man of twenty-eight. I'm pretty sure he can date anybody he wants."

Auntie Lee shakes her head. "That's where you're wrong. I'm his mama. I have final say here."

Suddenly, I realize that Davis was right on the money about the interfering mothers of Creek Water. Having said that, I'm totally on Auntie Lee's side. I don't want Shelby Wilcox to become a Frothingham, either. My God, it would make family gatherings positively unbearable. "What do you want us to do, Auntie Lee?"

She smiles at me deviously, "I want you to find Beau a nice young lady. Twenty times prettier and thirty times nicer than Shelby. Do I make myself clear?"

I look at Amelia. "You're going to have to lead this campaign, cousin. I don't know anybody in town anymore."

Amelia says, "Mama, this goes against everything I believe in. People need to make their own decisions and find their own relationships."

"Are you saying you're okay with Shelby being in the family?" she asks her daughter.

Amelia shakes her head adamantly. "Absolutely not, which is the only reason I'm going to help you. But just this once. If you get it into your head to set up Davis, or Emmie, or anyone else, I'm not going to be a party to it. Do you understand me, Mama?"

"Of course, baby. My goodness, the way you carry on, you'd think I was some kind of busybody or something." She waves her hand dismissively and says, "You'd better get on out there so the rest of them don't wonder what happened to us."

As soon as Amelia leaves, Auntie Lee sits next to me on the little love seat where I'm nursing the baby and says, "You understand I'm going to need your help with that one, don't you?"

"What happened to not getting tangled up in everyone else's love life?"

"Emmeline, Amelia is my daughter. It is my God-given duty to make sure she's settled well."

I roll my eyes. "So, now you're saying you want my help with both Beau *and* Amelia?"

"Davis too, eventually. But we can wait on him for the time-being. He's the baby, so I don't need to worry about him until the other two are settled."

"Auntie Lee, if I agree to help you, you need to make sure you stay out of *my* social life. Am I clear?"

She puts her hand across her chest like she's about to say the Pledge of Allegiance, and vows, "As God is my witness, honey!"

What in the world have I gotten myself involved in?

Chapter Twenty-Seven

Family is the biggest gift in life or the biggest challenge, depending on how you look at it. I love the care and concern our elders have for us; I really do. But, honest to goodness, at some point they need to remember that we've earned the right to make our own choices, and whether they're mistakes or not is something that time alone will determine.

After we get home from brunch, I tell Mama what Auntie Lee is up to. All she says is, "Can you blame her?"

"Not in the case of Shelby Wilcox, I can't. But she needs to leave Amelia and Davis alone. 'Cause you know, once she's done with them, she'll be working on me."

Mama pats my arm. "Not without my help, honey."

A chill of dread rushes through me like I'm sunbathing on a glacier. "Mama, you picked Daddy on your own. Don't I have the same right?"

"No, ma'am. I didn't pick your daddy. I thought he was too good for me. I didn't think a Frothingham would look twice at a country girl like me."

"Really? Why didn't you ever tell me that?" I ask.

"Because I never wanted you to doubt your worth like I did.

Thinking some folks are better than others based on whether they have a fancy house in town or live on a watermelon farm is plain stupid. People deserve to be judged on their actions, not the circumstances they're born into."

"So how did you and Daddy wind up together?" The story they told me is that they met up at the Fancy Freeze, an ice cream parlor in town.

"Granny Faye took one look at your daddy at a summer band concert after his junior year in college and decided he was the one. She paid a call on Granny Selia the next day." My grandmothers had known each other through the hospital auxiliary where they both volunteered, but they didn't start running in the same circle until Mama and Daddy became a couple.

"What in the world did Granny Selia make of that?" I ask. My daddy's mama was an iron girdle kind of gal. She loved us with a determination not seen outside of Grant's army.

"Selia said that if my mama felt so strongly about it that maybe she and I should join them for lunch at the club some afternoon. But Granny Faye told her that a war you wanted to win shouldn't be played on anyone's home turf. They needed a neutral location."

"So Selia suggested we rent pontoon boats on Creek Water Lake. She'd tell Reed she wanted to spend some time alone with him, and my mama should do the same with me. Then we'd meet at a set time and pretend it was a happy coincidence. Of course, we'd decide to share a boat at the last minute."

"Oh, Mama, that's awful! What did you and Daddy think?" I ask.

She smiles wistfully. "We knew immediately what they were

up to, but we were both okay with it because we'd noticed each other long before that. Your daddy and I used to run into each other quite a bit at the Fancy Freeze. If you'll recall, I worked there, and he seemed to always show up during my shifts. He never said much more than, 'I'll have a scoop of fudge ripple on a sugar cone,' but his eyes always promised more. So, you see, Emmie, mamas have a God-given duty to keep mothering long after their babies think they're no longer in need of such attention."

"I'd like to think you and Daddy would have found each other without any interference. In fact, it seems you already had. It's my belief that we come into this world with the name of the person we're meant to be with tattooed on our hearts, and those marks have a magnetism that pull us together when we get into close enough proximity to each another." How's that for hopelessly romantic? I think of Faye's daddy and realize that was different kind of magnetism altogether.

"That's very pretty thinking," Mama says. "But maybe sometimes you need your mama to help you start a conversation. What do you think of that?"

"Maybe," I concede. "But I still want to make my own decision."

"I wouldn't hear of it any other way, honey," Mama says while looking at me with such love in her eyes. Now that I'm a mother myself, I understand the need to do your best by your child no matter what. I worry about Faye growing up without a daddy. But I also know that a mama's love can be big enough for two parents when it needs to be.

"I'd like to go see Granny Selia at the home sometime this week. You want to come with me?"

Granny Selia is my only remaining grandparent, and unfortunately, she's neither of sound mind nor body. She has various physical complaints and advanced dementia, making it so she hasn't recognized any of us in more years than I care to recall. The uncles visit her every week regardless, even though sometimes she mistakes them for burglars and yells the place down.

Mama says, "I'd be happy to go with you. I think Selia would enjoy seeing the baby."

We decide to make the trip to her nursing home the following weekend. In the meantime, I'm going to head into town and look for inspiration again. Most stores are closed on Sundays, but I want to see what's out there anyway. I need to let Creek Water speak to me and tell me what she's lacking so I can help provide it.

"As soon as Faye wakes up, I'm going to take her into town for a look-see."

Mama says, "Why don't you go now? You've left enough breast milk in the freezer for seven babies, plus I told Sarah Jane I'd bring Faye over some time so she could get her cuddle on."

I don't argue. I change into a pair of Bermuda shorts and a t-shirt and hit the road to hear what my hometown has to say to me.

Chapter Twenty-Eight

I decide to ride my bike into town instead of driving. I figure a little exercise is the ticket to burning off some of the irritation I'm harboring against Zach. That man does not deserve to be the source of my preoccupation and I need to get him out of my system, stat.

The old bike path cutting through Creek Water woods has been cleared and paved over to make for a smoother ride. I fly through without the added adventure of dodging potholes and fallen logs. It's easier, but way less enjoyable.

As kids, we used to bump along this trail singing "I've be Workin' on the Railroad" as loud as our voices would allow, just so we could hear them warble like we were singing into the business end of an electric fan. Then we'd laugh so hard on the bouncier parts that we'd have to stop peddling long enough to catch our breath.

I spent hours in Creek Water woods as a kid with my cousins. We used to go frogging during the early summer months. Riding out when it was dark, armed with only our flashlights and gigs, which are long spear-like hunting forks. We'd sing "Froggy Went a Courtin'" the whole way. Which is kind of barbaric if you think about it, as it was our agenda to catch as many of the creatures as we could before cutting off their legs and putting them in the fridge.

Our mamas would mix up some flour and crushed saltine crackers tossed with salt, pepper, and sometimes a little garlic powder. They'd dip the legs in an egg wash before dredging them in the mixture and frying them in peanut oil. My mouth waters at the memory.

I'm sure some folks think frogging sounds backwoods, certainly not something the founding family of our town would engage in, but it's a rite of passage in our part of the world. I haven't been since the summer I turned twelve, but I'm sure I'll take Faye when she's old enough.

I whiz by several people, most whom smile or wave as they pass. Bicycling in Central Park was never a neighborly experience. It was more of a do or die situation, weaving in and out of bike lanes, avoiding pedestrians and stray children. It's probably why I didn't own a bike in the city, preferring to rent one on the few occasions I braved the cycling paths there.

The woods transport me back to childhood as surely as if I'd just stepped into a time machine. Daddy and I would walk this path to the river, where we'd get enough fish to fill the freezer for a year. Walleye, sauger, bluegill, catfish, and bass were just a few of the kinds we caught. I loved getting up in the wee hours and heading out while it was still dark. We used to pretend we were early adventurers exploring the Mississippi for the first time.

This terrain reminds me of my daddy more than even our house does. I'm lucky I had the uncles to step in when he was gone, but even with all of their love and guidance, there's no way they could have totally filled their brother's shoes.

I park my bike next to the big old tree we all used to carve our names into as kids. It's located right at the fork of the path—one way leading to the river, and the other to the creek. I walk around running my fingers across the engravings on the trunk looking for mine. I finally find it, but the years of weathering has made my imprint so faint that I feel the need to deepen the impression.

I pull out the nail kit I keep in my purse and dig out the thin metal file. It's the closest thing I have to a knife. I lean in and smell the earthiness of the wood before I begin scratching into the bark. When I'm done with my name, I make Daddy's and Mama's names stronger too, like by deepening the lines I'm assuring my fading memories are real and not just some fantasy I've concocted.

I turn around, intent on strolling over to the old boat dock we used to jump off as kids. The image of dozens of happy children yelling and screaming in delight as they leap into the cool water fills my brain like I'm watching it on a movie screen. I remember Beau threatening, "If you don't jump, I'm gonna throw ya in!"

I'd yell back, "Back off, you big bully, or I'll tell everyone you're a bed-wetter."

That would inevitably incite him to a full-out charge. I'd wind up jumping in just to keep him from having the satisfaction of pushing me.

My cousins were more like siblings during my formative years. Things shifted a bit when I went off to college and started to come home as infrequently as possible, but we seem to have picked up right where we left off, and I couldn't be more grateful.

I step over a fallen log and am just about to exit the woods toward the dock when I see Shelby and Zach approach from the other direction. A normal person would either say hello to them and walk past, or simply turn around and beat it out of Dodge, so she didn't have to interact with them at all. But not me. For some inexplicable reason I drop to the ground like I'm training on a military obstacle course and have hit that portion where I need to shimmy under low-strung barbed wire. In other words, I eat dirt.

The duo stops walking about ten feet in front of me and turns to look around like they'd heard my less-than-graceful maneuver. When they don't see anyone, they start to talk.

With hands on her hips, Shelby says, "I don't care if we are just pretending to be seeing each other, you cannot treat me like trash in front of Emmeline Frothingham. Do you understand?"

Hello, what's going on here?

"It seems to me that you're getting more out of this than I am, Shelby, so I don't think it's your place to tell me what I can and cannot do." I can't help but wonder what he's getting out of it.

"You promised you'd help me, Zach. It doesn't help to have you making eyes at Emmie."

"Beau wasn't even around," he insists.

"No, but if Emmie goes home and tells her family that you don't like me, then I'm sure as heck never going to make Beau jealous."

Zach scoffs, "Shelby, I don't know if you were paying attention at brunch, but Beau toasted our union. That doesn't sound like a guy who's pining away for you."

"He couldn't keep his eyes off of me!" she heatedly declares. "He traded places with Emmie just so he could glare at me. If that doesn't sound like a man regretting his decision to walk away, I don't know what does."

Zach rolls his eyes. "You're pie-in-the-sky dreaming, Shelby."

"What's going on with you and Emmie anyway?" she demands. "You were all over her like ticks on a hound dog at the country club and then at the yogurt shop you left me hanging so you could stay and eat with her. You can't seriously be interested. I mean, she's got a baby."

Before Zach can answer, I feel something crawl toward my mouth and I hurriedly spit at it to deter its entrance.

Zach glances at the tree right above where I'm lying but doesn't bother to look low enough to see me wallowing in the dirt under the brush. "Trust me, there's nothing going on between me and Emmeline Frothingham."

She asks, "Is this because of what happened in high school? I don't necessarily want you to go after her now, but you eventually have to let that go, Zach."

He takes Shelby's arm and leads her toward the pier. The only other thing I manage to hear before he walks away is, "You don't know what you're talking about."

Chapter Twenty-Nine

The bike path dumps me off into Frothingham Park. I ride through until I come to the old pavilion. I spent every Monday night here as a kid listening to our community band play a combination of patriotic songs, show tunes, and odd renderings of rock music from the seventies. I'll bring Faye back tomorrow night to hear her great uncles play.

I lean my bike up against the platformed bandstand before sitting at one of the wooden picnic tables nearby. *So, this is where Granny Faye decided to try her hand at matchmaking?*

I imagine my parents in the '80s—Mama in a Laura Ashely dress and Daddy with a mullet—it makes me smile. Sometimes I feel sorry for myself that I lost my daddy so young, but he's everywhere in this town. His ghost follows me as sure as if he were still flesh and blood.

I look up, surprised to see my cousin strolling across the grass in my direction. "Hey, Beau, what's going on?"

"Not much. Mama asked me to stop by to make sure the bunting got put up."

I look up and spy all the little patchwork flags that have been strung together and hung from the rafters. "I'd say you're good to go."

"You coming tomorrow night? It's the first concert of the season and promises to be a good time."

"You couldn't keep me away," I declare. I loved summer band concerts as a kid. They were just one big community party. The parents all stayed under the pavilion and sipped the cocktails they brought in their coolers. They listened attentively while the kids took off and played in the park—running in wild packs with no set destination. The humid summer air, the sound of music, and the act of being in motion were all ingredients in the heady recipe for the freedom of my youth.

Beau sits next to me and announces, "Mama hates Shelby."

With my mind on the conversation I just overheard by the creek, I say, "She's not always that likable."

He nods slowly. "It's Cootie's fault. The time I've spent with her, just the two of us, has been quite enjoyable, but as soon as she's within spitting distance of her mama, boy howdy, does she change."

"You like her a lot?" I ask, praying the answer is no.

"I wouldn't say that," he answers. "I'm just trying to figure her out."

"Why?" I mean, why would he care to try if he weren't interested in her?

He shrugs his shoulders. "I'm not sure. I guess there's something about her that draws me, but I can't figure out what."

An alarm goes off in my brain and I wonder if Beau and Shelby are meant to be. Maybe their heart magnets are pulling them together, but they aren't quite ready for each other. Damn, that would be a shame. If Shelby becomes one of us some day, then Cootie will as well, and that thought turns my stomach as surely as if I'd eaten a live earthworm.

Beau says, "You want to tell me what's going on with you?"

"What do you mean?" I ask.

"Oh, I don't know. How 'bout you start with coming home with a baby and then you can tell me about Zach."

"For the love of god, Beau, there's nothing going on with me and Zach." I wonder if I sound convincing to his ears, 'cause to mine, I sound like a big, fat liar.

"You've got eyes for him. I noticed at brunch that you couldn't eat your food for all the time you spent ogling him."

I release my breath so fast it sounds like a balloon popping. "He thinks I'm trash."

Beau's eyebrows knit together in anger and he declares, "I'll kick his backside six ways from Sunday. What's he said to you?"

"He didn't say anything exactly, it's just the way he treats me. Nice one minute and then out of nowhere you'd think I was something he stepped in at a busy dog park."

"You want me to talk to him?"

I manage to not yell, "Don't you dare. That's the last thing I need. I just want to slide right back into Creek Water without drawing any more attention to myself than I already have."

"Tell me about Faye," he changes the subject.

So, I do. I tell him about losing out on the Demitasse award and how I wound up in a bar and then a stranger's apartment. I leave out all the gory details, because well, he's as near to a brother as I have, and I can't imagine him being impressed by my behavior.

"You ever try to find the guy?" he asks.

I shake my head. I'm too ashamed to tell him I never bothered to pay attention to where I was at. "What's the point?

I mean, he was a stranger, not someone I was dating. I can't imagine he would have been too pleased by the news."

"He still has a right to know that he's a daddy."

It's my turn to change the subject. While I don't like Shelby, I love Beau and if his heart is calling him in her direction, I feel it my duty to warn him. "Your mama is on a campaign to find you a girl that's not related to Cootie."

He laughs. "You think I don't know that? Emmie, she's my mama, I know how that brain of hers works. She turns up all over town with new gals to introduce me to all the time. Why, just Friday, she showed up in my office with one of the club ladies' daughters, claiming to be helping her look for a cute little starter house in town."

"What makes you think she wasn't looking for a house?" I ask.

"Oh, she was looking, but she wanted a house for a family, and she kept hinting that all she needed was a nice husband to help her fill it."

"Well, just so you know, I think Auntie Lee has decided to up her game. She's dead set against Shelby and has enlisted the help of me and Amelia."

"Amelia's not going to help her." He eyes me as if to challenge my loyalty.

"I'm the one who just told you what she was up to," I defend. Then I ask, "Why won't Amelia help her?"

"'Cause if she interferes in my love life, I'll turn around and return the favor."

"How in the world do we keep our mamas out of our business?" I ask.

"We just got to give them enough room to feel like they're conspiring against us while making sure we don't actually give them any power over the situation. In some ways I envy your years away. It had to have been nice not to have the whole family up in your business all the time."

I don't agree. Instead, I say, "I missed you all."

He looks surprised. "Then why didn't you come home sooner?"

"I don't know. I guess I felt like I had something to prove."

"Not to us," he says. "As far as we're concerned Creek Water is where you belong."

I don't regret my years in New York City. It was good to get to know myself outside the confines of the small town I was raised in. I succeeded in business there, I had adventures. Heck, I conceived the best thing in my life there, but darn if I ever really felt at home.

Now all I have to do is shake off my conflicted feelings toward Zach and step into my new life. That shouldn't be too hard, right?

Chapter Thirty

I've managed to avoid Zach for most of the week. I skipped the band concert because Faye was feeling poorly, and I've avoided the sewing machine factory by staying home to do research and create a budget for Emmeline's. As the store is the uncles' first foray into retail, I want them to feel confident that I know what I'm talking about and I'm not squandering their money.

I'm sticking with the idea of a gourmet/kitchenware shop that has gift items scattered about. I've also contacted several local artisans and have worked out a consignment agreement with them. They'll put their merchandise in the store and will get paid once it sells. In addition to a local soap maker, and a potter who specializes in one-of-a-kind vases and pitchers, Amelia is going to stock her jewelry and Davis is going to supply his armoires. We'll use them as display cases, but we'll sell them as well.

I'm meeting with Jed and Jesse later this afternoon to present my concept to them. First, Mama and I are driving to Millersville to see Granny Selia this morning. I've been warned to expect the worst, but I still take pains to look as nice as possible. Granny always appreciated a lady looking like a lady.

On the ride over, Mama says, "It's been weeks since Selia has spoken to any of us. We go to visit, and she just stares off into space like we're not even there. It's plumb heart-breaking."

"I haven't even seen her since before I got pregnant with Faye." I feel horrible about that, too.

We're quiet for the rest of the twenty-minute drive, both lost in our thoughts. When we finally arrive, Mama pulls into a spot in the nursing home parking lot right next to a very familiar-looking vehicle. *Crabs and crackers, what in the world is Zachary Grant doing here?*

I ask Mama about it and she says, "Zach's Granny had a stroke last year, and she was admitted right after being released from the hospital. I'm not sure she'll ever get out of here."

This is the nicest nursing home in a sixty-mile radius of Creek Water, so I shouldn't be surprised there are other people we know here, but still, the whole thought of running into Zach gives me the heebie-jeebies. I can't help but feel a renewed something toward him. I'm not sure it's interest, as he's not treated me well enough to deserve my notice—like telling Shelby straight out he wasn't interested in me— but still it's something too close to that for my comfort. What's wrong with me?

We check in at the reception desk and find out that Granny is not herself today. She's accused the doctor of keeping her against her will and has threatened to have his medical license revoked if she isn't driven home immediately. Mama looks sad and asks, "Should we come back another time?"

"Stay," the nurse answers. "She might actually talk to you today."

We're ushered down a long corridor, past a gaming room and

the cafeteria. It's a nice environment that doesn't reek of disinfectant or illness. I'm not sure how they managed that, but it might have something to do with the giant flower arrangements everywhere.

The nurse knocks on Granny's door and greets, "Mrs. Frothingham, you have visitors."

I hear her before I see her, "Are those damn peasants back?"

I catch the nurse's eye and she shrugs but looks unsurprised. Apparently, this behavior isn't unusual for Granny even though it's not exactly normal.

She says, "No, ma'am, I have your family with me."

"What family? My family was murdered during the Bolshevik Revolution back in nineteen eighteen."

The nurse turns to us. "That means she's Anastasia Romanov right now."

Mama pats my arm. "She changes identity a lot. She's been Mary Queen of Scotts, Josephine Bonaparte, and Nefertiti, as well."

"I see." Which I don't. "Is she always royalty?" I ask.

"Always," Mama confirms. "Unless, of course, she's herself, which she hasn't been in ages."

The nurse says, "It's a good sign, actually. We'd much rather have her talking and interacting, than just lying around like a vegetable."

Granny is sitting up in her bed with a flowerpot on her head when we walk in. Luckily, it appears to have been emptied before she put it on. She smiles at us brightly and tells the nurse, "We'll take our tea in the solarium."

The nurse fusses around with the room, and asks if she can polish Granny's crown, and then curtsies to her and backs out of the room holding the flowerpot.

Mama greets, "Mama Selia, how are you?"

"Who is this Mama Selia?" Granny asks imperiously. "Is she some kind of herbalist or healer, voodoo priestess maybe?"

I approach the side of her bed and sit down next to her. I say, "I'm so happy to see you again, Granny."

She doesn't chastise me for calling her Granny, instead she stares at me for a long moment like she might remember me from somewhere. I forge on, "I brought my baby, Faye, to meet you." I lift the baby carrier onto the bed.

Her eyes brighten. "Faye is a beautiful name. I once had a good friend named Faye. We betrothed our children to each other."

Mama jumps like she's just received a jolt from the business end of a cattle prod. She says, "Faye was my mama."

Granny looks confused, "No, dear, Faye was a villager in the town where I'm from. I don't even know who you are." Mama looks defeated.

I say, "I named my baby after your friend Faye. She was my granny, too."

Granny creases her brow up as if to get a better look at me and tears start to form in her eyes. In a much smaller voice, she asks, "Emmeline, is that you?"

Mama drops into a chair by the door like a load of bricks.

"It's me, Granny." I don't know how, but my grandmother has come back to us. I suspect it'll be for a very short time, so I want to make the most of it. I kiss her before pulling Faye out of her contraption. Then, I hand my daughter over to the matriarch of my family.

Granny takes her and immediately breathes in the top of her head. She dreamily says, "She looks like Reed."

I turn to Mama, who has come over and joined me, and see tenderness. Selia looks up at her daughter-in-law and says, "Gracie, doesn't she look just like Reed?"

Mama chokes down a sob and says, "Yes, ma'am, she most certainly does."

Granny asks, "Who's her daddy?"

Oh lord, I hadn't thought about how I'd answer that question, as I didn't expect her to remember me at all. I answer, "He's at home," at the same time there's a knock on the door.

Mama walks over to answer it, and wouldn't you know it's none other than Zach Grant standing there with a big bouquet of flowers. He looks shocked to see us, but he comes in anyway. He bows to Granny and says, "Your Highness, I've brought flowers from the royal gardens."

Granny laughs, "Zach, boy, what are you going on about? Come here and give me some sugar."

Zach looks startled at Mama. "Mrs. Frothingham, how are you today?" He willingly follows her directive. Then he looks at me and says, "Emmie."

Granny claps her hands together and declares, "You married my Emmie! I thought Faye looked just like Reed, but now I see she looks just like her daddy."

Oh, dear heavens. I try to correct her and say, "No, Granny …" but Zach wraps his arm around me and says, "I sure did. How could I help but marry the prettiest girl in Creek Water?"

I decide to let his pronouncement ride. After all, there's no point in upsetting my grandmother when I don't even know how long we'll have her. So, I nod and say, "It was a beautiful wedding. You would have loved it."

Granny smiles wistfully and holds Emmie close. She whispers, "This is the most precious gift ever."

Then there's another knock on the door and the nurse comes in carrying a tray of teacups. She curtsies and announces, "I've brought the tea, ma'am."

Like the flick of a switch, Granny looks up at us like she doesn't know who we are, waves her hand, and dismisses us. "That will be all," she says as she holds Faye out for me to take.

Chapter Thirty-One

I'm shaken up as I put Faye back into her carrier. I want to throw myself into my grandmother's arms and beg her to remember me again, but the look on her face says that would be the wrong thing to do. I make a silent vow to come back often on the chance that we'll have some quality time together—even if I have to gain her friendship by pretending to be her maid.

Mama and Zach walk out of the room first, but it takes me longer. I dawdle a bit, hoping Granny might pop back into her skin, even if only long enough to share a knowing smile. I eventually accept she won't be reappearing today and stop at the door to stare at the woman who taught me how to properly carve a turkey, cut a watermelon, and slice a loaf of fresh-baked bread. Granny seemed to have a thing for cutting stuff up—right now she's doing a number on my heart.

In the hallway, Mama takes the baby carrier from me with wide-eyed wonder and says, "That was plain amazing. You brought her home, Emmie."

I try to smile but my mouth doesn't want to comply. Instead, I change the subject and ask Zach, "How's your grandma doing?"

He shakes his head. "Not good. The doctors say she's not going to get any better."

I almost ask if Mama and I should stop in to say hello to her, what with him apparently being a regular visitor to my granny, but his body language suggests he's ready to leave. So, I inquire, "Do you see Granny Frothingham every time you're here?"

He nods. "I do." But he doesn't say anything else.

Mama interjects, "You know Selia was good friends with Zach's grandma." I think of how sad it is that these good friends are right down the hall from each other but aren't able to enjoy one another.

I'm so full of emotion I'm not sure how to respond to Mama's comment. Plus, I'm still madder than a wet hen at Zach's previous treatment of me. One minute he seems ready to declare his attraction, and the next he's swatting me away like I'm an aggressive mosquito. Then I overheard him tell Shelby there's nothing going on between us. Boy, he's got that right. Although it seems that even Shelby knows I turned him down in high school, so more and more I'm thinking that's where his animosity toward me stems. I just don't know what to say at this late date to make things right. Ultimately, I say, "Thank you for being so nice to Granny. I'm sure she appreciates it."

"That's the first time she's recognized me. No matter who she thought she was, she's consistently thought I was the gardener."

"Do you always bring her flowers?" I ask.

"I do."

My heart flops around my chest like a newly caught fish. Why would Zach do that, and for so long even? What's the payoff for him unless he truly is a super nice guy? But if that's who he is, why is he so dang judgmental toward me about being a single mama? It doesn't add up.

Once we get to the parking lot, Mama says, "I want to stop by the nursery down the road to pick up some new flowers for my window boxes."

"Can you do it some other time, Mama? I'm meeting the uncles for my presentation."

She doesn't look pleased, but says, "I guess."

"I'm heading to the factory," Zach says. "Why don't you drive with me, Emmie?"

"Thank, you Zach," Mama responds before I have a chance to decline his offer. Now there's no way to get out of it without looking ungracious and raising Mama's suspicions that there's more going on between me and Zach than I've copped to. Crap.

I kiss Faye on the top of her head and tell Mama, "I should be home by three to feed her."

"Whenever. The freezer is full of breast milk, so you don't need to rush." Mama waves her hand as we drift toward Zach's car.

Like a gentleman, Zach opens the passenger door for me before walking around the car to get in himself. The radio blares Jakob Dylan's "One Headlight." He turns it down while explaining, "I picked up the CD at that used record store in town after hearing it on the radio the other night."

That would be the night of our business dinner/date. I figure I've got nothing to lose, so I ask, "What happened to that gal you told me about after we had frozen yogurt? You know, the one you said you had your eye on?"

Zach's foot hits the gas and the car accelerates as if it's trying to pick up enough speed to fly us back to town. He finally answers, "Turns out she doesn't share my feelings."

"How in the world did you come to that conclusion?" I demand. I mean if it was me he was talking about, and I'm pretty certain it was, I did nothing but encourage him.

"It doesn't matter how I figured it out," he says. "I just did."

"Did you tell her how you feel?" I ask ruthlessly. He shakes his head, so I continue, "You might want to do that. You'll never know her true feelings until you come right out and ask her."

"I'm not sure my heart could take the rejection," he responds.

For the love of god man, get your head out of the past! "What if she doesn't reject you? Isn't it worth the effort of finding out?"

Of course, if it *is* me, I'm tempted to reject him for treating me so poorly regarding my single mother status, but then again, I might just go ahead and give him a chance. I guess we won't know until he mans up and says something.

Chapter Thirty-Two

Zach pulls up in front of the building, unlocks the car doors, then jumps out to open my door. As I emerge, he says, "I guess I'll see you later," and then he speeds off before I can reply.

The uncles are already sitting at the table we've put in the space designated for Emmeline's. They're drinking coffee and fiddling on their phones. I don't sit down. Instead, I stand in front of them and announce, "I can open the store I want for seventy-five thousand dollars."

"What happened to the hundred thousand?" Jesse asks.

"I used my know-how and ingenuity and brought the price down." I declare, "I don't want to open a card shop. People don't send cards like they did twenty years ago. They text memes for free. I want to open a store this community needs. One that has legs to grow on and can withstand the test of time."

Jed asks, "And that's your gourmet kitchen shop?"

"A gift shop with a lot of gourmet and kitchen items. I don't think Creek Water has the demographic to pull off something like Silver Spoons, but I think we can certainly benefit from incorporating those kinds of things. Mostly, we're going to offer quality merchandise that spans from a mid to high price point, interspersed with one-of-a-kind objects d'art."

"And you can do that for seventy-five?" Jesse asks.

"I can. But just as importantly, I can do it in three months. I can be ready for a fall opening."

Jed nods his head enthusiastically. "We've been targeting September. We'd like to have an official grand-opening by mid-November. That ought to give everyone enough time to work out the kinks while still giving businesses plenty of time to benefit from Christmas sales."

"When do you think the second and third floors will be up and running?" I ask.

Jesse answers, "Beau is ready to move his company over as soon as his new space is set up—we'd like that to happen by the end of July. Then he'll start renting out the office space. We figure the condos won't realistically be ready to start selling until we have the model set up. We're hoping to have that done sometime in October. We'll sell the other spaces unfinished. That way, the new owners will be able to choose their own countertops, fixtures, etc."

I'm smiling so big I'm pretty sure they can count my molars. "This is super exciting, isn't it?

"Yes, ma'am, it sure is," Jed says. "Now how 'bout we hit the third floor and pick out the condo we plan to use for the model?"

Jesse picks up his phone. "I'll have Zach meet us up there."

When we step off the elevator, Zach's holding an armload of cardboard cylinders and says, "I think I've picked the perfect spot. Follow me."

He leads us to the side of the building that overlooks the river. He's taped off a large space in yellow and black construction tape. After dropping the cylinders on the table, he grabs one of the tubes and pulls out architectural plans. He unrolls them and lays them out for us to see. "I think the model we use should be one of the two-bedroom, two bath condos. If we shoot for the biggest and best and use the three-bedroom, buyers will feel let down if they can only afford the one-bedroom. But if we go with our mid-sized unit then it won't be that big of a stretch for buyers to imagine either the one or three-bedroom setup, depending on their budgets."

"Sounds reasonable," Jed says. "Plus, this view is going to knock their socks off."

I suggest, "We need to reach out to some of the bigger newspapers and decorating magazines in the area and send out press kits." I ask Zach, "How soon can we get some color three-D drawings of these plans so that I can start setting things up?"

"I could have simple drawings by the end of the week. It would be a better use of time and resources to pick up some interior decorating software. We can plug in our dimensions and details and design the space in a way that will really catch people's eye."

"Can you and Emmie take care of that?" Jesse asks.

Zach looks like he wishes he'd kept his mouth shut, but ultimately answers, "Sure thing." He walks us through the rest of the space where he's broken down the individual units for us to see.

When the tour ends, Jed asks, "How soon will you be done designing the space so we can get a model?"

"By next week," Zach tells him. "We've got all the infrastructure in place. I'd like to finish up the second floor first and then we can go full-steam up here."

I smile at Zach and suggest, "Why don't we meet tomorrow morning and get to work on the mock-ups? Most publications do their layouts three months in advance, so I want to get going on this as soon as possible."

I can't tell if he looks excited or uncomfortable about spending more time together, but he nods and smiles, "Sounds like a plan."

I excuse myself to go back downstairs and start sketching out the layout for Emmeline's. I can hardly wait to get this show on the road.

Chapter Thirty-Three

In my mind's eye, I visualize our store looking a lot like Silver Spoons with slight tweaks that will appeal to a country crowd. Davis's beautiful rustic furniture will be much more enticing than sleek steel shelving. I'm also going to focus on earthy colors for our brand instead of sterile white. Folks here respond to a homey vibe and in order to spend money, they need to feel at home at Emmeline's.

Hours pass as I troll my laptop for the perfect fixtures. If you can believe, the ones I want are from Silver Spoons, but due to personal reasons—like them laying me off—I'm loath to pay full price. I'd rather they not make any extra money off me.

I pick up my phone and call my old friend and former co-worker, Lexi. She answers, "Emmie, how are you? How's Faye?"

It's a rush of pure weirdness to hear my friend's voice. The last time we talked was the morning I left New York. We've been relying on texts to stay in touch. "We're so good. I miss you, though."

"I miss you, too. More importantly, Silver Spoons misses you. The two dingbats that have taken your place have no idea what they're doing."

"What do you mean?" I demand. "I trained Chelsea and Eli myself."

"They left! They've joined forces and are opening their own store in the SoHo. It's called Cheli."

"How exciting." I'm going to have to call them and cheer them on. It takes real gumption to open your own store in New York City. It also takes an enormous amount of capital.

Lexi asks, "Any particular reason you're calling and not messaging?"

"I want your employee discount," I declare. "I thought that request required a more personal touch."

"What's mine is yours," she replies. "What do you want me to order for you?"

I give her all the item numbers and quantities before telling her what I'm going to use them for. She says, "I haven't begun to reach my spending limit for the year, so let me know if you need anything else."

"If you're sure about that, I might just use their fixtures in the model condo. I'll get back to you by the end of the week."

"Sure thing," she answers. "I'd love to come down and visit sometime soon. Maybe this fall? I have a month of vacation time that's been accruing and if I don't use it by the end of the year, it'll go away."

I assure her that she's always welcome in my home before we hang up. It'll be a big culture shock for my friend as she was born and raised in Manhattan. She claims to have never been to the Southern states. Her mom is a college professor and her dad, an artist. When they took family vacations it was to places like London, Paris, and Florence.

It's after five by the time I finally close my laptop and look for someone to drive me back to Mama's. When I venture out of my little corner of the building, I discover Jesse is the only person left who's not part of the construction crew. They're all still hard at work.

"Hey, Jesse," I say. "Can you give me a lift?"

"You going to the club?" he asks.

"I'm going home. Why would I be going to the club?"

"Tonight is the event of the year—the first catfish fry of the summer! I thought you would be ready to get your bib on." The Players Grill hands out bibs on catfish night because it's one greasy and glorious affair: catfish, coleslaw, and hush puppies, primed and ready for mass consumption. I haven't been to a catfish fry in years.

"Are you going?" I ask.

"Yes, ma'am. I wore my pants that have a little extra wiggle room." He pulls his waistband out to spokesmodel his attire.

"Is the rest of the family going?"

"Pretty sure. I was going to ask you and Gracie if you wanted to drive with me, but the day got away from me. What do you think?"

My stomach growls in response. "I'd love to go. Just take me home to see how Faye's feeling and maybe change my clothes. She was grumpier than a prickly pear yesterday from all her teething. If she's still as sweet as she was this morning, I'm in."

My uncle smiles brightly before tossing me his keys. "Go ahead and take my car. Y'all can pick me up on your way. I should be done by six. If you decide to stay home, send your mama."

144

I head out to Jesse's bright red sports car and let the top down. I drive home with the music blaring, feeling more settled than I have since coming home. Catfish night at the club is one of my fondest childhood memories, and while Faye's way too young to eat anything, I'm thrilled at the thought of sharing it with her.

Creek Water and I seem to finally be embracing each other in a way I've always dreamed of.

Chapter Thirty-Four

Mama's dressed and ready to go when I get home. She says, "I totally forgot tonight was catfish night until Jesse called. You in?"

"Depends," I answer. "How's Faye doing?"

"She's been a delight. We played patty cake, peek-a-boo, and where-are-baby's-toes all afternoon. She's taking her afternoon nap right now."

Relieved, I tell her, "Let me grab a quick shower and throw on a sun dress and hopefully Faye will be awake."

Standing under a cool spray to perk myself up, I wonder if Zach and Shelby will be there. I kind of hope they will. Not because I want to see Cootie's gang, but because I think Zach is still interested in me, regardless of what he told Shelby down by the creek, and I want to lay eyes on them together to assure myself there's really nothing going on there. I'm not sure why he's running hot and cold on me, but I sure would like to find out once and for all.

I take extra pains to look gorgeous while Faye coos away, batting at her teddy bear mobile. When I'm ready, I pick her up from her crib. Regardless of what Mama says, I don't think I was the one who brought Granny back, I think it was Faye. Babies are nothing but pure magic. They're so unspoiled and fresh to our world, they're like rays of sunshine after a thunderstorm. It took something that bright to reach into Granny's darkness.

Mama wants to take her car, so we don't have to transfer the baby seat. She figures Jesse can pick up his ride when the night ends. My daddy's brother is waiting out front when we get to the sewing machine factory. I should probably call it the new Frothingham building, but like every other vintage commercial structure in town, I s'pose I'll always refer to it by its original designation. People don't call Amelia's shop Bead It. They still call it Whisper Willy's. I don't believe there's anyone in town who was alive when the building really was a chocolate shop.

Jesse jumps in back with Faye, and greets, "I didn't eat lunch in preparation for tonight."

Mama laughs. "I guess we'd better order you two bibs in case you go wild."

"Yes, ma'am," he says. "I think that's a mighty fine idea."

When we arrive, Mama pulls up to the valet stand instead of finding her own space. She tells us, "By the looks of it, we'd have to park a mile down the road to find a spot."

The whole front lawn of the club is filled with picnic tables. Folks are milling about as far as the eye can see. The excitement in the air is as thick as if we're here to witness the Second Coming.

I spy Uncle Jed, Auntie Lee, and the cousins at a table near the fryers. It's Jed's usual spot, so he can be first in line when the fish production starts, which is six thirty every year, like clockwork. They greet us with hugs, kisses, and warnings.

Auntie Lee cautions, "Cootie's on a tear. Watch your backs."

"What's up?" Mama wants to know.

"She says she's got the most delicious gossip and she can't wait to share it."

Mama groans, "Sweet Jesus, what now?"

"She won't say until the shortcake is served. She's enjoying building up everyone's excitement."

Mama shakes her head and announces, "That can only mean one thing."

"What's that?" I ask.

"It means she's got real dirt on someone," Auntie Lee declares.

Mama adds, "If Cootie doesn't start yacking right away, it's not just speculation, she has a reliable source to prove the authenticity of her news. She likes to draw out the anticipation as long as possible, then spill the beans when she's got a crowd foaming at the mouth in excitement."

Auntie Lee shakes her head. "I wonder what poor sucker she's set her sights on tonight?"

"I guess we'll know soon enough," I say. "In the meantime, check out Jed. It looks like we're about to get this party started."

My uncle is doing deep knee bends and lunges while checking his watch. He's preparing to launch himself at the food line as soon as Chef Jarvis fires his starter pistol, signaling the opening of this year's catfish fry.

Auntie Lee shakes her head. "I don't know why he always persists in doing this. They inevitably burn the first few fish while they try to get the oil just right."

Amelia walks over in her tie-dyed gypsy skirt in time to answer, "Daddy says he likes the burned ones, but I think he's compensating for never being any good at sports in school. Like if he can outrun every other man here, even if it means eating burned fish, he's some kind of latent track star."

Auntie Lee confirms, "Third trombone was his most impressive extracurricular activity. It's a good thing he had such a great personality."

Chef Jarvis blows the ceremonial whistle that's been hanging from his neck for the last thirty years of this event. He shouts out in excitement, "It's on in five, four, three, two, one!" He fires his pistol into the air and Jed, along with at least twenty other men, take off like their britches have just been hit by a live grenade.

It's all good-natured until Harold Wilcox trips Uncle Jed. He stops to say something to him before speeding past like a wannabe roadrunner in those old-timey cartoons.

Jed doesn't get up right away or make his move for the coveted first in line. Instead, he slowly stands up and walks back to us.

Auntie Lee asks, "Are you sick, Jed? Why aren't you up there fighting for your fish?"

He looks like a herd of elephants have just walked across his grave. "I don't think I'm in the mood for fish tonight. Why don't we all go over to Filene's? I'm buying."

"What in the world are you going on about, Jed?" Auntie Lee demands. "We want catfish."

My uncle shakes his head. "Harold just gave me a little head's up." At our expectant expressions he continues, "Looks like Cootie's gossip has something to do with our family."

Mama's eyes crease and she purses her lips tightly. "Cootie's nothing but a low-down bullying bitch. I say we stand our ground."

Personally, I'm more interested in running. I don't hold for intimidation, but darned if I want my family caught off guard. I can't think of a thing she could say against us, so I don't believe she can corroborate her meanness, whatever it is. At the same time, I think it's best to know what her lies are before we formulate our response.

Jesse sides with Uncle Jed, "I could sure go for a nice filet."

Davis and Beau have joined our throng and heard enough to weigh in. Davis decides, "I'm in the mood for a T-bone."

Beau announces, "I'm going to have a little chat with Shelby." He walks away with all of our eyes glued to his back.

Chapter Thirty-Five

Beau storms right past Cootie and takes Shelby's arm, leading her away from her mother. We can't tell what he's saying to her, but he's clearly giving her what for. Zach showed up after Beau and stands next to his make-believe girlfriend, but he doesn't come to Shelby's defense. Instead he takes a turn and has some words of his own for her. I wish I were a fly on the wall so I could hear what's going on.

Cootie finally notices that her child is getting a tongue lashing and storms across the lawn to Shelby's aid. She points a vicious finger at my cousin and joggles it back and forth like a metronome gone mad. Beau takes a step toward her as if to intimidate her by his stature, but the gossip queen of Creek Water, Missouri holds strong. She does not appear to be backing down.

Mama says, "Good lord, I wonder what they're saying."

Auntie Lee decides, "Maybe now's a good time for a steak, after all."

"Ladies, give the man a chance, will ya?" Davis drawls, smiling ear-to-ear, clearly enjoying the scene enfolding in front of us.

Jesse tries to remove himself by taking Mama's arm and saying, "Gracie, I'm not feeling too well. Would you mind driving me back to your place to pick up my car?"

Mama pulls away, "No, sir, if you're feeling poorly, you'd best take yourself off to the pool and lie down on a lounger. I'm not going anywhere."

Beau raises his voice and we hear him clear as day threaten, "You better watch your step, Ms. Wilcox, or I'll be coming after *you*." The whole club stares at them with their mouths hanging wide open and their eyes darting around to see if anyone has any idea what's going on.

Not one word is spoken until Cootie retaliates, "*You* are no position to threaten *me*, Beauregard Frothingham."

At that, Shelby steps forward and takes her mama's arm. She whispers something in her ear and then Cootie adds, "This isn't over."

Beau replies, "Yes, ma'am, it surely is." Then he nods his head once to Shelby before walking in our direction.

We twitch around while we wait. When he arrives, we demand, "What did you say to them? What's going on?"

Beau answers, "I just told them that we know Cootie's up to something and she'd best reconsider sharing it if she knows what's good for her."

Auntie Lee demands, "How'd she take that?"

Beau turns to his mama and answers, "She said that she had a score to settle with you and Auntie Grace and that she's gonna make you rue the day you messed with her. Something about ketchup?"

Mama looks mad enough to bite through steel. "I'm gonna

rip every last strand of hair out of that woman's ridiculous head!"

Uncle Jesse stands in front of her to block her path. "I don't think that's the best idea, Gracie. I say we take Jed up on his offer for steak and let the dust settle."

Chapter Thirty-Six

Mama squares her shoulders, steps around Jesse, and strides purposefully toward the buffet table. I guess she's not interested in going out for a steak. The rest of the family follows closely behind as though we're a battalion on our way to the front line. We're covering Mama's back against any surprise attacks.

Mama serves herself a mixed salad and one ear of corn before heading back to the family table. Her head is high and there's determination in every step. She's signaling to everyone watching that Cootie's in for the fight of her life if she decides to take on our family.

I wonder if someone is sneaking around with a little betting book, placing odds on the outcome of tonight's event. I can't pretend to know who would reign supreme in a knock-down drag-out with Cootie on one side and Mama and Auntie Lee on the other. The Frothingham gals have plenty of spunk, but Cootie Wilcox is full of spit and vinegar. I can say this though, if Mama and Auntie Lee don't win the battle, they'll wage another until they're the victors of the war. This could go on for years.

I sidle up to Beau and ask, "What did you say to Shelby?"

He looks like steam is still wafting off him. "I told her that once her family does harm to mine, there's no chance in hell I'll ever consider a relationship with her again."

"What did she say to that?" I feel like I'm in the middle of a junior high school pissing contest. I'm equal parts scared and invigorated. It's a heady mixture, for sure.

"She said she'd talk to her mama."

"She must like you a whole bunch, Beau. You still feel a pull?" I ask.

"I won't know the answer to that until I see how tonight works out," he replies, unknowingly giving away the truth that his feelings are already compromised.

I try to catch Zach's eye, but he seems determined not to look at me. Either that or he's too far away to notice me. I wonder if he knows something. While the fish smells like heaven on earth, my stomach is in such a whirl, I don't know how I'm going to safely swallow anything for fear it will come right back up on me.

Amelia saunters over next to me. "I think we need ourselves a cocktail. What do you say we hit the bar and come back for food later?"

Normally, I'd ask Mama to look after Faye, but given a rumble may break out, I fetch her before following my cousin up to the veranda where drinks are being served. I order an icy cold beer and drink half of it down before Amelia and I find a place to sit.

"I feel like we're being watched," I tell her.

"Ya think?" she laughs. "Everyone here's trying to decide if we're running scared from Cootie, giving credibility to her lies, or if we're going to stand up and spit in the eye of the devil."

"It would help if we knew what her gossip is."

"It surely would. I have an idea," she says. Amelia thinks I should talk to Zach, but he appears to be doing everything he can to steer clear of me. Which, to be honest, is annoying the crap out of me while making me feel even more determined to find him.

I drink down the rest of my beer and leave Amelia in charge of Faye before running into the clubhouse to freshen up. I attempt to fluff my hair and reapply my lipstick, but my eyes are drawn to the changing room where Zach and I hid from Mrs. Wilcox the day of my baby shower. Lordy, my body ignites at the memory. Zach has never so much as kissed my lips, but I feel like he's somehow laid claim to me. How in the world has that happened?

It takes me a solid ten minutes to still my racing heart and administer proper attention to my hair and face. I finally walk out of the locker room, determined to find out the answer once and for all, but after searching everywhere, I can't locate Zach. He's disappeared.

Shelby is sitting by herself under a tree, looking like someone just kicked her dog, so in a moment of crazy I walk over to her. She eyeballs me intently, clearly ready to do battle. But the last thing I want is a fight. I say, "So, you and Beau. I hear you're trying to get him interested again."

"Of course, I'm not," she declares. "Who've you been talking to?"

"Look, Shelby," I tell her, "I don't like you very much. You're too much like your mama for my taste." The look on her face tells me that my accusation hits a raw nerve. So, I drop the bomb,

"But just because I don't like you doesn't mean that Beau can't. Do you understand what I'm saying?"

Now she's totally confused. "No."

"I'm saying that Beau is a big boy and has the right to follow his own heart. If his heart leads him to you, so be it. But you'd better believe him when he says that if you mess with his family, he'll drop you faster than a fish fresh out of the fryer. And he won't give you a second chance, either. Beau is loyal to those he loves. If you're ever lucky enough to have him love you, you'll understand what an incredible gift that is."

I've definitely caught her off guard. She doesn't seem to know how to respond. She finally settles on, "I can't control my mama. I can't make her stay quiet about something if she's determined to say it."

"Maybe you can appeal to her motherly instincts, then. Let her know that she holds your happiness in her hands and that if she loves you, she'll back away from whatever nastiness is up her sleeve."

Shelby surprises me when she confesses, "I don't want folks to think I'm like her."

"Then don't be like her," I say. "Find the strength to be your own person and do the right thing."

Chapter Thirty-Seven

I'm pretty sure Zach has already gone. Back at the table with the family, I manage a few bites of catfish and coleslaw, scanning the crowd for him the whole while, but he never shows his face again. Cootie remains quiet after the shortcake dessert has been served, so it appears tonight's fireworks have been canceled. Thank the good Lord for that. Yet, I can't help but wonder how long we have until she decides she can't stay quiet any longer and starts peddling her trash to whomever will listen.

Beau and Shelby spend the night sending scorching glances back and forth to each other. Beau's looks are of the warning variety, while Shelby's are unadulterated longing. Davis has gone to the veranda for a drink, Mama and Auntie Lee are sitting on a bench under a tree plotting their defensive strategy, and the uncles are having a contest over who can eat the most. Amelia has been chattering non-stop in my ear, but I can't tell you one word she's said. My thoughts are one hundred percent on Cootie and her gossip.

At eight thirty, I inform my family that Faye and I are going home. Uncle Jed will take Mama and Jesse home with him and Auntie Lee. If I were having fun, I'd have stayed until they kicked me out, but this night has become a chore, plain and simple.

I place Faye in her carrier, say my goodbyes, and head toward the valet. It looks like I'm leaving at the perfect time 'cause a line starts to form behind me. Someone steps too close and I'm about to turn around and ask for space when I feel hot breath on my neck. My insides puddle and I know without looking that it's Zach. "Heya, Emmie," he purrs. He's close enough I can smell his intoxicating manly scent.

"Heya, Zach, where've you been?"

"Off, thinking."

"Why in the world would you do that when there's catfish to eat?"

He ignores my question and says, "Would you mind giving me a ride home? I think I may have had one too many."

"What about Shelby?" I ask.

"I s'pose she'll ride home with her folks."

"Didn't she come with you?"

He disregards my question again and repeats his. "Will you give me a ride or not?"

If my insides weren't flying around like I was on some sketchy carnival ride before, they sure are now. "Sure," I say, as one of the parking attendants pulls up with Mama's car.

Zach holds opens the backdoor before taking Faye's carrier from me and securing the contraption just like I taught him the night of our non-date. He doesn't seem the least bit incapacitated. Then he opens the passenger side door and gets in while I climb into the recently vacated driver's seat.

"Where to?" I ask.

"Just take me to your house. I'll walk from there."

"What do you mean you'll walk from there? It'll take you twenty-five minutes to walk into town from Mama's place. Just give me your address and I'll drive you."

"I don't live in town," he says.

I'm not sure why I thought he did. I guess because most of the younger, single folks who reside in Creek Water live in the heart of our growing downtown. "Where do you live?" I ask.

"On the other side of your aunt and uncle."

"No, you don't! I've never seen your car over there."

"I park in the garage," he says.

"But I've never even seen you drive by."

"How often do you hang out in front of your house?" he asks.

He's got a point. I'm out back plenty, but the only time I'm in the front of the house is when I'm coming or going. But still, you'd think I'd have seen him before now, or someone would have mentioned he was our neighbor. "Are you renting?" I ask.

"Nope. I bought the place right after I returned to Creek Water."

"Why in the world?" I demand. My best friend from grade school used to live there so I know for a fact the house has four bedrooms and three bathrooms. It's not ostentatious, but it's big, and not the kind of home you'd expect a bachelor to purchase.

"I liked the house," he answers.

"It's a great street," I agree. "But isn't it a tad much for just you?"

"I don't plan on being there by myself forever," Zach says.

A lump forms in my throat at the thought of him living only two houses away from Mama with a wife and kids. I know that wife won't be Shelby, but still.

I keep peeking at his profile while driving down the road that leads out of the club. He looks swoon-worthy handsome despite being ruffled and tired. I ask, "Do you know what Cootie had up her sleeve tonight?"

He shakes his head, "No, ma'am, I sure don't. I expect it was nothing good, though."

"She'd sure be one heck of a mother-in-law."

"That would be my guess," he answers, but he doesn't say any more than that.

We drive the rest of the way home in silence. My brain is full of questions that I want to ask, but I get a vibe that Zach doesn't want me to ask them.

By the time I pull into Mama's driveway, I feel all kinds of conflicting emotions, ranging from intense attraction to frustration. Stating the obvious, I announce, "We're here."

I'm about to open the car door when Zach grabs my arm to stop me. I hear crickets chirping through his open window; they sound like they're trying to convey an urgent message. He checks over his shoulder, "Faye's asleep, let's sit awhile," he says.

The summer air combined with my current company is keeping the car's internal temperature far warmer than I'm comfortable with. "Okay. What do you want to talk about?"

He eyes me longingly and whispers, "I don't want to talk."

Chapter Thirty-Eight

"If you don't want to talk, what do you want to do?" I ask softly, not realizing I've been holding my breath until I start to feel lightheaded.

Zach doesn't answer with words. Instead, with the hand that's still holding my arm, he pulls me toward him. I go willingly, hypnotized by his hazel eyes. He groans, "I've wanted to do this since I first saw you in your uncles' office." A split second later his lips are on mine, telling me a story of their own.

His kiss is hot and hungry, while somehow sweet and searching. I taste the beer on his breath, but more prominently I taste desire. He declares ownership as surely as Christopher Columbus did when setting foot on the new world. I nearly hand off the keys to the kingdom.

I come to my senses a tad later than I should and pull back with a jolt. Zach looks totally perplexed. "What are you doing?" I demand.

"I was kissing you," he says. "You seemed to be enjoying it."

"Zach, you can't just kiss me after the way you treated me the other night at dinner. You were just awful to me!"

He looks down and his lap for a moment and replies, "I guess

I was just upset about something."

"What?" I demand. "Are you still mad at me for not going to that dance with you when we were in high school?" His eyes bug open like he's surprised I'm bringing it up. "For your information I wanted to go out with you, I just didn't want to go to a dance at the club."

"Why?" he seems totally taken aback.

"You see how Cootie is around my family. Well, she was worse when I was a kid. She made my mama feel so bad that we quit the club all together. I used to do everything in my power to stay out of the way of her and her gang. Going to a dance there would have put me right in their sights."

"Why didn't you just tell me that. We could have done something else."

"I might have done that, but you went out of your way to avoid me. I couldn't seem to catch your eye for anything in this world after I said no to the dance."

"You could have called me," he says.

"I suppose I could have. But Zach, I was sixteen years old and had pretty limited experience with the opposite sex. I was scared to call, especially because you started acting like I was a contagious disease."

"I'll have you know, Emmie, that it took all the courage I could muster to ask you out. I wasn't much to look at in high school. I was crushed when you said no."

"I'm sorry, Zach. I really am. Can we finally put that episode behind us? More than anything I'd like to go out with you, but not if you can't forgive me."

Zach leans in again and very slowly touches his lips to mine.

It's just a hint of contact before he says, "I forgive you, but only if you'll forgive me for acting like such a class A jackass."

This time I'm the one who initiates intimacy. I say everything I can think of in my touch. Including, "I forgive you," "I'm sorry," and "If you play your cards right, I might just let you take me to another dance."

My daughter seems to open a psychic channel and wakes up, letting out a squawk so loud that Zach jumps back like he's tripped an alarm. Which maybe he has. Maybe Faye, unable to say what's on her mind, is suggesting we cool it a bit until things are more settled between us. If that isn't a fanciful notion, I don't know what is.

Zach kisses me one more time before letting go of me and getting out of the car. He comforts Faye, "Hello, sweetheart. What do you say we get you inside and put you to bed properly?"

Faye makes an adorable cooing sound as if agreeing to his suggestion.

He carries my baby onto the porch while I haul her diaper bag. Once I unlock the door, we go inside, and Zach takes the baby straight into the back of the house where the bedrooms are. He correctly guesses which room is mine—I'm guessing the old movie posters on the wall were a giveaway—and places her carrier gently on my bed. He unbuckles her, picks her up, and holds her close while singing a lullaby in her ear the whole while. In no time, she's sound asleep again. This time with her head on his shoulder.

"She likes you," I tell him.

"I like her," he replies. "I like her mama, too." He says this in a way that causes the hair on my arms to stand on end and my central nervous system to feel like it's been invaded by butterflies.

I boldly ask, "And you're not mad at me anymore?"

"I promise I'm not. I'm going to start acting like a grown-up from this moment on."

"No more games?" I demand.

"Remember when I told you about the woman I liked who didn't feel the same way about me. I guess I feel like once bitten twice shy."

"But I wasn't the one who bit you, Zach."

He doesn't answer right away. Instead, he smiles almost like it hurts to do so. After a long moment, he says, "What about you? You have a baby with another man. Are you sure you're ready for another relationship after losing Armand?"

Gah, Armand! I keep forgetting about him. I want to tell Zach the truth, but I dare not until I know I can trust him. He's obviously friends with Shelby, although god knows what he's getting out of the relationship. I can't tell anyone outside the family before I know they can be trusted. And sadly, I don't trust Zach yet. What in the world does that say about me that I'd kiss a man I don't fully trust?

"So, what do we do now?" I ask.

"Let's just take it one day at a time."

"I guess that'll be okay," I say.

Zach lays Faye down in her crib and gently tucks her blanket around her. He stares at her for a long moment and then says, "I'm sorry her daddy never got to meet her. She's as sweet as they come."

I feel guilty that her daddy never got to meet her too, but I can't say I'm sorry about it. I can't imagine how hard it would be to raise my child with a total stranger. And if he didn't want to be a part of her life, I'd feel even worse knowing that I conceived her with a deadbeat.

I follow Zach to the front door, and announce, "Armand is part of my past. I would not have agreed to go out to dinner with you the other night if I weren't ready to move on, and I sure as heck wouldn't have kissed you tonight if that weren't the case."

Zach says, "I'm glad to hear it. I'll pick you up for work tomorrow morning at nine."

"Okay," I agree. "But you don't have a car. I'll pick you up and drive you over to the club to get it."

"I forgot about that," he says. "Okay, you pick me up, but let's go into town together. You can drop me to get my car after work."

I open the door to see him out, but he doesn't go right away. Instead, he pulls me back into his arms and ever so lightly touches his lips to my forehead. It's as gentle as a whisper.

I replay the image all night long and hope against hope that Zach is telling the truth and doesn't start acting all weird again. I'm not sure I can handle much more drama.

Chapter Thirty-Nine

I ring Zach's doorbell the next morning at nine o'clock sharp. His house is a classic craftsman-style with a wide front porch and a low-pitched gable roof. There are exposed wood beams and tapered square columns in a dark brown that contrast the lighter blue-gray color of the paint. The clean masculine lines are softened by blooming scarlet buckeye shrubs out front and the Portside wicker rocking chairs on the porch.

I hear him yell, "Come on in!"

I tentatively peek through the front door and call out, "It's me, Emmie."

"Come on back. I'm in the kitchen."

I would never have recognized this house as the one my girlfriend's family lived in. Zach has done a monumental amount of work. The interior beams used to be painted white to match the color of the ceiling, but Zach's had them stripped and stained back to their original glory. He's done the same to the built-in cabinetry.

I walk through a dining room furnished with a mission-style table and chairs and a large built-in window seat, then into the kitchen. In contrast to the rest of the house, the kitchen is light and airy. Zach is standing next to the stove, stirring something in a saucepan. "You haven't eaten yet, have you?"

He turns around all freshly showered and snazzy in his pressed chinos and linen shirt. His feet are bare, and I stare at his toes like they're an intimate appendage. He says, "I figured we could work over breakfast. I've got all the measurements we need to get started. We can head over to the factory when we're done."

I sit down on a stool at the counter and ask, "What are you making?"

"I've got a German apple pancake in the oven and I'm whipping up a caramelized pecan and maple syrup for the top."

Drool pools in my mouth for a multitude of reasons. "That sounds delicious. Do you cook a lot?"

"Only when I'm trying to impress someone." He smiles at me coyly.

This morning's Zach is very different from the Zach of previous encounters. He's open and warm, which makes me think he meant what he said last night and has finally forgiven me. "Lucky me," I say. "As far as I'm concerned, you can show off any time you want."

He comes around from the stove to stand next to me. Then he gives me the sweetest kiss imaginable. My blood turns hot like molten lava and my body suddenly feels like it weighs a thousand pounds—I couldn't move from this spot if my life depended on it. "Thank you for driving me home last night," he says afterwards.

"You're welcome," I answer breathlessly. "So last night wasn't just a one off? We're kissing now?"

He groans deep in the back of his throat like he's in pain. "We're definitely kissing now."

"What about Shelby?" I ask. I'm all for kissing, but I'm not if he's going to keep going around town pretending to be her boyfriend.

"I called her when I got home last night and told her she needed to find someone else to make Beau jealous with."

"I bet that didn't go over well," I say, trying to keep happiness out of my voice.

"Like a lead balloon," he confirms. "But she knows I'm serious."

"Why are you friends with her, anyway?" I want to know.

"Shelby was the first person to welcome me back to town when I came home. She brought a pie," he says.

I arch my eyebrow questioningly. "You sure she wasn't just trying to get into your pants?" I blush as soon as the words come out of my mouth.

He looks shocked by my bold question and answers, "No, ma'am. She was busy trying to get into Beau's."

"Ah," I say. "So, she was using you for information about my cousin."

"Probably. But she really is a nice girl when you get to know her. It can't have been easy growing up with a mother like Cootie."

"If you say so." But I'm still not convinced she isn't Cootie's mini me, despite what she said last night.

Zach serves up the most delicious breakfast I've ever eaten. I didn't even think I was hungry until I take my first bite. When the forkful of puffed pancake and caramelized apple hits my mouth, I eat like I haven't eaten in a month. I barely keep up my part of the conversation, I'm that busy appreciating his efforts.

When Zach clears our dishes, he says, "I went ahead and downloaded some software last night and plugged in the measurements of the model unit."

I'm surprised. "I thought we were going to do that together?"

"It's tedious work, so I figured I'd get it done so we didn't feel guilty about not going right in to work."

"That's sweet," I tell him. I mean, first he does my work and then he feeds me? Zachary Grant has all the earmarks of a winner boyfriend. Although, we have a way to go before we hit that point. I'll have to tell him about Armand for sure and I don't look forward to that. I fret he'll take the news as well as he did when he learned of my tequila intolerance. I can't imagine him being impressed by my loose behavior. But that's a bridge I'll have to cross when I get to it. It the meantime, I'm going to enjoy the ride there.

Chapter Forty

Zach and I go straight to the third floor when we arrive at the old sewing machine factory. We start to conceptualize the space by adding as many details as we can to make our model look warm and welcoming while still portraying it as a cool millennial loft. Let's face it, our buyers probably aren't going to have families yet.

The uncles arrive shortly after noon. They both look considerably less perky than normal. I greet them, "I thought we wouldn't see you until after lunch."

"I'm not sure we're ever going to eat again," Jesse groans.

"I doubled up on my cholesterol medication this morning," Jed adds. "I feel like my innards have been deep fried."

"How long did you stay at the club last night?" Zach asks.

"We closed the place down at midnight," Jesse answers. "And before you tell us they close at eleven, we know. The staff wasn't too pleased with us, but we tipped them enough to make it worth their while."

"Did Cootie do anything after I left?" I inquire. I don't say "we" because my family doesn't need to know anything about me and Zach yet. Certainly not before I know what we are to each other.

Jed shakes his head. "No, ma'am. She left shortly after you did. I think Beau ruined her fun."

"What about Beau and Shelby?" I ask. "Did they spend any time together?"

Jesse answers this one. "They sniffed around each other all night like dogs in heat, but nothing came of it."

Jed says, "Auntie Lee made sure of that. Every time it looked like they were homing in on each other, she'd ask Beau to do something for her that would take him as far away from Shelby as possible. Then she kept Shelby locked in her sights so Shelby couldn't follow him without her knowing about it."

No one seems to be concerned that they're discussing Shelby's interest in Beau right in front of Zach, her supposed boyfriend. So, for sake of fun or stirring the pot, I look at Zach and say, "Well, Shelby's with Zach anyway, so I'm sure she's not even interested in Beau." All three men laugh out loud at my pronouncement.

Jed says, "Please, the whole town knows that Zach's just helping Shelby out to make Beau jealous."

The men confirm this by nodding their heads.

"Well then, what was the point of pretending?" I demand.

Zach comes over to me and puts his arm around me in a very proprietary manner and answers, "As you know, it was all for show." Then he pulls me close and kisses me tenderly on the mouth before adding, "But that show's over."

My uncles are enthusiastic about Zach's display of interest.

Jesse hoots out loud and exclaims, "I approve!"

"So, do I," Jed adds.

I ask Zach, "What happened to not 'defining us' and keeping everything on the down-low?"

"I didn't take out an ad in the newspaper," he says. "But there's no way we can sneak around behind your family's backs; they'd sniff us out for sure."

"We're seeing each other?" I ask. It seems that Zach has made a few decisions without discussing them with me. Although, he's rightly interpreted my interest.

"Well, yeah," he answers. "I figured that if we're kissing, we're seeing each other." My face turns beet red. The uncles are enthralled by the conversation we're having in front of them.

"Wait until Lee hears!" Jed exclaims.

"Please don't tell Mama or Auntie Lee," I beg.

Jesse looks up from his phone guiltily. "Too late," he says.

"You've been texting them?" I demand.

"Well, yeah," he answers. "Don't get all worked up, Emmie. They've been placing bets on whether or not something would happen with Zach."

"They have?" I demand. "Why?"

Jed answers, "I don't know, two attractive young people working together, living nearly next door, seems like the perfect storm, dontcha think?"

When he puts it that way, I start to worry that maybe the trouble might not be over. I sure as heck am not looking for a storm. I want peace with plenty of sunshine and maybe a donut. But Zach is smiling like he's on top of the world, so maybe he wants the same thing I do. Only time will tell.

Chapter Forty-One

Zach has a meeting with the plumbers on the second floor, so he heads off shortly after Jed and Jesse come up to check on things. He boldly kisses me right in front of my uncles again. It's one thing to be kissing, it's another entirely to be doing so in front of an audience. We'll have to discuss the difference when we're private.

Once Zach walks out the door, Jesse makes his way over to me and says, "Well, well, well, Miss Emmeline, it looks like you've got yourself a suitor."

"I guess so," I reply, unable to control the smile on my face.

"Your mama's going to flip a biscuit."

"Hand me your phone," I order. I look at his texts to Mama and Auntie Lee.

Jesse: Y'all, Zach's just gone and told us that he and Emmie are a thing. They kissed right in front of us!

Mama: I knew it! I knew that boy was interested ever since that brunch at the Steamboat. He couldn't keep his eyes to himself.

Auntie Lee: He *has* been asking about Emmie an awful lot.

Jesse: Whoops, she just caught me texting … more later.

Trills of excitement ripple through me as soon as I read that Zach has been asking about me. I feel so light that if I jumped up, I figure I'd float right through the air.

Jesse asks, "You going to tell him about Armand?"

Talk about a buzz kill. "Yes. But do me a favor and alert the family that I'll do it when I'm ready. I don't want anyone jumping the gun like they did when they invented Armand."

"If you say so, but I think that all turned out pretty well. It's sure kept Cootie and her club ladies off your back."

"I guess," I agree. "But now I have to figure out how to tell Zach that Armand never was. It adds a whole new layer of anxiety I'd just as soon not have to deal with."

"Why anxiety?" he asks.

"What if he judges me harshly and doesn't want to be involved with me?" I ask.

"Emmie girl, you think that boy hasn't had a bedmate or two in his time?"

I grimace. "I'm sure he has, but he didn't get anyone pregnant."

"First of all, how do you know that? And secondly, a baby outside of marriage isn't just the mama's doing. It isn't shameful, it's just harder, that's all."

"Jesse, women take the brunt of folk's judgment when there's a baby and no ring. As unfair as that is, it's the plain truth. Have you ever heard anyone talk about unwed fathers?"

He truly thinks before answering, "I guess not."

"Yet they discuss unwed mothers like they're discussing diarrhea or something."

"Emmie, I don't think anyone is looking down on you because of Faye."

"Only because Auntie Lee concocted a fake fiancé for me. A dead daddy makes my baby's start in life acceptable. Why else would Auntie Lee have bothered to make him up?"

Jesse sighs. "Girl, you got me there. Just know the family has your back and we're not going to let anyone talk bad about you."

"How are you going to stop them?" I demand.

"You want me to tell Zach about Armand?" he asks.

"Dear god, no! In fact, I want you to text Mama and Auntie Lee and tell them to keep their yaps shut about it. I'll tell Zach when I'm good and ready."

He nods his head. "Okay, but you let us know if you need our help."

The best part of coming home is being back in the bosom of folks who love you so much they'd do anything for you. It's also the worst part. Sometimes they do too much, like creating a phantom fiancé named after a famous movie star.

After Jed and Jesse get back to work, I open up my laptop and start looking for fixtures to decorate our model. It's the perfect distraction. I finalize the order I'll send to Lexi, then I choose furniture and artwork. I even order bath towels and dishes. I want the place so finished looking that when we open it to the public, prospective buyers feel like they're arriving at a dinner party.

As soon as I finish up, I shut down my laptop and grab my purse. I take the service elevator down to the first floor and go out the backdoor. I head over to Davis's workshop to look over his inventory, to see what we can use. Davis is the elusive one in the family. Even after getting caught in a compromising position with one of the club ladies, he managed to stay unaffected by the gossip. I wonder if he has any suggestions for me about how to tell Zach the truth about Armand, and whether or not I should go public with the information.

Outside, the majesty of the mighty Mississippi keeps me company and fuels my confidence that everything is going to work out. Strolling next to such a mighty thoroughfare makes me feel positive and bold. Surely my little drama isn't even a blip compared to all the living that's taken place on her banks. I let this rush of optimism wash over me and hope against hope that I'll come out on top once the truth is known.

Chapter Forty-Two

Davis's workshop is in the old Creeky Button Factory. The uncles plan to renovate it after they're done with the sewing machine factory. I walk through the sliding barn door out back and immediately hear old Southern rock and roll blaring. Davis is here. It's his signature sound.

The building looks like it hasn't been touched in decades. It's one big wide-open space filled with partially built furniture. There are sawhorses and workbenches throughout. I see my cousin sanding down an armoire wearing safety goggles and a bandanna across his face. I wave as he looks up.

He stops his electric sander and greets, "Hey, Emmie. You here for the grand tour?"

I smile back. "I am. I'm also looking for a little bit of advice."

"Good, cause everything you see here is the whole tour. What's on your mind?"

"First of all," I say, "I need a great piece for our model condominium at the sewing machine factory. What do you have?"

He leads me across the expanse of the first floor, which is a similar size to the building we're currently renovating. Behind several partitions, he says, "Pick whatever you want that doesn't have a red tag on in. Those are all sold."

There must be forty pieces and most of them are marked. "I love the light stain you use. It looks so natural."

"It looks so natural because I don't use stain, I use linseed oil. It's a more rustic and organic finish which fits my aesthetic better."

I walk over to a light-grained craftsman-style armoire. "Tell me about this one."

"That one's built out of maple. It's a standard design that works well in either bedrooms or living rooms. I can install a wardrobe bar or shelving, depending on what you want it for."

"I'll take it," I say. "I also need to choose some pieces for Emmeline's. What do you have?"

"Same armoires, I just won't put doors on them. Then you can design the shelving however you see fit."

After picking out four more pieces for the store, I say, "Now, about that advice."

He arches an eyebrow. "I'm all ears."

"You know the truth about Faye's start in life," I say. He nods once, so I continue. "And you know how your mama saw fit to invent a fiancé for me?"

"I do."

"Well, say I start dating someone. How do you figure I tell them that Armand isn't real and that Faye's daddy is a stranger to me?"

"You talking about Zach?" he asks.

"How do you know about that already?" I demand.

He lifts his phone in the air. "Uncle Jesse. It cuts down time on having to tell everyone what's going on."

"My god, y'all are like a bunch of gossipy hens. What did he tell you?"

"Just that you and Zach had reached the kissing portion of your courtship. He added me and Amelia to the text after he told our mamas."

Lord, these people are going to be the end of me. I say, "I'm trying to figure out when to tell Zach about Armand."

"You're better off doing it sooner than later, I suspect. Trouble has a way of multiplying if you wait too long."

"But how do I tell him? I mean, just coming out and saying it would make me look bad."

"Emmie, I don't have a script for you, but I know you best hurry up and come clean. No one likes to hear a truth different than the one they've been led to believe, especially when there are feelings involved."

"You speaking from experience?" I ask.

"Yes, ma'am."

"What happened to you, Davis?"

"If I want folks to know, I'll send out a group text, okay?"

"You don't have to be snotty about it," I say. "Besides, I didn't get to decide for myself."

He runs his hand through his wavy hair. "I'm not bein' snotty, I'm just endeavoring to keep some things to myself. As you've recently been reminded, that's kind of hard to do in this family."

"Do you know Zach well?" I change the subject.

"Not really, but from what I understand he's a pretty upright guy. Just sit him down and tell him it was my mama's fault."

"Thanks, Davis." I give him a hug. "If you ever feel like talking, I promise to listen and not send out a family message telling everyone what's going on with you."

"I'll keep that in mind," he says. "In the meantime, when do you want me to have your furniture delivered?"

"It'll probably be a couple weeks; I'll keep you posted."

I say goodbye and decide to head home to continue ordering stock for Emmeline's. Mama's taken Faye over to visit with Zach's mom. I expect the two of them will have plenty to discuss after Jesse gets done with his little text-a-thon this morning. I'm suddenly looking forward to some peace and quiet while I try to figure out how to tell Zach about everything. In a perfect world, I'd want to wait a few weeks before I say anything, but I'm not sure it's wise to wait that long.

Chapter Forty-Three

By the time Mama brings Faye home, I've already spent twenty thousand dollars on merchandise for the store. I'm purchasing from companies I already have a relationship with from my years at Silver Spoons. I'll eventually have to make a trip to New York and go to the Merchandise Mart to choose a few focal pieces, but that can probably wait a couple of weeks. Once the walls go up and the space gets laid out, I'll know how I'm going to display the merchandise. The thought of leaving Faye makes my heart hurt. And I know I can't take her with me and accomplish everything I need to.

Mama walks through the front door looking like she's about to burst from happiness. She hands me my baby girl and says, "Zachary Grant, huh? I had a feeling about that boy."

"You did? Why didn't you say anything to me about it?"

"I didn't want to jinx it," Mama says.

I roll my eyes. "If you say so. Meanwhile, thanks to Auntie Lee, I need to figure out how to tell Zach about Armand."

"Why?" Mama asks.

"Oh, I don't know. Maybe so we don't start a relationship built on a lie."

"Seems to me it doesn't matter who Faye's daddy is. The only thing that matters is that he's not in the picture to cause any trouble."

I'm about to tell her that a lie of omission is still a lie when the doorbell rings. Mama claps her hand together. "I wonder if it's Zach."

I suppose it could be, although I think he's tied up in meetings all day. Mama turns around and nearly sprints to the door in excitement, but when she opens it, her whole posture slumps almost as if it's the grim reaper himself. "Shelby, what are you doing here?"

Shelby Wilcox is the last person I expected to show up on our doorstop. She looks positively deranged. Her blonde hair has escaped its confines and her clothes look like she slept in them last night. She doesn't wait for Mama to ask her in, she just charges forth like she's occupying enemy territory. She stalks right over to me and declares, "You!"

"Hi, Shelby, what are you doing here?"

"You've gone and stolen Zach from me," she accuses.

"I've done no such thing. Zach was never yours to steal. You were just using him to get to Beau."

"But now I'll never make Beau jealous, and it's all your fault."

"Why do you need to make him jealous?" I ask. "Why can't he just like you on your own merit?"

The concept seems to confound her. She finally says, "He didn't like me enough on my own merit to stay with me."

"The way I hear it, he just didn't want to make a declaration of undying love after only three dates," I tell her.

I'm not sure what I expect Shelby to do, but I do not expect her to break down and start crying. And she's no delicate crier, either. She's snuffling and snorting and carrying on like she's at the funeral of everybody she loves.

"Oh, dear," Mama says. She's not big on uncomfortable emotional scenes. She runs off to get a box of tissue and for some reason brings along a bottle of wine when she returns.

"Who's the wine for, Mama?" I ask her.

"Me. If this girl doesn't settle down, I'm gonna need a little something."

Shelby takes the tissues and grabs a handful before blowing her nose. She wilts in the middle of the floor instead of moving a few steps to a chair. "I don't know what to do," she says between hiccups.

Mama pulls the cork out of the wine and very uncharacteristically swigs from the bottle. I take it out of her hands and replace it with the baby. "Why don't you go put Faye down in her crib? I'll take over here."

She happily takes the baby and exits the room. I reach my hand out to Shelby. "Get up," I order. I pull her up to her feet then lead her over to the couch. Once she's settled, I add, "You gotta pull yourself together, girl." But from her quivering chin to her pained eyes, it doesn't look like that's going to happen anytime soon.

I try to divert her from her own concerns by asking, "What kind of gossip does your mama think she has on my family?"

Shelby cries even harder. She finally says, "I can't tell you."

"Why?"

"I just can't. Mama would kill me dead. But I promise I'm doing everything I can to keep her quiet. Although, I'm just not sure why I should bother now that Beau's gonna know there was nothing going on between me and Zach."

"I hate to be the one to break it to you, Shelby, but he's known from the start."

The look on her face is priceless, part deer in the headlights and part slug in her salad. "How do you know that?"

"He told me when I moved home."

"Oh, my god! What do I do now?" She starts bawling all over again.

I'm not sure how to handle this situation. I can't call Cootie, that's for sure. So, I do the next best thing, I pick up the phone and call Beau.

Chapter Forty-Four

"Hello?" Beau answers the phone.

"It's me, Emmie," I tell him by way of greeting.

"Zach Grant, huh?" he asks. Someone must have added Beau to the family text regarding the details of my love life.

"Yes, now shut up. I need you to do me a favor. Can you be over at Filene's at six o'clock tonight?"

"Sure. But why? If you want to chat about something, we can do it now."

"I don't need anything. I want you to meet a friend of mine. She needs some help and I think you might have the information she's looking for."

He asks, "You got a friend moving to town looking for real-estate?"

"Something like that," I reply. Shelby already lives here, but she is looking to acquire something, just not a house. "Give the hostess my name. I'll make the reservation."

"Thanks, cuz," Beau says. Of course, he may not be thanking me when the night is over, but there's only one way to clear the air between him and Shelby and that's for them to talk. We hang up before I share any of that with him, though.

Shelby has stopped crying and is now looking at me with wild-eyed fear. "What was that all about?"

"That was about you and Beau finally sitting down like adults and clearing the air," I tell her.

"We can't do that!" she practically yells.

"Why not?"

"Because, because, I don't know why, but I don't think it's a good idea. We already broke up once."

I remind her, "You broke up with him because you let your mama interfere and tell you to break up with him. Why don't you just explain that to Beau, and let him know that you want to date him, and you don't need him to pledge to forever just yet?"

"But Mama will freak out if I start dating him again and he hasn't committed to me exclusively."

"Why is it her business?" I ask.

She looks confused by my question. "Because she's my mama?"

"Look, Shelby, it's okay to have your own life and not share everything with your family." I know I'm pie-in-the-sky dreaming. But who knows, it might be possible to keep some things from them.

She eyes me dubiously, so I add, "You're a grown woman. Your mama already made her choice. She doesn't get to make yours as well." It's like I'm speaking Swahili or something.

She finally answers, "I've never thought about it like that. Mama's always made the decisions for our family."

"Because you've let her. Take back control of your life."

Shelby startles like a full-grown yeti has just walked into the room. "I look like heck in a hurricane. I can't meet Beau looking like this."

I pick up my phone and tell Siri to connect me to Filene's. After making a reservation for Shelby and Beau under my name, I say, "Come on into the bathroom with me. I'll help make you look presentable."

"Why would you do that?" she asks cautiously. "I mean, it's not like we're exactly friends."

"No, we're not," I confirm. "But Beau's my cousin and I love him. For some reason he's drawn to you. I'm doing this so he can either find some closure or get on with dating you, already. Limbo is no place for anyone to live."

"But you're still helping me," she says.

"You can't be all bad if Beau likes you," I tell her. "My cousin has good taste, but he's not one to suffer fools." I reach out to take her hand and pull her off the couch. She puts up as much resistance as a rag doll that's lost all of its stuffing.

I lead her into my bathroom and hand her a washcloth. "Splash some cool water on your face. I'll be right back."

I hurry into Mama's room to let her know what's up. There's no way I can involve myself in this without her knowing. She's lying on the bed playing with Faye. "Shelby's still here."

Mama looks up. "Show that girl the door, honey. We don't need one of Cootie's kind over here."

I ignore her and say, "I'm helping her get ready to meet Beau tonight at Filene's. Those two need to get a few things straight."

"Why in the world?" she demands. "As far as I can see, Shelby's digging her own grave with Beau and that's for the best. We don't want to help them reconcile," she reminds me as if I could've somehow forgotten where she stands on the issue.

"I think we want two different things, Mama. I want Beau to be happy. For some reason he thinks Shelby makes him happy. I want to make sure he really wants to walk away before whatever is between them ends for good."

"But Cootie …" Mama starts to say.

"Cootie nothing, Mama. I don't want that woman in our lives any more than you do. But maybe she'll give up targeting us if she's one of us."

"Do not underestimate that woman's degree of danger, honey," Mama says.

"I'm not," I assure her. "But the bottom line is that Beau is an adult and he should make his own choice without any interference from us."

Mama shakes her head. "Auntie Lee is going to scream the house down when she hears this."

"Then don't tell her. This isn't her business just as it isn't yours or mine. Stay quiet and let things unfold without trying to control the situation. And no gossiping about this, either."

"I am not a gossip," Mama defends. "I love my family and want to do right by them, is all."

"I know. But sometimes you and Auntie Lee get a little too involved. You can love and support us without steering the ship. You know what I'm saying?"

She cocks one eyebrow in response. She knows exactly what I'm saying. Now, she just needs to trust that the world will work out as it should without her interference. I'm so not holding my breath.

Chapter Forty-Five

By the time Shelby leaves to meet Beau, Mama's barely speaking to me. She walks into the kitchen while I'm washing lettuce. I ask, "Is Faye asleep?"

She shrugs her shoulders and answers, "Maybe."

"Maybe? What kind of answer is that?" I demand.

"I don't want to gossip about the people I love. She's either asleep or not. I guess you'll have to figure that out for yourself."

"Mama, you're being childish," I tell her. She's wearing a fresh dress and her makeup has been touched up, so I ask, "Where are you going?"

"Out." That's all she says.

"You aren't by any chance going out to dinner with Auntie Lee?" I ask.

"We have to eat," she declares defensively.

"Then eat here," I tell her. "I'm going to make you that salad I had at Filene's the other night."

"Sorry, we already have reservations. Lee's picking me up."

There are only two places in town that require dinner reservations. One is at the club, the other is Filene's. "Mama," I warn, "stay out of this. It's none of your affair."

She huffs dramatically, "My dinner is most certainly my affair." Then she grabs her purse and is out the door before I can respond. I do the only thing I can think of. I find my phone and call Beau. When his voicemail picks up, I say, "Change of plans, Beau. My friend will meet you at Mama's house. Come on over here instead of Filene's." Then I call Shelby to share the news.

She says, "But I just sat down."

"Get right back up," I tell her. "My mama and Beau's mama are on their way over there. I'm pretty sure they're looking to cause trouble."

Shelby sighs. "Maybe we shouldn't even bother. With all of our mamas against us, it'd be easier to ride a horse all the way to Paris, France."

"Give up if you want," I tell. "But I think Beau's worth fighting for."

After several beats, she says, "I'm on my way."

I hurry to set the table for two, going so far as lighting candles. I put the steaks I defrosted under the broiler and throw the salad together. By the time the doorbell rings, I have the baby in her car seat and I'm ready to walk out the door.

My cousin greets, "Hey, Emmie, where are you going? I thought you told me to come over here."

"I did," I tell him. "I just have to run to the store real quick. Watch the steaks under the broiler and take them out when the timer rings." I've got the baby in Mama's car and I'm pulled out of the driveway before he knows what's hit him.

I drive over to Zach's and lay on the horn as soon I see his car out front. He opens the door and waves. "Come on in. I was just going to put on some dinner."

I hang my head out the window and reply, "No, sir, dinner's on me. I got us reservations at Filene's."

I fill him in on what's going on as soon as he gets in the car. He asks, "Why are you helping them? I thought you didn't like Shelby."

"I don't," I tell him. "But I love Beau and he needs to make a decision about what he's going to do. He can't keep leading Shelby on, for her sake as well as the family's."

"What about us? If your mama and auntie Lee are at Filene's, surely they're going to be watching us like hawks out for a fresh kill."

"I'm counting on it," I say. "If we can keep them entertained enough, then hopefully they'll forget about Beau and Shelby."

Zach smiles brightly and declares, "I'm pleased to do my part."

I smile back. "Good. But just be warned, now that you've outed us to my family, they're going to get themselves involved in every little thing we do."

"Hopefully, not everything," he teases. My body gets all hot at the implication that we have some fun times in our future.

I warn, "I'm not the one who kissed you in front of them. Just so you know, they're going to consider anything we do fair game until we declare ourselves before the preacher." The words are out of my mouth before I can pull them back. *What have I just said?* No man wants his dating yacking about matrimony their first real time out. I figure our first trip to Filene's doesn't count and while we left last night's fish fry together, we sure didn't arrive that way.

But instead of getting twitchy at my words, Zach jokes,

"Then we'd best schedule the wedding now."

I try to laugh that off, but the sound comes out as more of a groan of longing. When I moved home, I thought it would be ages, if ever, before I found a man I wanted to date. But I ran into Zach, and our encounters have been building to the point where I'm full-on longing for his companionship. Either I've crossed the line and have become easy since Faye's conception, or there's something special going on here. I guess only time will tell.

I pull into the parking lot at Filene's and park in a spot right next to Auntie Lee. Those ladies don't know who they're messing with. But I'm about to show them.

Chapter Forty-Six

The hostess who greets us is the same one that flirted with Zach the night of our non-date. She doesn't look overly thrilled to see us.

Zach puts his arms around my waist with one hand while carrying the baby carrier in the other. "Frothingham, party of two," he tells her. She looks at her book for a moment too long, so he adds, "My girlfriend made the reservation earlier today."

Little earthquakes erupt all over my body. I'm not going to tell you where the epicenter is, but I'm pretty sure you can guess.

The hostess glares at us both before looking back at her book. "I'm sorry I don't see it and we don't have an opening until eight."

I tell her. "My reservation was for two at six o'clock."

She looks down again and says, "That table has already been seated."

"Who's sitting there?" I ask, although I'm pretty sure she means Shelby. But Shelby should be on the way to Mama's house.

The hostess says, "Two ladies who I happen to know are Frothinghams," she says.

Ah, so Mama and Auntie Lee have taken my table. Zach says, "They're expecting us."

I look at him like he's just decided to take a stroll through an active mine field. I lean in and whisper, "Do you have any idea what you're doing?"

He replies, "I think I do." Then he smiles at the hostess and adds, "Should we follow you or would you like us to find our own way?"

She grabs two more menus while muttering, "I'm not sure there's room for four at that table."

Zach assures her, "'Course there is. We like each other enough to be in close quarters." That woman is going spit in his drink if he doesn't calm down.

It appears she's decided to do her job even though she looks none too happy about it. "Follow me."

And we do. We walk straight through the dining room to the doors that lead outside. She takes us to the table I requested and drops the menus unceremoniously. "Here you go."

Mama and Auntie Lee look up, astonished. "What are you doing here?" Mama demands.

"Having dinner. Imagine my surprise when we got here and found our table had been taken."

Zach adds, "I hope you don't mind if we join you." He pulls out a chair for me next to Mama.

Auntie Lee seems to be at a loss for words. Then she finds some. "What about Beau and Shelby? I thought they were eating here."

"Really? Wherever did you get that idea?" I glare at Mama.

"Where are they?" Mama wants to know. "Did you send

them over to the club?" She moves as if to push her chair out so she can stand up.

Zach takes that as his cue to lean over me and lay one on me. It's not a chaste kiss either. It's hot and steamy and very thorough. *Heavens. This man is like a drug.* Even though I know he's kissing me to distract our audience, he's doing a number diverting me as well.

Auntie Lee interrupts us by saying, "I understand you two are an item now."

I'm about to tell her that we've just started to date, when Zach says, "Yes, ma'am, we sure are."

I want to laugh at this whole crazy situation. The mamas are torn between tearing out of here to find Beau and Shelby and staying right where they are to witness whatever is going on between me and Zach.

Mama asks again, "Are you going to tell us where Beau and Shelby are?"

"No, ma'am," I tell her.

Auntie Lee decides, "Then we're going to stay here and have our dinner with you."

Zach throws his hands up in the air like an overly excited cheerleader. "How wonderful! I'll order us a nice bottle of wine and we can settle in." When the server comes over, he asks for a highchair and bottle of Merlot, then he orders the sautéed mushrooms as an appetizer.

I excuse myself to use the ladies' room. But instead of powdering my nose, I walk outside and pull out my phone. The call is answered after only one ring.

"Emmie, what are you up to?" Beau demands.

I ignore his question. "The steak should be nice and rested. Go ahead and serve it with the salad on the counter. The dressing is in a Mason jar in the fridge."

"Emmie," he warns.

"Beau, I love you," I tell him. "You told me there was something about Shelby that called to you. Find out what that is and either get on with it or let her know you're serious about things being over. No more games."

"I'm not the only one playing games," he answers.

"You surely aren't. That's why you need to tell Shelby what you want, so she knows how to respond to you. Right now, you're both dancing to Cootie's tune. Don't you think it's time you dance to your own?"

After several moments, my cousin says, "I love you too, Emmie. Thank you."

"Sure thing," I tell him. "But I can't keep Mama busy for more than two hours, so make sure you're out of there by then." More than anything I wish I could be a fly on the wall to see how Beau and Shelby do with each other. But, I realize it's none of my business. I just hope they can find their way and finally regain control of their relationship, whatever it is. Right now, though, I need to go face the music in the form of Mama and Auntie Lee. Saints preserve us, it could be a long night.

Chapter Forty-Seven

I get back to the table in time to hear Auntie Lee say, "Armand was like a son to us all."

Jesus, Mary, and Joseph, this has to end. I sit down clear my throat. "Zach, there's something I need to tell you about Armand."

Mama interrupts, "What Emmie's trying to say is that while she's grateful for the time she had with the dear boy, she's ready to move on." She pats my hand as if trying to console me.

"Mama," I tell her. "That's not what I'm trying to say, and you know it. What I'm trying to say is …"

"Are you ready to order?" our server interrupts me.

Zach looks at me expectantly, clearly interested in what I was going to share with him, but he addresses our server's question first. "Mrs. Frothingham, do you know what you'd like?"

Mama opens her mouth to answer, but Auntie Lee beats her to it. "I'd like the petite filet with herb butter and asparagus, please." After all, she's a Mrs. Frothingham, too.

We all order after that, but our conversation never gets back on track. Instead, Zach tells us about the shed he's building at the back of his property. "I wanted to have a place to start my seeds before transplanting them to the garden and the only places inside the house that get enough sunlight are living spaces, so I'm building a half-shed/half-greenhouse."

"I've always wanted a greenhouse!" Auntie Lee claps her hands in approval. "But Jed's always telling me that I don't plant enough to make it worth his while to build me one."

"Good thing I live next door, then. You're welcome to use mine," Zach tells her.

Auntie Lee beams like he's just offered to loan her the Taj Mahal for a luncheon. I'm not sure Zach knows what he's getting himself into, but I do know he's ingratiating himself with my family like nobody's business.

Auntie Lee says, "You're too kind, Zach. I thank you and I'll most certainly be availing myself of your generous offer." Then she says to Mama, "Let's go through the seed catalog later and pick out the flowers we want to grow next year."

Mama replies, "Honey, if we let ourselves go wild, Zach might rescind his offer."

Auntie Lee shoots him the side-eye. "I bet he won't."

As much as I don't care about gardening, I'm happy the conversation isn't all about Zach's and my fledgling relationship. Over salads, Auntie Lee demands, "What do you think you're up to, Emmie?"

"Pardon me?" I say.

"With Beau and Shelby," she clarifies. "I thought you were on my side."

"I'm on love's side," I tell her. "I think Beau is a big enough boy to make up his own mind, and if his mind is telling him that Shelby is the one, then that's his choice."

"Cootie!" Mama jumps like she's just been shot by a taser gun or she's suddenly developed Tourette's or something.

"Cootie, nothing," I tell her. "Shelby's mama has nothing to do with this, it's none of her business, just like it's none of ours."

Zach agrees, while still trying valiantly not to alienate Mama and Auntie Lee. "Shelby really is a nice girl. I've spent a lot of time with her in the last year. On her own, she's quite lovely."

Auntie Lee demands, "You sure you never had any interest in dating her for yourself? 'Cause let me tell you, son, I will not stand for you messing with Emmie's heart. She's been through enough."

Zach shakes his head. "No, ma'am. I promise I've only ever been Shelby's friend. As such, I offered to spend time with her to see if Beau would change his mind about being exclusive with her."

"Cootie!" Mama nearly shouts again.

Auntie Lee looks at her and says, "Good lord, Gracie, are you stroking out on us or something?"

Mama shakes her head and points. "Over there. Cootie just walked in with Harold. They're sitting on the other side of the deck."

Auntie Lee wipes her mouth on her napkin. "Well, that was a lovely meal," she says. "Why don't you all head out to the car and Gracie and I will pick up the check?"

"Auntie Lee," I tell her. "We haven't eaten yet."

Mama says, "I'm just stuffed. I'll get doggy bags for our entrees."

There's no way we're leaving here just because Cootie Wilcox has walked in. I've got Beau and Shelby back at Mama's house, and they need some uninterrupted time. I need to think of something fast that will settle them back down.

Zach beats me to it. "When do you ladies think the best time is to get married in Missouri?"

All three of us nearly choke on our wine.

"Married?" Auntie Lee gasps. "Are you proposing to Emmie already?"

Now it's Zach's turn to lose his words. Clearly, this isn't what he was alluding to with his question.

Mama intervenes, "Honey, you only just started dating and while Lee and I would love to plan a wedding, this does seem a little fast."

Zach finally manages, "I didn't mean for Emmie and me," he says. Then he looks at me and smiles sweetly, "Of course that might be in the cards someday." Glancing back at Mama, he says, "My cousin, Mandy, just got engaged."

"Oh, that's right, Sarah Jane did say something about that," Mama replies, seemingly relieved and disappointed at the same time. "I guess I'd have to go with early June. You know, before it gets too hot and muggy but after all the rain. What do you think, Lee?"

Auntie Lee suddenly looks green. She stares across the room and says, "I think we either need to get out of here or prepare for battle. Cootie's spotted us."

Chapter Forty-Eight

Cootie Wilcox struts across the deck like a general charging the enemy. I hope and pray that woman minds her tongue, or all my hard work to give Beau and Shelby a chance will be for naught. If Cootie alienates my family any more, Beau will wash his hands of Shelby entirely, no matter his true feelings.

I gulp my wine for some liquid fortification as Mama and Auntie Lee both prepare to pounce. Seriously, they're sitting on the edge of their chairs with their shoulders back, their chins high, and wearing identical expressions of determination. They look like they're about to burst into a synchronized swimming routine.

I try to diffuse whatever is about to occur as soon as Cootie is upon us. "Mrs. Wilcox, don't you look nice tonight."

She stares at me like she's trying to telepathically dismember me. "Don't try to sweeten me up, you little slut." She says loud enough to attract the attention of several other nearby tables.

"Pardon me?" I ask.

Before she has a chance to answer, Zach stands up as though prepared to physically defend me, should Cootie try something. "Mrs. Wilcox," he says in a quiet, but forceful tone, "I think you need to hold your tongue."

"You!" she hisses. "How dare you be seen in public with this, this, tramp? You're dating my daughter, and I will not allow you to shame her!"

"I'm not seeing your daughter, ma'am," he says. "Shelby is my friend, but nothing more."

"That's not true," she insists. "You and Shelby have been seeing each other for weeks. She says things are starting to get serious."

He shakes his head. "Shelby is trying to make Beau jealous, and I've been helping her out. That's all that's been going on."

Not knowing what to believe, Cootie declares, "Shelby and I decided that she's too good for the likes of a Frothingham." Then she trains her eyes back on me. "You're nothing but a lying, scheming little whore."

Mama and Auntie Lee are on their feet in a flash, ready to rumble. Mama says, "Cootie, I'll give you to the count of three to walk out of here before I rip every hair off your stupid head. One," she starts the count.

"Don't you dare threaten me, Gracie Lynn Frothingham. You're nothing but a piece of trash, just like your daughter!"

"TWO!" Mama yells while Auntie Lee starts flexing her fingers like she's preparing them for combat.

Cootie shakes a fisted finger at Mama. "Reed only married you because he knocked you up."

"That is not the truth and you know it, Cootie. Reed never looked twice at you because you were as big of a bitch back then as you are now," Mama retaliates with stealth speed.

Auntie Lee decides to get in on the action. "Actually, you're a bigger bitch now. Reed was never interested in you, Cootie, and you know it, he knew the kind of woman you'd become."

"That's not so," she responds. "He and I had a lovely first date until this, this"—she gestures wildly at Mama—"piece of garbage showed up."

"One date does not a relationship make, Cootie," Auntie Lee tells her.

Cootie defends, "One date is enough when you've known each other your whole lives and your mamas have expectations."

"Selia threatened to disinherit Reed if he ever saw you again," Auntie Lee says.

"You're making that up," Cootie says. "Reed would have asked me out again, and mark my words, we would have gotten married, too."

"Doc Chester's nurse was a big gossip like you, Cootie," Auntie Lee cuts her off.

Not taking her meaning, Cootie demands, "So what?"

"So, what about that time you came home from visiting colleges with your sister during your senior year of high school?"

Cootie's eyes go as round as dinner plates. "You wouldn't dare!"

"Wouldn't I?" Auntie Lee asks.

I don't know what's going on, but I feel like we're on a dangerous precipice that there will be no coming back from if this conversation goes any farther. "Mrs. Wilcox," I say, "why don't we all just decide to call this one a draw and let it go? You go on back to your table and we'll stay here and forget this bit of nastiness ever happened."

"You'd like that wouldn't you?" she sneers.

As a matter of fact, I would, but she clearly doesn't agree. "I think it would be for the best," I say, thinking of Beau and Shelby.

"I bet you do. I bet you don't want your boyfriend here," she smacks Zach on the arm, hard, "to know about your fiancé, do you?"

"Zach knows all about him." Well, not *all* about him, but he knows of him.

I swear if steam could really pour out of a person, Cootie would be dehydrated by now, like the dried-up old prune she really is. "Does he know that the army hasn't any record of an Armand Hammer among its ranks in decades? Neither has the navy, air force, or marines."

Before I have a chance to answer, Auntie Lee yells at the top of her lungs, "How's your herpes doing, Cootie? Had any outbreaks lately?"

Oh. My. God. It's on. I can't bear to look at Zach to see how he's reacting to this news about Armand. I don't know where to look, actually. This is the biggest scene I've ever been party to, if you don't count the night of *the event* and me hitting old Allison Conrad over the head when she stole my award out from under me.

Faye lets out a shriek but she's not crying, she's staring around at everyone like she wants in on the action. I hand her a teething biscuit to distract her before picking her up and walking out of the dining room.

Once I'm free of the restaurant's four walls, Faye and I sit on a bench out front and take several breaths. Then I pull out my telephone. Things may have just ended with Zach before they've even started. He's bound to think a lot less of me now that he knows the truth about Armand. But there's something more immediate I need to take care of.

I dial Beau's number, but he doesn't answer. I have no idea what's going on over there, but I need to warn him. When his voicemail picks up, I say, "It's hit the fan with Cootie. I don't know what's going to happen now, but I'm pretty sure our families have made a future for you and Shelby impossible. I'm so sorry, Beau. I really tried to let this be your decision alone. Also, I don't know how much longer I can keep Mama and Auntie Lee occupied, so you might want to skedaddle."

As I walk back into Filene's, Cootie nearly knocks me over on her way out. She stops long enough to spit, "This is not over, Emmeline Frothingham. You tell your mama and Auntie Lee *that* for me." Then she pokes me in the chest for good measure. It's all I can do not to break off her finger and shove it up her nose.

Suddenly, single motherhood in New York City looks like a picnic compared to coming home to the safety and security of my family. I cross the dining room with my eyes trained on Zach, trying to discern his expression. But for the life of me, I can't determine what he's thinking. One thing's for certain, I'm about to find out.

Chapter Forty-Nine

As soon as I sit back down, Auntie Lee says, "That wasn't as bad as I'd anticipated."

Mama agrees, "As far as scenes go, it could have been a lot worse."

"I'm sorry," I say, "you think that asking after Cootie's VD in a crowded restaurant was a better result than you'd expected? How much worse could it have been?" I purposely don't bring up her accusations regarding me and Armie.

"We could have mentioned Harold's affair with the ladies' tennis coach," Auntie Lee replies.

"Or the time Cootie walked in on him with her hairdresser," Mama adds.

I halfway feel sorry for Mrs. Wilcox due to her husband's philandering, but not sorry enough to let her slander me or my family. I turn to Zach and say, "I guess you have some questions."

He looks uncertain about how to proceed. He finally settles on, "You must have your reasons for making up a fiancé."

"I do," I tell him. "But you're entitled to answers if you want them."

"Do they change how you feel about me?" he asks.

"They don't."

"Well, then," he says, "I don't suppose I have any questions right now." He looks pointedly at Mama and Auntie Lee as if to suggest he doesn't want to carry on with this conversation in front of them, which leads me to believe we'll be talking about it later. Damn. I wanted to tell him, but I hoped to do so on my terms and not because I was forced into it.

The rest of our meal is stilted at best. We spend an awful lot of time chewing our food amid an awkward silence. If Zach still wants to see me after tonight, I vow that we should avoid Filene's like the plague. We do not do well here.

When it's time to go, I reach for the check but Zach beats me to it. I say, "This one was on me, remember?"

He shakes his head. "No, ma'am, the pleasure is all mine." He pulls a credit card out of his wallet. Neither Mama nor Auntie Lee even try to make a grab for the bill. Which honestly, is the least they could do after what just transpired here.

Mama says, "I have a pie at home. Why don't we all go back to my place?" She adds, "Emmie, after we're done, you can leave the baby with me and go off with Zach." She winks as if a little romance might be in order. As if such a thing is likely after the night we've had.

There's no reason to stay at the restaurant any longer. I've warned Beau, so he'll know to expect us, if he checks his voicemail, that is. I just don't have the energy to try to keep Mama and Auntie Lee away any longer. We've reached the point where whatever will be, will be.

In the car on the way home, I tell Zach, "Auntie Lee made

up my fiancé because she didn't think the gossips would treat me kindly if they knew the truth."

"Which is?" he asks.

"I didn't know Faye's daddy. It was just one night. I chose to come home to avoid raising my baby on my own in New York." It feels good to finally get that off my chest. Although, I'm not looking forward to the rest of the town finding out.

"You weren't dating the guy or anything?"

"No," I tell him. I feel shame course through me. This isn't the way I was raised to behave, but still and all the same, the whole thing was consensual. It's nobody's concern who I have relations with or how well I know them, especially not someone I wasn't even involved with at the time. After all, this *is* the age of Tinder where folks swipe right or left—I don't know which—to hook up all the time. Just cause I've never done that before doesn't mean half my generation doesn't. I'm starting to get a little annoyed.

Zach must sense that because he says, "It's none of my business who you were with before now. To be honest, I'm relieved that Armie wasn't real."

"Why?" I ask.

"Because it means you're not trying to get over a broken heart. Believe me, no man wants to be the rebound guy."

"No woman, either," I say. "You want to tell me about the gal who broke your heart?"

"I want there to be clear air between us, I'm just not ready quite yet," he says.

I respect that. After all, I didn't tell him about Armie until Cootie spewed her venom. I'm assuming that was the gossip she'd planned on announcing the night of the catfish fry. I shudder to think of the scene she would have caused at the club. Mama and Auntie Lee would have probably retaliated with everything they had on Cootie, and god knows where that would have led. Probably to a girl-on-girl fist fight that would have resulted in someone behind bars.

We pull into Mama's driveway as she and Auntie Lee park next door. Beau and Shelby's cars are still here, which I assume means Beau didn't get my message. Mama and Auntie Lee have noticed as well and are full-on sprinting across our front lawns to find out what's going on.

I've got to do something to alert Beau, so I lay on the horn. Mama and Auntie Lee let out simultaneous screams of surprise and I say, "Zach, can you get the baby? I've got to get inside before they do." I don't wait to hear whether he says yes, I just tear out of the car so I can try to give my cousin five seconds warning.

Chapter Fifty

Mama and Auntie Lee are already at the front door with a key in the lock, so I hightail it around to the back of the house hoping to signal Shelby and Beau by waving in a window or something. But by the time I open the sliding door that leads to the living room, it's too late. The mamas are already standing in the entryway, bosoms heaving. "Where are they?" Auntie Lee demands.

We split up and search the bedrooms, the rumpus room, and Mama even looks in the pantry, but nothing. I thank the Good Lord they're not in the bedrooms. That would have been a catastrophic scene the likes of which one does not recover from too easily. Auntie Lee is busy looking under the sofa cushions; for what, I do not know.

Suddenly, I hear a muted sniffling sound coming from the bathroom in my bedroom. As casually as I can, I hurry to investigate. The door is closed, which is not how I usually leave it, so I put my ear to it. I'd like to say I'm doing it for a reason other than blatant snooping, but I'm not.

I can't hear much more than murmuring voices and crying, so I know that more than one person is inside. I use my brilliance to deduce that Beau and Shelby are in my bathroom. Several interesting questions come to mind, but there's only one real way to find out what's going on.

I knock gently on the door. "We're home," I say by way of greeting.

The voices stop but no one opens up. So, I continue, "Me, Mama, *and* Auntie Lee." I assume Zach and Faye will be of little interest to them given that Beau's mama is in the house.

The door finally opens, and Beau stands there looking like a slice of white bread. He's pale as can be and seems a bit wobbly. "Emmie ..." is all he manages to say before Mama and Auntie Lee storm in the room.

"Where is she?" Auntie Lee demands.

Mama opens my closet door and when she doesn't find anything, she looks like she's ready to drop to the floor and check under the bed.

Auntie Lee walks right over to my cousin and demands, "Beauregard Frothingham, you'd better tell me what's going on right this minute."

Beau doesn't say a word, he just steps aside to let his mama walk into the bathroom with him. Several moments of silence occur, which makes me wonder what the heck is going on in there. Then I hear Shelby's soft sobbing.

Auntie Lee calls out, "Gracie, can you come in here, please?"

All sorts of things fly through my head like toothpicks in a tornado. They're sharp and jabby enough that I know they're there, but nothing stands still long enough for me to hang on to. I do briefly ponder the image of Beau standing over Shelby, clutching a knife while she's lying in the bathtub dying. *Where did that come from?*

Auntie Lee says, "Beau, I need you to go put some hot water on the stove for tea." He doesn't move quickly enough, so she says, "Now!"

Once he's gone, I take his place. Shelby is sitting on the toilet, doubled over with her face in her hands. Auntie Lee says, "Honey, you feel up to talking and telling us what's going on?" She's gentle as a lamb, which does not all fit her most recent mood. But, it's clear Shelby is in distress.

Shelby hiccups and coughs and finally manages, "I'm bleeding all over the place."

Mama asks, "You want me to get you some feminine supplies?"

Shaking her head, Shelby answers, "No, ma'am."

"It's not your period, is it?" Auntie Lee inquires.

Again, Shelby shakes her head. I'm not quite sure what's going on. All I know is that Shelby is bleeding into my toilet, claiming not to be having her period. What happened? Did she fall and cut her lady business?

Auntie Lee asks, "How far along are you, honey?"

She answers, "Eight weeks."

Holy crap. Shelby's pregnant!

"Did the bleeding just start?" Mama asks.

"Yes, ma'am. About thirty minutes ago."

Auntie Lee wants to know, "Is it Beau's?"

The tears flow down Shelby's face like a faucet as she nods her head.

Auntie Lee takes charge, "Okay, young lady, first things first. We're going to get you out of here and lay you down in bed while I call the doctor."

"You can't call the doctor!" Shelby shrieks. "Nobody knows yet."

"I'm not going to say it's you," she comforts her. "But this has happened to me before and I need to make sure what I did back then is still what they're doing now."

Shelby shakes her head, "I'm losing the baby, Mrs. Frothingham. I don't think there's more than one way it's going to come out of me."

Mama scurries out of the room to pull the covers down on my bed, while Auntie Lee says, "Honey, I bled through all three of my pregnancies. So, I'm going to consider this a live baby until we have confirmation otherwise."

She gently helps Shelby to her feet and leads her out of the bathroom. Once she's settled on my bed, Auntie Lee says, "Emmie, I want some pillows under this girl's feet to elevate them," then she leaves the room.

Shelby groans, "I'm so embarrassed."

"Why?" I ask, although clearly I understand this isn't an ideal way to tell your baby's future grandmother that you're expecting.

"Emmie, I'm pregnant and I'm not even seeing the baby's daddy. My mama is going to have a fit the likes of which I can't even imagine."

I consider mentioning that I know what it's like to be in the family way without being in a relationship with the baby's daddy, but instead I ask, "Cootie doesn't know yet?" I wonder what's up with my family. We aren't doing things in the right order at all.

Shelby shakes her head indicating that her mama is clueless about the current situation. I think back to the scene that just took place at Filene's, and I cannot imagine how this is all going to work out without serious casualties. I just hope against hope that this baby isn't one of them.

Chapter Fifty-One

After fetching her phone, Auntie Lee comes back into my room, talking to someone. "I'm wondering what we do for a pregnant woman who starts to bleed. Do we take her to the emergency room?"

Auntie Lee listens for a moment and then asks Shelby, "Honey, have you been to the doctor yet?"

She shakes her head. "I've been too afraid my mama would find out, but I've been taking my prenatal vitamins and I've been eating really healthy food." Auntie Lee relays the information and listens some more.

When she finally hangs up the phone, she says, "They want you to stay off your feet until tomorrow morning and see if the bleeding stops. Then we need to get you to a doctor and find out if there's a heartbeat."

Shelby looks like you could knock her over with the slightest touch. "Once I started to bleed, I thought that was it. I didn't even consider there was still a chance."

Auntie Lee sits next to her on the bed and gently consoles, "You've got a Frothingham inside you, and I can guarantee they like to come into this world as dramatically as possible."

Mama laughs. "Isn't that the truth? Emmie decided to come

early while Reed and I were away enjoying a last getaway together before becoming parents."

I remember what Cootie accused Mama of at Filene's and ask, "Was I really early or were you pregnant before the wedding?" Not that it matters, but I am kind of curious.

"You were only five pounds, honey, and you spent two weeks in the hospital after you were born. You were nearly a month early. You were our honeymoon baby." She smiles at me so tenderly I can tell she's reliving those moments in her head.

Beau finally comes back into the room still looking a little wobbly around the edges. He says, "I put the water on for tea. Is there any special kind I should make?"

Auntie Lee shakes her head. "I was just trying to get you out of the way." Then she says, "Shelby's going to stay here. We'll get her to the doctor in the morning to see what's going on."

Beau stares at Shelby in disbelief and a bit of awe, like she's a rainbow unicorn or something. "Why didn't you tell me?"

"I didn't want you to think I was trapping you. I wanted you to want to come back on your own, not out of duty."

"Jeez, Shelby, this is a mess," he says.

She bursts into loud, gut-wrenching sobs. I intervene and demand, "For the love of god, Beau, don't you think she knows that? We need to keep her calm and quiet and your being here isn't going to help with that. I think you'd better leave."

He stands his ground. "I'm not going anywhere. Shelby's pregnant with my baby, and I belong here at her side." He doesn't even question if the baby is his which leads me to believe two things: he knows it is and he really does have strong feelings for Shelby.

Auntie Lee says, "Then go back to the kitchen and do the dishes. You can stay in the house, but you cannot upset Shelby. Do you understand me, young man?"

Beau nods his head as he leaves the room again. Auntie Lee is being so nice, I hardly know what to say. Just an hour ago she was bent on doing everything possible to keep Beau and Shelby apart, but now she's full on championing her.

"What do we tell Cootie?" I ask.

Auntie Lee looks at Shelby and says, "You need to call your mama and tell her that you've decided to spend some time in St. Louis shopping or something. Can you do that?"

Shelby nods. "I'll call my daddy and let him tell her. I need to do something with my car though, or she might find out that I'm here."

Folks in small towns are hyper-aware of every little thing going on around them. When there isn't enough drama, they're happy to manufacture it. Just ask the club ladies. Those gals are the very hub of fabricated news in our town.

I ask, "Where are your keys? I'll pull it into the garage." Once I have them in hand, I leave the room and run smack into Zach in the hallway. He looks kind of sketchy.

He's gently bouncing Faye on his hip and nervously asks, "Is she okay?"

"We don't know yet," I tell him. "She's going to stay here tonight, we'll take her to the doctor in the morning, let's hope the bleeding stops."

"Did you have any troubles like this with Faye?" he demands.

I shake my head. "I didn't spot or anything. I had an ideal, if lonely, pregnancy with her."

"I'm sorry you were alone," he says.

"Mama visited a couple times, so that was nice."

"I'm sorry Faye's daddy wasn't there to support you."

I'm glad he wasn't because how uncomfortable would that have been being that I didn't even know him. I don't want to remind Zach of that, so I say, "You're sweet, you know that?"

He smiles almost painfully and says, "I just know how hard it is to grow up without a father; all kids deserve one. I tell you what though, I'm going to make sure Shelby's baby's daddy is a part of its life."

He seems so adamant that for a crazy flash I wonder if he isn't really the daddy instead of Beau. He hands me Faye before continuing on into the bedroom. As I try to squelch that uncomfortable thought, I once again worry if I did the right thing by not trying to find Faye's daddy earlier. Life is one complicated affair.

Chapter Fifty-Two

There's no way Zach is the daddy of Shelby's baby. That's foolish. I've believed him all along that they were just friends. I even overheard them talking about how he was trying to get her back with Beau that day at the creek. So why would this idea even pop into my head? It's just there was a look on his face that made me feel like there's something bigger going on in his head that he's not sharing with me.

I tell myself I'm being silly and go on outside to move Shelby's car. Beau is sitting on the porch looking like he's just lost his best friend. I plop down on the rocking chair next to him and ask, "You didn't have any idea?"

He shakes his head. "I sure didn't."

"How do feel about it?" I ask.

"Confused," is all he says.

"You do know how babies are made, right?"

"Don't be a smart aleck, Emmie. Of course, I know how babies are made. That's not the part I'm confused about."

"I'm sorry," I say. "That was uncalled for. I'm sure you're confused. I was confused after I found out I was pregnant with Faye."

"At least you don't have the complications of her daddy."

"You're the one who told me he had a right to know," I exclaim. "Are you suddenly wishing you didn't know?"

"Not at all. I'm saying that maybe you made the right choice is all. It's complicated enough for me and Shelby, and we were actually dating at the time. I just wish she'd told me sooner so we could have discussed this like two adults. It's silly that she's been trying to make me jealous with Zach all the while pregnant with my baby."

"She's afraid of her mama," I say.

"We all are. God, that Cootie is a real nightmare, and that's before she knows about Shelby's pregnancy. Can you imagine how she's going to act when she finds out?"

I grimace. "You don't know the worst of it."

"What now?" he demands with a look of primal fear etched across his face.

"We ran into Cootie at Filene's and she was a real terror. Your mama retaliated by asking after her herpes. Loudly."

"You're kidding? How in the world are we ever going to tell her about *this*?"

"Maybe she'll drop dead from a heart attack when you do and you won't have to worry about her after that," I say.

"That's just wishful thinking, Emmie. Life never turns out that easy."

"It sure doesn't," I tell him. "But take it from me, once you get through the hard bits, the rewards are pretty sweet."

Beau stands up and starts to pace. Back and forth he goes with his hands shoved deep in his pockets and his head hung so low it looks like it's growing out of his chest. "Should I ask her to marry me?" he wonders.

"Do you want to marry her?" I ask. "And not just for the baby's sake, but for hers?"

"I don't know her well enough to say. How crazy is that? We made a baby, but I don't know her well enough to know if I want a long-term relationship with her."

"Who are you telling? I don't even know who my baby's daddy is."

Beau looks at me and suddenly bursts out laughing. "This whole town is going to think the Frothinghams are nothing but trash."

I start laughing too, and reply, "That's not even funny. Why are we laughing?" But we're both doubled over, holding our sides like we're trying to keep our guts from spilling out.

When we finally settle down a bit, I say, "We've been held up to some crazy standards that I'm not sure that even I think exist anymore outside of the country club set."

He looks at me closely and says, "You know, you're right. Our parents didn't care one whit about you being a single mama. They're only worried about how the town would treat you. And by the town, I mean Cootie and her henchmen. Now that it's done and Shelby is pregnant, Cootie can no longer hold her family above everyone else."

"Poor Shelby," I say. "Her mama's going to come down on her like a house of bricks."

"Which is why we have to keep them apart for as long as possible. I hate to say it, but if the baby doesn't make it, at least we can keep Shelby from ever having to tell her."

"Life never is easy, is it?"

"Not usually," Beau replies. "But times like this sure do have a way of making you grateful for the boring times."

"How do you feel about becoming a daddy?" I ask.

"I don't know. I mean, I always knew I wanted to be one. I just figured the circumstances would be a lot different. You know, like I'd be married first."

"Tell me about it," I say. "That's how I saw it too, but I wouldn't trade Faye for all the tacos in Mexico. That baby is the brightest spot in my whole life."

"I wonder if it's a girl or a boy," he says.

"Do you have a preference?" I ask.

"No, ma'am. Right now, my only preference is for the baby to live. I don't know what the future holds for me and Shelby, but I do know I want to be its daddy." My cousin breaks down and cries like a little boy who just lost his puppy.

I fold him up in my arms to offer my love and support. Then I say, "You need to go tell Shelby that. I think that's she's feeling pretty lonely right now. You need to lean on each other."

As Beau walks back into the house, my mind goes straight to Faye's daddy, and suddenly I feel lower than a swamp snake that I never told him about her.

Chapter Fifty-Three

Beau and Shelby both stay with us, so I move into the nursery and sleep on the day bed in there. Staring up at the white, dotted-swiss canopy above me, I'm full of doubts about my life. Will Faye hate me when she grows up and discovers that I never knew her father? Will she blame that for every little thing that's out of whack in her life?

All I know is that the guy lived in Brooklyn and was drinking at a bar near the Met in Manhattan. That's seriously nothing to go on. I vaguely remember the block he lived on, but it's been well over a year since I was there. Who's to say he still lives in the same neighborhood? Maybe he got married and lives there with a wife. He could even have six other kids out in the world in the same predicament as Faye.

Once my brain hops on the what-if train, I'm always hard-pressed to fall asleep. I finally succumb to the sandman long after I should, being that I have to work in the morning. When I wake up, Faye is cooing away in her crib. I quickly nurse and change her before heading down to make a pot of coffee.

Beau is already in the kitchen doing just that when I arrive. "How'd you sleep?" I ask.

"Who slept?" he responds. "I stayed awake all night offering God all kinds of deals to let the baby live."

"How's Shelby?" I ask.

"She finally fell asleep sometime after one. She's still bleeding but she says it's not as heavy."

"When are you going to take her to the doctor?"

"I'm going to call this morning and schedule something. Unfortunately, there's very little that can be done at this stage in the game. Studies show that nearly twenty-five percent of early pregnancies end in miscarriage."

"Someone was on the internet last night," I say.

"That's what I did in between praying and staring at Shelby. I'm now the owner of statistics that would scare the crap out of you."

"Hang tough, Beau. Call me if you need anything."

"You're heading in to work?" he asks.

"Yeah, I'm trying to finalize the design for Emmeline's so I can finish ordering the inventory."

I hurry to get cleaned up and then let Mama know I'm leaving. She takes Faye and informs me, "I'm planning on sticking close to home."

"I'll be at the sewing machine factory. You can drop the baby off with me if you need to." For some reason I'm having a hard time leaving my daughter today. I suddenly realize how much could have gone wrong and how very lucky I am that she's here.

Mama gives me a big hug and says, "Everything will work out as it should, honey." I know she's talking about Shelby's pregnancy, but still I find her words comforting.

Up until last night, I rarely even thought about Faye's daddy, and when I did, I'd half begun to believe the lies that he was my dearly departed fiancé. Suddenly, guilt is hanging off me like a pack of monkeys. I do not like how this feels, but for the life of me, I don't know how to make the situation right.

When I get to the factory, the uncles and Zach are already there. Zach spots me and comes right over. He gives me the sweetest kiss and asks, "How'd you sleep?"

"Like hell. How about you?"

"Same," he says. "How's Shelby?"

"She was sleeping when I left. Mama said she'd keep me posted. What are you working on today?" I ask.

"We're finishing the second floor and then we'll get going on the model condo. Have you ordered the furnishings for it yet?"

"Not all of them," I say. "I thought I'd pick up a few things when I go to New York to finish shopping for the store."

His eyes open wide. "I didn't know you were going back to New York."

"I have to hit the Merchandise Mart and finish purchasing for the store. I suppose I could have gone to St. Louis or Atlanta, but I have longstanding relationships in New York. I'm hoping they'll be willing to swing me some deals."

"I wish I could come with you," he says. I'm not sure how I feel about that. I mean, we've only just started dating. After the whole Armie Hammer incident—otherwise known as getting myself in the family way—I'm not sure I want to rush things with Zach. Firstly, because I don't want to get pregnant again until I'm lawfully wed, and secondly, I'm being careful with my heart. I think it's for the best if we don't do the horizontal hokey pokey for a long while. As hard as that might be to resist.

"Do you like New York?" I ask, avoiding his comment about joining me.

"I like what I've seen in my limited time there," he says.

"I miss the restaurants," I tell him. "There's this darling place in Central Park called the Boat House. They make the best crab cakes in the entire world."

He smiles sweetly, "Maybe we can go there together some day."

"That would be nice," I tell him. And I mean it. Just not during this trip. This time I need to go alone. I have a lot to think about while I'm there. First and foremost, I need to decide if there's anything to be done about finding Faye's daddy. Suddenly, I think it may be worth a try. If for no other reason than to get rid of this overwhelming guilt that's started smothering me.

Chapter Fifty-Four

Mama calls at two. "She lost the baby."

"Oh, my word, that poor thing. How's she doing?" I ask. I can only imagine all that Shelby has gone through in the last two months and what's ahead of her. I don't care what some folks say about it not being a baby until the third trimester. When that child is inside you and you already love it, it's your baby, plain and simple.

"She's been crying her heart out for the better part of an hour," Mama says. "She's in your room with Beau. Auntie Lee is making soup."

"How's Faye?" I ask, suddenly longing for her like she's the air I need to breathe.

"She's napping right now."

"Mama," I ask, "would you be willing to go to New York with me and Faye next week? I need someone to keep an eye on her while I'm shopping for the new store."

"Why don't you just leave her at home, honey? There's no reason to drag her along."

"I don't think I can be apart from her just yet," I tell her. Shelby losing her baby has put shaky ground beneath my feet.

Mama says, "Of course I'll come. Faye and I can go exploring together. Maybe even do a little shopping of our own."

"Thanks, Mama. Is there anything I can pick up for you or Shelby on my way home?"

"Beau's gonna take her over to his place so he can take care of her for a few days, and I don't need a thing. Just come home when you're done there."

I text Zach the news and he comes right down from where he's working on the second floor. He opens his arms and I rush right in. The warmth of him, the smell of him, everything about him makes me feel secure. I could stand here all day.

"You heading home?" he asks.

"Pretty soon. I've barely gotten a thing done today." My brain is totally occupied with thoughts about the fragility of life. "All I've managed to do is make hotel and airline reservations for my trip. I'm leaving for New York on Monday. I'll be back Thursday."

Zach looks sad to see me go. "Maybe I *can* get a couple days off and join you."

I shake my head. "Mama and Faye are coming. Let's plan another time for us."

"Okay," he agrees. "I'll take you out for crab cakes and you can give me the grand tour."

"It's a date," I tell him.

"What are you doing tonight?" he asks.

"Probably sitting around feeling bad for Shelby and Beau. You want to join me?"

"Yes, ma'am, I sure do. How about I pick up dinner and bring it to your house?" he asks.

"Mama will be there," I tell him.

"That's okay. This is the kind of time when family should stick together, dontcha think?"

"I do." I like that he knows this, and I like that he considers himself part of that family. If Zach and I wind up together, he'll be the only daddy that Faye will know. Maybe that's enough. I know it's a lot of pressure to put on our future, but it seems a much better chance of occurring than finding a needle in a haystack like locating her sperm donor.

When I get home, I discover Faye lying in her playpen sucking on her toes. I pick her up and love on her for a good long while. Mama comes into the living room and says, "I just changed the sheets in your room. Beau and Shelby have already gone."

"How are they doing?" I ask, knowing full well they aren't doing great.

"They have a lot to figure out," Mama says.

"I guess so. I can't help but wonder if this will pull them closer together or cement a wedge between them."

Mama grimaces a bit. "I guess it could go either way."

"I selfishly liked the idea of Faye having a cousin close in age to her," I say.

"Well, then you'd best get busy helping to find someone for Amelia and Davis, then. I'm pretty sure Beau isn't thinking along those lines right now."

"Mama, I told you before, I'm not going to stick my nose into anyone's relationship business. Their hearts will lead them in the direction they're meant to go."

"Like your heart did with Zach?" she asks.

"Exactly."

Mama smiles like she's telling herself a whopper of an inside joke. She asks, "Are you seeing him tonight?"

"He's coming over in an hour. He's bringing dinner for us."

"Sorry," Mama says. "I told Jesse I'd have dinner with him. He's got relationship troubles again."

I ask, "Are you just saying that to give me and Zach time alone?"

"No. Your uncle is truly in a spot with a certain lady right now and he doesn't know what to do. Although I'm happy to take Faye with me if you want some private time with your young man."

I hold my daughter tighter. "No, ma'am, I don't need anything as much as I need her. You go on along and give Jesse the benefit of your extremely limited dating experience."

She smiles. "Just 'cause I never dated much before your daddy, doesn't mean I don't have good sense when it comes to relationships," she says.

"I just think it'd be nice if you worried about your own social life as much as you worry about everyone else's. Maybe instead of me getting all worked up trying to help my cousins find love, I'll start working on you."

"Don't you dare!" she says. "I'll have you know I'm still your mama and I could still take you over my knee."

I laugh at her threats. "You and what army?" I ask. Then I say, "Don't worry, Mama, I'll leave you alone as long as you leave the cousins alone."

She stares at me for so long without saying anything, I wonder if her mind has gone wandering. She finally says, "We'll see." Which makes it clear she's going to do whatever she darn well pleases.

Chapter Fifty-Five

The week flies by like it booked a trip on the space shuttle. No one sees Beau or Shelby, so we can only hope they're working their stuff out. We sent flowers and left messages of support, which is all we can do. The hard part, grieving their baby, is all on them.

Zach and I have dinner together every night and I feel us growing stronger, like we're becoming a real couple. He's gone from a super judgmental semi-stranger to someone I feel myself blending with. I still don't know about his relationship with the gal who sent him running home, but it no longer matters. I told him about Armie Hammer, and the truth doesn't bother him in the least. I'm sure I'd feel the same way about his past. In fact, I owe a debt of thanks to the woman who didn't return his feelings. What a moron, huh?

The afternoon before I leave for New York, Zach and I go for a quiet stroll through the woods. He confesses, "I hated my daddy when he left. I hated him, but I cried myself to sleep every single night."

"How old were you?" I asked.

"Four. I was four years old. I remember wondering what I did wrong that my own daddy chose to leave me."

"Oh, Zach," I say with tears springing up in my eyes, "you know it wasn't you."

"I do now, but I still wonder why he never tried to see me. What kind of man has a child and doesn't move heaven and earth to be a part of its life? Your daddy would have sold his soul to stay alive and watch you grow into the amazing woman you are today."

I love that he knows that, but I hate that he still hurts so much over an abandonment he couldn't control. "Did your mama ever hear from him?

"Nope. She had to hunt him down through a private investigator to serve divorce papers," he says.

"Maybe he was ashamed," I offer.

"He should have been. But no amount of shame should keep a man from his child. Could you walk away from Faye?"

The question alone is an arrow to my heart. I barely managed to whisper, "Never."

"When your daddy died, I wanted to talk to you. I wanted to tell you that I knew what it was like to lose your daddy, and I wanted to tell you that it was going to be okay."

"Why didn't you?" I ask, so full of awe that he even considered such a thing.

"Because I was a ten-year-old boy who wasn't mature enough to follow through with a good plan."

I ask, "I know it's early days, but if you and I wind up together long term, you'd be a father figure to Faye. How does that make you feel?"

He stops walking and turns to look me in the eyes, before

squeezing my hands. "Honored. It would make me feel honored."

"Even though she isn't yours?" I ask.

"Emmie, people can choose to be parents regardless of DNA. Parenthood is about love and trust and wanting to be there. Family is a choice. My father just didn't choose us."

We continue to walk quietly sharing a thoughtful silence. My daddy didn't have a choice, Zach's did. We both grew up without fathers and we have both been greatly affected by that deficit. At least I was lucky enough to have the uncles.

Once again, I think about Faye's daddy, and I feel the weight of the whole world on me.

Zach drives us to the airport the following morning. I watch as he puts our suitcases in the back of his car and feel like I'm looking into the future. Mama gets Faye all situated in the seat next to her and I climb in front with my boyfriend. I'm calling him that now.

Zach pulls out of our driveway and says, "We could drive, then I could go with you."

"No, thank you," I laugh. "That would take days and I just want to get this trip over with."

Mama says, "I remember driving to Florida when Emmie was a baby and I really don't want to relive the experience."

"Mama," I admonish. "What kind of thing is that to say about your most cherished daughter?"

"Girl, you were sick as dog and threw up everything we put into you. The car smelled like something died in it."

Zach teases, "That thought makes it a little easier to say goodbye to y'all for a few days."

When we get to Cape Girardeau airport, he drops us off at

the curb. He wanted to park and walk us in, but I don't want to make this a dramatic scene. We've packed lightly, as we'll only be gone for four days. I can easily manage our bags if Mama pushes Faye in her stroller.

Zach gives Mama a hug and instructs, "Take good care of our girls." Ripples of pleasure rush through me that he considers us "his girls." Then he kisses Faye on the top of her head and says, "Bye, sweet baby, you be good for your mama and gran." He opens his arms to me, and I rush in to his embrace. He whispers in my ear, "I'm gonna miss you. Don't go deciding you want to stay in New York again, okay?"

"As if," I laugh. "No, sir, this is an in-and-out kind of trip. I wish I didn't even have to go."

He squeezes me tight. "I have a feeling it's going to be good closure for you."

I reach up and give him a tender kiss before saying, "I'm ready to put the past to bed and move forward." Then I step out of his arms and lead the Frothingham gals through the airport to our gate.

I loved my years in New York City. The energy was exhilarating. There's something about being able to order Chinese food at midnight that sends a shot of excitement through me. But I'm a mama now and if I'm still up at midnight, I'm going to be tired the whole next day. Babies have a way of shifting your priorities to more mundane pleasures, like sleeping.

Our flight is a breeze, and we arrive at the hotel well before dinner time. We're staying at a boutique hotel on the Upper East Side, not too far away from the Metropolitan Museum of Art— home of *The Event* that started my new life.

Once we check in and get everything sorted in our room, I suggest, "Let's head out to dinner. We shouldn't have to deal with big crowds if we eat early."

Mama says, "I want Thai food. I love Creek Water, but it's not exactly a hotbed of ethnic cuisine, if you know what I mean?"

I do know. It's one of the things I miss about city living. Actually, now that I'm here, I realize it might be the only thing. I've adjusted to a calm and quiet life. The car horns, the crush of people, the constant motion—it's all too much.

We take an Uber downtown to my favorite Thai restaurant, Uncle Boon's, on Spring Street. I swear we could have walked there faster. We should have just ridden the subway, but Mama has a fear of them. She claims she feels like she's in a scene from a movie called *Blade Runner*, whatever that is. So, we stay above ground and creep along like snails on a skating pond. After a delicious meal that has Mama claiming she needs to eat here three more times before we go home, we take a car back to the hotel.

When we're a few blocks away, I see the bar where I met Faye's daddy. I ask Mama, "Would you mind taking Faye back to the hotel by yourself?"

"Not at all, honey. Where are you going?"

"You see that place up ahead called Cezanne's?" When she nods, I continue, "That's where I met Faye's daddy. I just want to go in for a minute."

"Why in the world?" Mama asks. "You hoping to run into him or something?"

"The chances of that would be slim to none. Plus, I have Zach now, so it's not like I'm interested in anything. I just feel like I need to go in, is all." The truth is I do kind of want to see if he shows up. I just can't let go the idea of telling him that he has a daughter. But then if I do tell him, I wonder how that would mess things up with Zach. It's a lot to consider. Truthfully, it's such a long shot I'm sure it won't even matter.

The Uber drops me at the curb and I just stand there staring at the entrance like it leads to another world. I try to remember what I was feeling the night I came here after losing the award. I swear I see a version of myself all dressed walking up the street in my direction. She hurries into the bar. I wonder if I'm being fanciful or if my doppelgänger is real. Either way, I follow her.

It's much darker here than at the restaurant I just came from. The tealights and dim chandelier glow cast a mood over the place that makes it feel like I'm walking into a dream. I watch the vision of my other self sit down at the bar. She bats her eyes at the bartender before ordering two shots of tequila.

Is this what I looked like the night I came in here—all cool and collected with an air of recklessness? I can't imagine. I felt devastated and borderline desperate after losing out on the award I was expecting to receive.

I sit a few stools away from the phantom me and watch as she salts her hand, knocks back a shot and then sucks on a lime. When the bartender asks me what I'd like, I order a glass of white wine. I take a sip when it arrives, all the while keeping my eyes on the mirage that brought me here.

I see a man take notice of her and I realize I know him. At least I think he's the one. He looks an awful lot like Armie Hammer. Again, I wonder if this is real or I'm just imagining him?

He smiles down at my twin and leans in to say something to her. At the same time, I feel hot breath against my neck. Delicious waves of lust shoot through my body like a bottle rocket going off. Then I hear a familiar voice say, "You came back."

Chapter Fifty-Six

Familiar hazel green eyes meet mine as I turn around and my worlds collide. "I wondered if you'd ever come back," he says. "I came here every night for a week after we met. I even postponed my trip home to do so, but you stayed away."

"Zach?" I demand. "What are you doing here? What are you talking about?"

"I think you know what I'm talking about," he says. "I'm talking about that night fifteen months ago when I was sitting over there," he points to a corner table, "having a beer on my way back to my Airbnb from a late meeting."

I cannot seem to connect the dots to what's going on here. Why is Zach in the bar I met Emmie's daddy in? He continues, "I watched this beautiful woman stroll past me and I thought to myself, 'she looks familiar.' Imagine my surprise when I walked over, and you introduced yourself as the one and only Emmeline Frothingham."

"That was you?" I demand.

"You really don't remember, do you?"

"I don't. I told you what I was like when I drink tequila. Why … why didn't you try to find me?" I ask.

"Because you told me that you'd call me. I gave you my card with all my information on it. When I never heard from you, I came back here every night in hopes of running into you. But you never showed, and I had to go back to Chicago."

The inside of my head feels like one of those Ninja blenders turned on high. Everything is flying around at supersonic speed, and I can't seem to hang on to a single thought before it's obliterated. "Why didn't you say anything when you saw me in Creek Water?"

"Because that's when I learned you had a fiancé, and a baby. I didn't know what to say. I figured you were ignoring what happened between us because you were embarrassed and wanted to forget."

"Oh, my god, Zach, you must have thought I was real trash."

"I thought you were real something. I was hurt that you didn't say anything about what happened between us, but then you agreed to have dinner with me, and I thought maybe we'd talk about it then."

"Then I told you I don't remember anything that happens when I drink tequila," I say.

"I remembered and I was mad at you for forgetting. That night in Brooklyn was the most amazing experience of my life, and you didn't even remember it. We didn't only make love, we talked. We talked a lot. I told you things that I never told anyone else about, and you just walked out like I didn't exist."

"Oh, Zach, I didn't even remember where you lived. I didn't remember your name, nothing."

"Why didn't you come back here to find me? Why did you sneak out before I even woke up?"

"I was embarrassed," I tell him. "I was horrified I'd done such a thing. In all my years, I've never had a one-night stand. It just isn't how I operate."

He sits down next to me looking like I've just kicked him in the gut. "Wait, I'm the only one-nighter you've ever had?"

I nod my head as things start to fall into place in my head.

"You know what this means, don't you?" he asks.

I nod again. "I do."

"If Faye isn't your fake fiancé's baby, and she's not the product of another one off, then she's mine."

Tears fill my eyes as a feeling of pure awe and astonishment rushes through me. "I hadn't been with anyone since my last boyfriend, and we broke up two years before, well, you know."

Zach starts to tear up. "But the math doesn't add up, and believe me, I did the math."

"Faye was twenty-six days early, same as me."

He drops to the stool beside me and says, "I'm a daddy."

"You are," I tell him. "Why did you move back to Creek Water?" I ask.

"I'd been toying with relocating for quite a while. I'd thought about moving to New York, which is why I was here. I was interviewing with a new company, but after our night together, and then not hearing from you, I didn't think I could live here. I decided to just go home."

"And move two houses away from my mama?" I ask. "That doesn't seem like very sound logic."

"I loved the house. Plus, I figured the chances of us running into each other were slim to none during your infrequent visits."

"How do you know how often I visited?" I ask.

"You told me that night we were together. You told me you despised Creek Water and that you barely even went home to visit."

"You must have hated me," I conclude.

He shrugs. "Love and hate are pretty close emotions. I can honestly say, I wasn't feeling too keen on you when you came back and acted like you didn't know me. And then to find out you'd been engaged to Armie Hammer at the time of our encounter … it didn't speak well for you."

"And had a baby to boot," I add. Then I ask, "Why did you come to New York now?"

"I didn't want to be away from you for four whole days."

"And?" I ask, because it feels like there's something more.

"And because I thought that maybe you'd remember me if we were here together. I was going to bring you here one night for drinks."

"Mama knew you were coming, didn't she?" I ask. She's been acting suspicious lately. It suddenly makes sense.

"She did. She told me where you'd be staying so I could book a room in the same hotel."

Too many things are hitting too fast and I have to take a moment to breathe. It finally occurs to me, "Mama is going to flip her biscuit when she finds out that you're Faye's daddy!"

"My mama will as well. She's fallen in love with Faye and keeps telling me I'd better hurry up and get married so she can be a grandma."

"Zach," I say as another humongous wave hits me. "Granny Frothingham said Faye looked just like you. It's like she knew."

Zach gets up and steps so close to me he's nearly standing

242

between my legs. Then he leans down and kisses me so sweetly and so tenderly that I barely feel the touch of him even though my whole body erupts in flames of desire. When he's through, I need to hang on to him, so I don't fall right off my bar stool.

He says, "Wait until Cootie hears."

"When are we going to tell our mamas?"

Suddenly, I cannot wait to go home.

Chapter Fifty-Seven

When we get back to the hotel, Mama winks and says, "I just need you to feed the baby if you plan on sleeping elsewhere tonight."

"Mama," I say, avoiding her comment, "did it ever occur to you that Zach looks a lot like that movie actor, Armie Hammer?"

Mama looks confused. "I guess. I mean I don't really know what Armie Hammer looks like, but I'll take your word for it."

Zach asks Mama, "Did I ever tell you that I used to visit New York for work?"

She shakes her head. "I don't believe I knew that, but I imagine there's a lot I don't know about you yet, Zach."

"The last time I was in New York, I stayed in Brooklyn."

"That's charming," she says. "You'll have to tell me about that some time." She's clearly wondering why he's bothering to tell her about it now.

"Turns out I ran into Emmie during that trip."

Mama finally seems interested. "Emmie, why didn't you ever tell me that?"

I shrug my shoulders, while Zach says, "We just came from the bar where we met."

Mama looks at me closely. "You must have gone there quite a bit, Emmeline."

"Nope, I was there just the once."

"But you told me in the car that was the place where you met …" She stops talking mid-sentence and looks at Zach. Then she looks at Faye. Then she looks at me and demands, "And you didn't remember it was Zachary Grant, from Creek Water, Missouri?"

"You know how I am when I drink tequila, Mama," I remind her.

"Hand me my phone," she declares while pointing to it on the nightstand.

I push it farther away. "No, ma'am. This isn't news that gets put out via a family text. This is something Zach and I are going to tell everyone ourselves, in person."

Mama stands up and throws her arms out and declares, "I need a hug. This is the most exciting thing I've ever heard! Wait until Sarah Jane finds out!"

Zach and I step into Mama's embrace and we all hang on to each other like long-lost relatives. Zach is the first one to pull away. He goes to the crib and picks up Faye. He holds her like she's delicate china and says, "Hey, baby, I'm your daddy."

Faye grabs onto his nose and pulls it toward her so she can bite it.

"She's hungry," I laughingly say. "Hand her over to me."

Zach sits next to me on the bed and watches as I feed our daughter. He's completely mesmerized as he says, "Can I stay up here with you tonight?"

Mama asks, "With the baby?"

Zach smiles. "I want to be with my family."

Mama chokes up and says, "If that isn't the sweetest thing ever." She puts her hand out, "Give me your key. I'll just grab my suitcase and head to your room."

After Mama leaves, Zach and I lie on the bed and talk for hours. I tell him everything I can think of about my pregnancy, from taking the pregnancy test to throwing up my breakfast for three months straight, to deciding to leave New York to come home.

"It's like you were being pulled to where you belonged, to my side."

I think of what I told Mama about believing people have heart magnets that draw them to the person they were meant to be with. I feel more certain than ever that it's true. Zach and I didn't really know each other as kids, but we still managed to find each other in a city of seven million people. The chances of us both being in that bar, on the same night, at the same time are virtually non-existent. Yet, there we were.

When I totally blew the opportunity of getting to know him after our *encounter*, our magnets brought us back together in our hometown.

Zach and I don't relive the night we met at Cezanne's in the physical sense. Instead, we lay in bed and fall asleep with our baby between us, relishing the beauty of our creation. I'm going to raise my baby with her daddy after all.

The rest of the trip flies by in the blink of an eye. Zach accompanies Mama and Faye on a tour of New York, which includes a trip to the Statue of Liberty, a carriage ride in Central Park, a visit to the Metropolitan Museum of Art, more Thai food, and even a drive-by the Airbnb in Brooklyn where Faye got her start in life.

Everything seems to be working out perfectly for us. Now all we need to do is go home and come clean to the rest of the town. I know most people will be thrilled for us. There's only one person I dread telling and that, of course, is Cootie Wilcox. She's capable of creating a stink the likes of which isn't seen outside a skunk convention.

Chapter Fifty-Eight

Trying to keep Mama quiet about Zach's and my history *and* Faye's parentage is going to be as challenging as teaching a whale how to waltz. For that reason alone, we've set the date to share our news at the next community band concert in the park, two days after we get back from New York.

Zach and I are busy at the old sewing machine factory during the day. We promise Mama a big reward if she keeps our secret. What that will be, I have no idea, but we'll think of something.

The uncles are thrilled to have us back and can't wait to hear about all the merchandise for the Emmeline's. Jed says, "I'm getting really excited about our opening."

Jesse agrees, "The ladies around town seem pretty jazzed as well. I ran into Bella Hopps at Bobbie Jean's cafe when I was there having pie the other day. She said the gals in her circle are all excited about getting their highlights done, having lunch, and doing a little shopping all under the same roof."

I ask, "How's Beau doing?"

Jed grimaces. "It's been tough."

"Are he and Shelby back together?" I ask.

Jesse says, "We saw them eating lunch together one afternoon, but no one knows if they're dating again."

"Doesn't Auntie Lee know?" I wonder.

"No, ma'am. She's vowed to stay out of it, which has me a little bit concerned."

"I think it hit her pretty hard," I say. "You know, from thinking she might have a grandbaby on the way to having no such thing."

"Amelia says she's been acting downright spooky. I guess Lee told Amelia that she was done prying in the lives of her children," Jed say. "I can't imagine such a thing myself. Good lord, that woman has been one hundred percent involved in trying to find her children their life mates since they started preschool."

Jesse says, "I hope that doesn't mean she'll be gunning for me next," he warns. "That's not going to fly, Jed."

I say, "I think she may find herself happily diverted by another topic very soon."

Both my uncles ask at the same time, "You getting married?"

"No. But I'm going to be sharing some pretty interesting news soon."

"You're not pregnant again, are you?" Jed asks, looking a little green around the edges.

"No, sir, I'm not," I tell him. "But I've still got news."

Jesse asks, "If you're not getting married and you're not pregnant, what else could it be?"

"I guess you'll just have to show up to the band concert on Monday night to find out."

Jed pulls out his phone and starts texting. I say, "Make sure to tell them not to be late." Of course, he's sending out word to the family.

I pull out my phone and text Mama to remind her to keep her mouth shut. But suddenly that doesn't feel like enough. I say, "I need to run home and feed the baby. I'll be back in about an hour."

Jed says, "Take your time. You worked your butt off getting our ordering done while you were away. Take the rest of the afternoon off if you want."

I don't tell him the ordering was a breeze. Instead, I smile gratefully. "Thank you." Then I run out the back door to the parking lot.

When I get home, I discover two other cars in our driveway, one of which is Auntie Lee's. I'm guessing she wasn't home when Mama invited her over or she would have just walked across the front yard. The other car belongs to Zach's mom. I know this because she gets out of it as I pull in.

There is only one reason Mama could have invited Auntie Lee and Sarah Jane over, and that is to spill our news. I quickly call Zach on the phone on my way into the house and say, "Get to my Mama's house right now. It's about to hit the fan!" I hang up before he can say anything.

I rush in right after Sarah Jane and see that Mama has set up a little tea party. When she sees me, she startles so bad she drops a teacup. "Emmie, what are you doing here?" she demands.

"I'm here to make sure you keep your end of our bargain."

"What bargain is that?" Auntie Lee asks.

Ignoring her question, I give my aunt a kiss on the cheek and ask, "Why are y'all here?"

Sarah Jane answers, "Your mama said she had some news she couldn't wait to share with us."

I just bet she did. I turn to Mama, "You feeling a little gossipy, Mama?"

She looks like she's trying to look offended. "No. I just wanted to tell the gals about our trip is all."

"Anything in particular?" I ask.

Sarah Jean says, "Apparently, life as we know it is about to change. What did y'all do in that city, anyway?"

I don't answer, instead I call Zach again. "Hurry up!"

I sit down on the couch and answer Zach's mama's question. "I was working most of the time, while Zach kept Mama and Faye company."

"That was sweet of him," Auntie Lee says.

Sarah Jane offers, "Zach used to visit New York once in a while. He even thought about living there."

Mama smiles manically at Sarah Jean and says, "We could have gotten the kids together back then." By her wild-eyed look, she appears to be trying to tell her friend there's something more to what she's saying, but Sarah Jane doesn't seem to be grasping it.

I say, "I'd love a cup of tea, Mama. Thanks for offering."

Mama storms into the kitchen, clearly annoyed that I'm pooping on her party. She comes back a few minutes later and announces, "Faye's hungry, Emmie. You better go into the bedroom and feed her."

"I didn't hear her cry, Mama."

"Well, she's about to. She cries every afternoon at the same time. You'd best hurry."

"Why don't you bring her to me?" I ask as I hear not one, not two, but *six* car doors slam out front.

"Who's here now?" Mama demands.

I have no idea as I'm only expecting Zach. That's when I see them. He's brought reinforcements. Jed, Jesse, Amelia, Beau, and Davis all follow him through the front door. When they get into the living room, Amelia demands, "What's wrong? Why did I have to rush over here so fast?"

Zach says, "Emmie and I have some news for you." And then he tells them.

"Zach is Faye's daddy?" Davis asks. "I did not see that coming."

Sarah Jane is on her feet running into the nursery before she says a thing. She comes out holding Faye and she's crying her eyes out. "I'm a grandma. This perfect little love is my grandbaby!"

Zach puts his arms around his mom and says, "You're welcome."

Sarah Jane smacks him hard and demands, "Why didn't you tell me?"

I answer, "He didn't know." Then I explain my tequila intolerance, for what I hope is the last time.

Amelia turns to Zach, "That's why you kept asking after Emmie."

He nods his head. "That's why." Then he puts his arm around me and holds me tight.

Mama looks so excited I'm afraid she's going to bust right open. She says, "Davis, I have champagne in the garage refrigerator. Go get it, will you?"

The rest of the afternoon is spent celebrating Zach's contribution to Faye's life. Sarah Jane has yet to relinquish hold on the baby for longer than it takes for me to feed her. She wants to know, "Are you two getting married? Are you moving in together?"

Zach answers, "We'll let you know when we have news."

We talked about getting married when we were in New York but decided to keep dating and getting to know each other before moving on to that step. We want to build as solid a foundation as possible for our baby. We both feel strongly that we're destined to be together, but we don't want to rush things. No more than we already have.

Zach even suggested we don't do what we did to make Faye until we get engaged. I'm not sure I agree with him as it's about all I can do not to jump him every time we're in the same room together, but I love that he wants me to feel that I'm important enough on my own without that side of things.

We spend the afternoon answering the bajillion questions our families have. By the time their curiosity well runs dry, there's only one thing left to do: decide how we're going to spin this so Cootie doesn't rake us over the hot coals of her judgment.

Beau declares, "I'll take care of it." He leaves the house to get busy on his plan before we can ask what he has in mind. As he's currently the closest Frothingham to Cootie's family, I'm pretty sure it will be a sound one.

All I know is that my life seems to have worked out in a way I could have never imagined, and I'm full to bursting with joy. I'm home with my baby, her daddy, and my whole family. My heart magnet has pulled me to the exact place where I belong, and I'm going to cherish every moment.

Epilogue

My entire family is under the pavilion in Frothingham Park on Monday night. Jesse and Jed are on the bandstand warming up along with the band, and the rest of us are assembled at a picnic table. We're sipping sweet tea and eating the picnic supper we packed. We're as nervous as grasshoppers at a bonfire.

Beau hasn't told anyone what's going to happen. All we know is that tonight is the night his plan gets executed. It feels like Hulk and Thor are battling it out in my stomach for world domination. Cootie is across the way from us and has not once looked in our direction. Normally, she'd have been over here making snide comments by now.

Shelby gets up and walks across the bandstand before the music can start and taps into the microphone. She says, "I don't know about you all, but I'm pretty excited about our concert tonight. I feel fortunate to be part of Creek Water, and I'm so proud of our fine citizens who volunteer their time for our listening pleasure."

Shelby isn't acting at all like herself. She's being nice and it scares me. I know she's been through a lot, and if her actions are to be believed, it's changed her for the better.

She announces, "We're about to get underway here, but my mama has a few words she wants to say first." Shelby motions to Cootie, who looks like she's been sucking on a cut lemon again.

Cootie still hasn't made eye contact with any of us Frothinghams, and I fear for what she has to say. Beau leans over and puts my mind at rest. "Don't worry, Emmie. It's gonna be fine."

Cootie taps the microphone and unconvincingly says, "What a nice night this is." In truth, it looks like she'd rather be climbing a tree stark naked with a spotlight on her bum than standing where she is. She's quiet for several moments and the townsfolk start to murmur like there might be something wrong with her. She finally mumbles, "I have an apology to make."

Cootie apologizing for anything is about as surprising as Jesus Himself announcing the Rapture while impersonating Elvis in a white bell-bottomed jumpsuit, thank you very much. The rest of the town seems to agree because the whispering blossoms into a loud rumbling. Cootie looks like she wants to drop to the ground and try to shimmy out of here unnoticed, but Shelby gestures for her to keep going.

She clears her throat loudly. "I want to apologize to Emmeline Frothingham. It has come to my attention that some folks are crediting me with some nasty gossip regarding Emmie's late boyfriend and I wanted to take a moment to clear the air."

What in the hell is going on here? I look at Beau in a panic, but he just puts his hand on my arm as if to calm me down.

Cootie continues, "I'm sorry if I made you feel the need to invent a fiancé. Your baby is darling, and it doesn't matter one whit whether or not you're married to her daddy." She says the last bit so quietly, I'm not sure everyone without a hearing aid heard her.

Those who did, turn to stare at me. I should probably respond, but my voice has disappeared. Zach, bless his heart, stands up and speaks for me. "That's very nice of you, Mrs. Wilcox. In fact, you did cause a bit of trouble for us. Emmie's Auntie Lee made up a future husband for her because she knew you'd create a stink. She invented Armie to protect Emmie from you." Cootie looks like she wants to kick Zach in the teeth.

He continues, "The thing is that Emmie's family didn't know about our relationship when they told folks about Armie. That's why Emmie and I have had to keep quiet about the fact that I'm Faye's real daddy."

I guess this is one way of making sure everyone hears it straight from the horse's mouth. But heaven help us, I would not have chosen a scene like this on my own.

Cootie decides to go off script and shout, "You big liar! There's no way you and Emmie had a baby together."

Zach replies, "I assure you, Mrs. Wilcox, we have all the right parts to make a baby." The crowd giggles at his words. *Shoot me now.*

If this isn't excruciating enough, Shelby takes the microphone out of her mama's hand and says, "A lot of us have the right parts to make a baby, Mama."

Cootie yells, "Shelby Marie, don't you dare!"

Shelby continues, "I was pregnant myself." The crowd look like they're playing that old game "statue maker," where nobody so much as twitches.

I look at Beau and see that this wasn't part of his plan. Shelby tears up and continues, "I was pregnant, but I miscarried my baby just last week." She breaks down and starts to sob her heart out. Beau runs to her and pulls her into his arms and lets her cry on his shoulder.

Cootie grabs the microphone back and says, "Shelby's just making that up to be nice. My daughter isn't trash like Emmeline Frothingham."

Auntie Lee stands up and walks toward the podium with a deliberation that quite frankly scares me. She strides right past Cootie and opens her arms to give Shelby a hug. Then she whispers something into her ear. Once Beau leads Shelby away, Auntie Lee reaches out to take the microphone from Cootie.

Here's a little something I've learned over the years that I've known Auntie Lee—it's pointless to try to keep her from getting something if she really wants it. And she really wants that microphone. Once she gets a grip on it, she rips it out of Cootie's hand in one fell swoop. Cootie nearly topples over trying to hang on to it, but she has to let it go to keep herself from falling off the bandstand.

Auntie Lee addresses the crowd. "I don't know about y'all, but I'm sick of bullies." The pavilion is so quiet the sweat trickling down my neck sounds like a waterfall. Okay, no it doesn't, but you get my meaning.

When no one says anything, Auntie Lee adds, "I don't mind folks talking about other folks." She points out into the audience at Winnifred Simpson and says, "Like I didn't know Winnie won a poetry writing contest until Sally Swathmore told me down at the club. And I thought to myself, that's a nice bit of information. So, you know what I did? I told everyone else I saw that day about it. Why do you think I did that?"

The crowd stares at her as though she's wearing a disco ball on her head. They're positively enthralled. Auntie Lee continues,

"I told everyone because I was darn proud of Winnie. To have such talent and a way with words, why, I was breathless at her accomplishment. Now, would you say I was gossiping about Winnie by sharing her news?" Auntie Lee pauses for a moment. "Some might say I was. But I didn't see it that way because I was sharing happy tidings that were pleasing to hear."

Cootie screeches from the sidelines, "For God's sake, Lee, what's your point?"

"My point," Auntie Lee turns to her, "is that some of us never bother sharing the good things. Someone us like to flap our gums telling tales to shame or embarrass others. Those people, Cootie, are malicious, no-account gossips." Then she turns to the crowd and says, "And I don't know about you, but I don't listen to those people. I don't take pleasure in the misfortunes of others, and I sure as heck don't spend one second of my life making up stories in order to make people feel bad about themselves."

Mama stands up and confidently makes her way to Auntie Lee. When she gets there, she takes the microphone from her. Then she turns to the crowd and says, "Lee's right. The only reason gossip has any power is because we give it power by listening to it and by sharing it with others. I pledge that if you come to me with a story that isn't your business to share, I'm gonna close my ears and walk away."

Auntie Lee steps up, "I want to hear how my neighbors are doing. I want to know if someone could use my help, but I don't want to hear unkindness."

Mama says, "Creek Water is our home and it's only as good as the hearts of the people in it. Who's with us? Who's willing to stand up against the hurtful nonsense that plagues a certain portion of our community?" They both look at Cootie.

Sarah Jane stands up and starts a slow clap. I jump in and so does the rest of the family, and before you know it, every audience member is on their feet, smacking their hands together affirming that they're tired of the mean-spiritedness, too.

Cootie slinks back as far as she can in the other direction without falling off the bandstand.

Uncle Jed stands up and addresses the band, "I think this calls for our special song. On the count of three, one … two … three …" They bust forth with Queen's, "We Are the Champions."

It's an odd and moving scene to watch our community band tackle such a big number. Let's face it, the talent isn't there, but they more than make up for their lack of skill with heart. Uncle Jesse stands up and walks close to the microphone, riffing like he knows what he's doing. But one thing is for sure, he's giving us our money's worth.

Zach takes my hand and squeezes it tightly before leaning down and saying, "I'm glad we're home." Then he lays one on me. It's a kiss so toe-curlingly sweet I cannot imagine myself being anywhere else on this planet.

With Mama and Auntie Lee leading the fight against gossip, I feel sure that Cootie's reign is at an end. Creek Water, Missouri is my home. It's the town I'm going to raise my daughter in, and hopefully the town where I give her some siblings someday. I'm proud that we've finally made our peace.

Keep reading for a sneak peak of book 2 in
The Creek Water series, The Move!

About the Author

Whitney Dineen is an award-winning author of romantic comedies, non-fiction humor, thrillers, and middle reader fiction. She lives in the beautiful Pacific Northwest with her husband and two daughters. When not weaving stories, Whitney can be found gardening, wrangling free-range chickens, or eating french fries. Not always in that order. She loves to hear from her fans and can be reached through her website at https://whitneydineen.com/.

Join me!

Mailing List Sign Up
whitneydineen.com/newsletter/

BookBub
www.bookbub.com/authors/whitney-dineen

Facebook
www.facebook.com/Whitney-Dineen-11687019412/

Twitter

twitter.com/WhitneyDineen

Email

WhitneyDineenAuthor@gmail.com

Goodreads

www.goodreads.com/author/show/8145525.Whitney_Dineen

Blog

whitneydineen.com/blog/

Please write a review on Amazon, Goodreads, or BookBub. Reviews are the best way you can support a story you love!

Other Books By Whitney Dineen

Romantic Comedies
Relatively Normal
Relatively Sane
Relatively Happy
She Sins at Midnight
The Reinvention of Mimi Finnegan
Mimi Plus Two
Kindred Spirits
Going Up?

Thrillers
See No More

Non-Fiction Humor
Motherhood, Martyrdom & Costco Runs

Middle Reader
Wilhelmina and the Willamette Wig Factory
Who the Heck is Harvey Stingle?

Children's Books
The Friendship Bench

Prologue

I don't believe in voodoo as a rule. I'm not superstitious or particularly gullible, and I sure as heck don't think anyone can predict the future. Why am I telling you this? Because when I was twelve years old, my grandmother took me to see a fortune teller in Harlem, right down the street from where she lived. The old lady with the Rastafarian braids, nose ring, and skunky smelling aura, read my palm and told me the following, "In your thirtieth year of life, right after the dog jumps over you, your whole world will change in the most unexpected ways. Be open to the change or you will always regret it."

Mimi wrote the message down verbatim and gave me the scrap of paper, making me promise to keep it in my little jewelry box with the dancing ballerina. She said, "Baby girl, that old bat might have been stoned, but she's given me priceless words of wisdom during my lifetime. I have no idea what's in store for you, but I know it was important for you to hear that."

I've long since lost the jewelry box, and Mimi died a handful of years after that, but I always remembered the message, just like I promised I'd do. I haven't thought about in years, but suddenly I'm awash with the memory ...

Chapter 1

"Incoming!" I hit the ground as soon as I heard the warning.

One of my all-time favorite pastimes is walking through Central Park in the fall. The air is crisp and the colors mind-blowingly gorgeous. Unfortunately, I have to share this miracle of nature with several million people who inhabit the seven-mile stretch of land with me.

The sheer volume of all those bodies can be dangerous. It can also seriously hinder my enjoyment. I'm currently feeling hindered, laying prone in a pile of damp leaves watching as a German Shepard jumps over me. He's chasing the frisbee that was destined to decapitate me.

I hear the old Jamaican woman's words like she's sitting next to me, "In your thirtieth year of life, after the dog flies over you, your whole world will change in the most unexpected ways."

A very attractive doggy daddy comes running toward me calling, "Nice catch, Hanzie!" He whizzes right by me to give his buddy a vigorous rub. I eagerly wait my turn. Just kidding, I don't really expect Mr. Hotty Pants to rub me down, but offering a hand up would have been nice. Clearly that's not going to happen as I watch him jog away with his furry friend. There isn't as much as a backward glance in my direction.

"Loser!" I yell at his retreating back.

Dear New York, I love you like the native I am, but you gotta quit letting the riff raff move in. How do I know he's riff raff? He was wearing an "I Heart Akron" sweatshirt. No real New Yorker hearts anywhere other than New York.

An authentic New Yorker would have run over to help me up before apologizing profusely for the near miss. He would have probably even offered to buy me a hot dog for my troubles. Stereotypes aside, born and bred locals are nice. Sure, they give you hell when you deserve it, but when something like this happens, they own it.

I lay still for a moment trying to regain my equilibrium, thanks to the jolt of adrenaline that just shot through me. I adore this island with my whole being. It's the only home I've ever known, but suddenly I wonder what life is like for the rest of the world. You know, the people who can enjoy the great outdoors with a modicum of elbow room.

I finally get up and buy my own hot dog to snack on as I walk home. Out of the corner of my eye I see a leaf sticking out of a ringlet of hair. Pulling at it, I realize I'll be picking bits of nature out of my hair for the next couple of days. My corkscrew curly brown tresses attract and conceal all manner of things, leaves in the fall, flower petals in the spring, probably small rodents if I ever let them near my head, which I don't.

As soon as I get to my building, I head down to the basement to get the rest of my cold weather clothes from storage. An Indian summer has been visiting, so I haven't been in a rush, but suddenly the bite of fall is upon us.

After retrieving two boxes marked, "Pumpkin Muffin Clothes"—I labeled them in anticipation of the season where I organically increase my carb intake—I head back to my apartment on the fourth floor.

I probably should have brought up one box at a time, but I really didn't want to make another trip. As I stagger down the hallway, I hear, "Hey Lexi, need a hand?" Timothy Sanders, my neighbor and all-around stud muffin, asks.

"Hi Tim, that would be great." I happily transfer half of my load into his very capable arms. "When did you get back into the city?"

"Last night. Sadly, Fire Island becomes nothing but a fond memory for another year."

He sighs in such a way that I feel an overpowering urge to wrap up Fire Island in a big red bow and gift it to him. Tim is a handsomely preppy brunette who dresses impeccably. Simply put, he would complete me if he ever bothered to ask me out. And believe me, I release all my single girl pheromones into the ether when he's around. So far, to no avail.

"Did you come back at all this summer?" I ask, already knowing the answer is no. I've been scoping out his unit with the dedication of a confirmed busybody.

"Nah, I worked remotely. It's nice being home though. What have you been up to?" he asks.

"Same old, same old. Doing my darndest to turn Silver Spoons into the next Williams Sonoma." My official job title of "Growth Manager" requires that I closely follow trends around the country looking for the next best fit to take our chain of kitchenware boutiques nationwide. I love my job for the most part, but I've gotten bored. When Emmeline, my good friend and fellow Silver Spoons employee, left several months ago, some of the joy went out of going to work. Actually, a lot. Her departure started a string of upsets we haven't quite recovered from.

"I forgot you worked there. Listen, can I come in and see you sometime next week? Maybe you can show me around, if you're available." Do fish swim? Do Yankee fans flip you the bird if you accidentally cheer for the other team? *I'm always available for the likes of Tim Sanders. Always.*

I've suddenly developed lockjaw, and I forget to swallow an excess of saliva that fills my mouth. *Tim is going to ask me out.* Why else would he want me to show him around my work? Granted, it's a weird kind of build up to courtship, but whatever gets the job done, right? After five long years my dreams are about to come true. OMG, that fortune teller was right! I'm thirty, a dog just jumped over me—I always thought that was some kind of metaphor, but I guess I was wrong—and now Tim is finally going to ask me out. My life is changing.

I inelegantly choke on my spit as I answer, "For you, anything. What day works best?"

"Don't know yet. Let me call Tiffany and find out when she's available."

"Tiffany?" I ask, hoping that she's his sister. I have no idea why he would need his sister to tag along.

"Oh, my gosh, that's right, you wouldn't know." I await explanation as tingles of dread crawl across my scalp like a spider infestation. "Tiff and I got engaged last month. Can you believe it?"

Imagine how you'd feel if the Big Friendly Giant wasn't truly friendly after all but was more of a Big Savage Giant. Visualize him shoving his meaty fist right through your solar plexus before ripping out your still beating heart. That's how I feel; all the hope and anticipation that this time of year stirs within me, mixed with the unadulterated joy of seeing Tim again, has evaporated, leaving nothing but debilitating emptiness.

After several silent moments, where it doesn't ever occur to me to congratulate him, I finally say, "I didn't know you were seeing anyone."

He looks surprised. "Really? That's weird. We've been together for over a year."

A whole year wasted, hungering for the unattainable. Three hundred and sixty-five days of my life I suddenly want back with the same yearning I used to feel for Christmas morning when my age was in single digits.

"Strange I haven't seen her before. Why's that?" I demand as though he's making her up.

He shrugs, blissfully unaware of my breaking heart. "We decided to get married when I got the notice about the building going condo."

All romantic angst is put on hold. "What building's turning into condos?" It has to be Tiffany's —I say her name in my head like it's Hitler or Satan— because I never received a notice.

"Lexi, didn't you get the letter from the management company alerting us that the owner is giving us the option to buy our apartments? Surely you've heard the rumors over the last few years."

Of course, I've heard the rumors. My last three apartments

were rumored to either be going co-op or condo and none of them ever never did. That's par for the course when you live in the Big Apple. "I didn't get the notice," I tell him. "When is it happening?"

"Not for six months, but that's going to fly by in the blink of an eye. You're going to buy, aren't you?"

"I don't know." My head is suddenly filled with sharp jabbing pains, like an acupuncturist is sticking needles directly into my brain. "How much are our units going for?" I ask even though I know it will be outside of my budget. I've managed to save seventy-two thousand dollars in the last nine years, but that won't be anywhere near the twenty percent down payment I'll need. Even if it was, there will be condo fees on top of a staggering mortgage payment.

"They're offering current residents, who have lived here more than three years, a ten percent discount. We should be able to buy in for about five hundred thousand. Too good an offer to pass up, don't you think?"

He must be high. How in the world does he imagine I'll be able to afford such a hefty sum on my own? He needs to marry *Tiffany* to afford it. And while I'd make decent money if I lived in Tulsa or Des Moines, living in New York City, conscientiously tucking money aside for future homeownership, I barely get by.

My one-bedroom, one-bath apartment on the Upper West Side has a view of Central Park, if you're not afraid to hang out the bathroom window and crane your neck so far to the left you look like you're performing extreme yoga. A view of any kind of park pushes the price point up, even though the whole space is under five hundred square feet, and that includes the closets. It's tiny, but it's my home. The home I can no longer afford to live in.

Defeatedly, I answer, "I don't have enough for the down payment."

"That's too bad," he says sounding genuinely sorry. "You've been a great neighbor."

Clearly, I've been the only one doing any pining in this relationship.

When we arrive at my door, I unlock it and lead the way in. Tim puts my box on the dining room table. "So about next week, I'll let you know when Tiff and I can come in to register for our wedding. I really appreciate you helping us out."

That's why he wanted to come into my work? I mean, obviously in light of his engagement, but still, so disappointing. "I don't know anything about the gift registry, but our sales staff will be more than happy to help you and *Tiffany*." Satan.

"Oh, sure. Makes sense," he says. "I'm really sorry to be the one to tell you about the building. If I were you, I'd call the management company asap to find out how much time you have before you need to move out. Maybe they'll let you stay longer."

I nod my head dumbly and show him to the door. My enthusiasm over Tim being home, the cooler weather arriving, my sweaters being unearthed, and the start of pumpkin muffin season has disappeared into a soulless abyss.

I'm thirty-years-old, a dog has recently jumped over me, and if I wasn't enough, I now believe the old kook from Harlem, that my life is about to change in the most unexpected ways. It already has.

Chapter 2

My mom fills two wine glasses with a hearty Beaujolais. "You'll just have to move back home with us. Think about how much money you'll save if you stay here for a couple of years."

I look around my parent's loft, my childhood home, and observe that nothing has changed. While the vast majority of SoHo has been renovated in the last several decades, adding marble and granite, expensive cabinetry, and gleaming fixtures, my parents place is an homage to the nineties. My dad's art supplies fill the entire living area, with huge canvases resting against walls and furniture. Books and assorted clutter fill every surface. The kitchen? Good grief, the kitchen, it looks like something straight out of a flea market, but not in a chic, designer kind of way— more like a garage sale meets your grandmother's castoffs.

Lambertos Blake, or Bertie as he's known to his friends and family, is an artist of some repute. He's had fits and bursts of success during his thirty-five-year long career that has cemented his name as one of the longest standing artists of his time. My dad is currently experiencing a drought though, declaring that the oppressiveness of the world's political climate is interfering with his creative mojo. Historically, these periods have always been followed by a burst of genius that leads to a record-breaking commission. He makes himself and everyone around him miserable while he waits.

"Where would you like me to sleep? Perhaps on the window ledge?" I ask, while pointing to one of the best features in the apartment. Giant ten-foot windows fill the majority of the east facing wall, making this an ideal artists lair.

"No one likes a smart ass, dear," my mom says while cutting up a plate of figs.

Regina Cohen is a professor of women's studies at NYU. My friends used to wonder why she didn't take my dad's name when they got married, until I informed them that my parents never got married. Regina felt strongly, and still does, that she is queen of her own destiny and that marriage is nothing more than letting our patriarchal forefathers enslave her. She wanted no part of it, even though she and my dad have been a devoted couple for thirty-five years.

Her fierce belief that women have been screwed over since Eve radiates from her like a furnace. Her mass of curly brown hair often bounces in a righteous indignation that can easily be perceived as hostile to those who don't know her. Though enormously passionate about her beliefs, she's remarkably kind to the majority of people, you just have to hang out with her long enough to get past her intimidating exterior. It's not a challenge everyone is up to.

I answer, "Have you seen the state of my room lately?" My dad has been using it as a storage room for half-finished paintings and supplies. "It smells like turpentine. I'd probably develop a brain tumor if I slept in there."

"Psh," she says. "Bertie would be so happy to have you home that he'd clear it out for you."

"Mom, I love you guys with my whole heart. But two days back here would have me jumping out the nearest window." With a Vanna White like flourish, I showcase the alarming selection of exits at my disposal.

She rolls her gray wolf-like eyes at me and declares, "Beggars can't be choosers."

"I'm not a beggar, yet," I inform her. "I'm going to start looking around for something else. Maybe I can find a widow on Fifth Avenue to rent out her maid's quarters to me for a song."

"I'd rather you move into a youth hostel. Those snooty Park Avenue types wouldn't treat you well at all."

"Why do you say that?" I ask, fully aware that I'm poking the bear.

"Because they didn't earn their money, they inherited it. They have no idea what it takes to hold down a job and raise a family with the sweat from their own brow. They're nothing but entitled …"

I interrupt, "Lords of the manner pulling the strings of the puppet peasantry."

My mom squints her eyes like she's trying to decipher whose side I'm on. She ultimately decides that no offense was meant, and continues, "I do not like entitled people."

"I was just teasing you, Mom." Not that I wouldn't rent the maid quarters in one of those penthouses. I would, but I don't realistically expect those folks are looking for tenants.

"You disappoint me, Lexi," she says.

"Why, because I don't have a chip on my shoulder? Because

I don't hate rich people on principal?"

She shakes her head, "Don't make light of the struggles that came before you, Alexis. Women who refused to be cast in the shadows of history are the reason we have the degree of equality we have today. Those who hunt out the wealthiest mate they can to bring forth new generations of privilege do not have my respect."

"The sisterhood was tough, so I could be soft, huh?" I ask with a hint of attitude. "It's not that I don't appreciate what's been done, Mom, it's just that I have a lot of other things on my plate right now. You know, like impending homelessness."

Regina changes the subject as she knows this could explode into something. "Where do you want to order dinner from?" She pulls out a bunch of menus from the kitchen drawer.

"I want Kung Pao something. Chicken, shrimp, goat, I don't care." My current mood calls for something spicy to help burn through the cloud of frustration that's filling my head.

"Excellent, I'll have the Sichuan Beef, Bertie will have the Cashew Chicken. We can share."

Apparently, I like to fight with my mom, and because I'm feeling a myriad of aggressive emotions, I say, "I'm not sharing."

She comes around the counter and stands right in front of me. Putting her hands on my shoulders, she says, "Lexi, you're going to be fine. You've moved before, you'll probably move again. You have to trust in your strength, keep your chin up, and plow through. I promise you'll be better off than you are now."

I don't want to believe her, but that's the super annoying thing about my mom, she's usually right. Not that I'll ever say that to her face. "I've been thinking about finally taking my accrued vacation time at work. If I don't use it by the end of December, I'll lose it."

"How much time do you have?" she asks.

"Five weeks. Maybe I need to get out of dodge for a while to help clear my head."

"You mean, leave New York City? Why don't you just stay and do all the things you want to do but never have time for?"

"Like what?" I ask. "I grew up here. I've pretty much done it all."

She releases a bark of laughter. "You haven't even begun." Then she asks, "Where would you like to go?"

"I want to visit Emmie in Missouri. I miss her and the baby so much, I think spending time with a friend will be good for me."

My mom nods her head once, but she looks concerned. "Missouri, huh? I've never been there. I can't imagine there's much to see." My parents have been all over the world for art shows and lectures, but they know very little about small town America. As a result, I don't either, but it's time for me to find out.

Chapter 3

Jameson Diamante, my boss, calls me into his office as soon as I get to work the next morning. He's good looking in the same way a friend's dad was good looking when you were in high school. You know, elegantly graying hair with crinkly laugh lines that hint at unknown adventures. You could appreciate his handsomeness without ever feeling anything remotely like attraction.

Unfortunately, Jameson is oblivious that his appeal doesn't transcend generations and he spends copious amount of time flirting with his staff, of which a solid ninety percent are women who are much younger than him and not at all interested in his overtures.

He stands when I walk through the door and gestures gallantly for me to take a seat next to him on the loveseat situated in a small seating area adjacent to his deck. "Alexis, how are you this fine day?"

"I'm doing well, Jameson. I'm glad you wanted to see me. As you know, I made an appointment to speak with you, as well."

"Me first!" he declares excitedly while clapping his hands together. "I have the happy news of telling you that you're being promoted to the position of East Coast relocation scout." The clueless look on my face prompts him to explain, "You'll be in charge of relocating our existing stores to different addresses, should it be beneficial to do so."

Huh. That doesn't sound like much of a promotion. I point out, "I'm currently in charge of finding new locations nationwide. How is regional relocation scout more prestigious than that?"

Jameson walks to the door, which I left open when I came in. He closes it. Then he sits next to me and very inappropriately places his hand on my knee. He leans in and says, "Confidentially, we've decided to stop branching out so aggressively."

"Why? I ask, even though there's only one reason a company ever cuts back on expansion – financial difficulties.

"We feel that it's in the best interest of the brand to slow things down and make sure the existing stores are performing optimally before we continue with our growth plan."

"Is there a raise involved?" I ask. I mean, he did say it was a promotion.

My boss clears his throat and refuses to meet my gaze while he adjusts a pile of magazines sitting on the side table next to him. "Not as such. But the good news is, it's only a slight decrease in salary."

"Decrease?" I demand. "Jameson, my apartment building is going condo. If I'm going to buy in, I need more money, not less." Not that it's even within the realm of possibility that they'll give me the amount I need to stay in my current digs.

"Ah, yes, but the promotion isn't the only good news I have for you." What? Are they going to buy my apartment for me as a signing bonus or something? It's all I can do not to let the sarcasm shoot out of me like a bottle rocket.

"The position is based out of our Atlanta store. Your cost of living will be much lower down there, so even with the decrease in pay, you'll be able to live a lot better than you do here in Manhattan. Isn't that exciting?"

As exciting as a root canal. "You want me to move to Atlanta? When?"

"We realize you'll have a bit of work to do here, so we will give you to the end of October to wrap things up. This way you can give notice on your apartment and fly down to Georgia to set up your new living situation. We'd like you to begin in Atlanta on November first."

"Jameson, my parents live in New York. I've lived here my whole life. You expect me to just pick up and move to the South?"

"People move for work all the time, Alexis." He raises an eyebrow at me like I'm supposed to shrink beneath his superiority. Clearly, he's never met the woman who raised me. Cowering to "the man" is not something within my DNA.

"We need to discuss why I made an appointment to talk to you," I tell him. He nods his head imperiously as though I should keep talking. So, I do. "I haven't taken a vacation in the last two years and I currently have five weeks of paid time that I'll lose at the first of the year."

"Ah, yes," he says as though he gives a crap about my vacation. "But you'll accrue vacation in your new position."

"I would expect so, but meanwhile I'd like to take the time I've already banked in my old position."

Confusion furrows his brow as if I'm not speaking plain

English. He finally asks, "What would you think if I could get the company to buy out your vacation time at half-pay?"

"I'd think that I'm already getting a fully paid vacation, so I'd most certainly have to pass on your offer to reduce that."

"Lexi." Jamison never uses my nickname. "The company is in financial difficulty at the moment. I could pay you at half rate for your vacation now and then write in a more substantial package for you in your next contract. How does that sound?"

With the company in trouble, I'd have to be an idiot to agree to move to Atlanta with decreased pay before taking the vacation I've already earned. I tell him, "I think I'll stay with my current contract. I'll tie up my workload and then I'll take my time at the beginning of November." If the company is still alive and kicking, then I'll consider if I'll accept a new position with them in Atlanta.

Jameson is clearly displeased that I'm not going to dance to his tune, but I'm letting him know loud and clear that I'm no pushover. My mother didn't raise a stupid child. I'm prepared to unleash *the full Regina* if he doesn't go for it, but he eventually stands and puts out his hand to shake mine.

"You've got yourself a deal, Alexis. I'll write up a new offer detailing our agreement and let you know when it's ready to be signed."

As I walk back to my desk, I can't help but wonder if Silver Spoons is a house of cards in a windstorm or if they're simply being fiscally responsible by not overextending themselves. There's no way to know. I'll just have to sit back and keep my eyes open. Meanwhile, I need to give some serious consideration to my housing situation. I can't keep my current place if I move to Atlanta, and I sure can't keep it as an unemployed New Yorker, which is what I'll be if I don't take the job in Georgia.

I decide to forgo actual work and walk down the street to the new bakery that just opened. Even if a pumpkin muffin doesn't help me think more clearly, it will surely offer a degree of comfort, which is one thing I could use in spades right now.

I stir one packet of fake sugar into my latte before turning around to try to find a place to sit. With no seating open, I walk outside and cross the street to Central Park and find an empty bench almost immediately. My life is turning into something of a shit show. I'm losing my apartment, my job, and my hope that Tim might have some interest in me. All crushed within three days. I watch as people buzz around me. Time on my little corner of the bench has totally stopped, and the rest of the world has hit fast forward.

I take two bites of my muffin before realizing I can't even taste it. I eventually pick up my phone and punch in Emmie's number. She answers on the third ring, mid-laugh, "Hey Lexi, what's up?" And so, I tell her. Halfway through Tim's engagement story, I uncharacteristically burst into tears. By the time I relay that my apartment is going condo I'm so stuffed up I'm not sure if she has any idea what I'm saying. I don't even know who I am in this moment.

Before snot runs uncontrollably down my nose, she interrupts me. "Come to Creek Water and see us. Faye and I miss you to the moon and back."

I tell her I've already decided to do just that and give her my dates, asking if they work.

"A whole month!" she squeals in my ear. "You're never going

to want to leave after you've been here for that amount of time."
I want to remind her that she lives in Missouri, and Missouri is
pretty much a nothing location from a New Yorker's perspective.
But I don't want to hurt her feelings. Also, I'm starting to
wonder if my life in New York is all it's cracked up to be. Just
don't tell Regina I said that or she's liable to give birth to a cow.

Buy the book!

Four Years Ago

My best friend is a vision straight out of one of those glossy bridal magazines that costs more than a macchiato and breakfast sandwich at Starbucks. She's well over six feet tall in her heels, slim as a fashion model—except she's sporting a C-cup no emaciated supermodel would be caught dead with—and her silky brown hair is currently twisted in an impossibly complicated up-do that probably required four professional hair stylists and a drag queen to execute. She's elegant beyond words.

I gasp as she spins around, so I can behold her in all her splendor. The sleeveless, beaded-bodice trumpet gown fits her like a glove. "Jasmine Marie, you're glorious!"

She giggles, which is a sound you wouldn't expect to come out of such a stunningly ethereal creature. She spins again, "I've never felt so girly! And that's saying something being that I'm this tall."

"Whoever said a month's paycheck was too much to spend on a wedding dress clearly never saw you in this one. I feel like a proud mother right now."

Jazz heaves a sigh. "Speaking of mothers, you have to do me a favor." My eyebrows raise in interest. She continues, "Watch out for mine and make sure she doesn't murder my dad's new wife during dinner."

I snort. "Puh-leeze, your mom is every ounce a lady. She'd no more commit murder than I would."

"Alas, Brandee—with two e's— the latest of my dad's spouses, has just announced she's pregnant. My mom isn't taking the news gracefully."

"You're kidding me? You're going to have a new brother or sister at twenty-nine?" Then I ask, "How old is Brandee again?"

My friend rolls her big brown eyes. "My dearest stepmother has just turned twenty-four."

"I don't know, Jazz. I think your dad is the one who needs offing in this scenario. I might be persuaded to help."

"I would appreciate if no murders were committed at my nuptials." Then she hugs me, and says, "But I love you for offering."

"Oh, Jazzy," I exclaim, "this day is going to be so wonderful. You deserve every minute of happiness. Dylan is one lucky guy."

Brushing a non-existent wrinkle out of her skirt, she declares, "Now all we need to do is find you the perfect man. Three of the groomsmen are single. You've met two of them, and the third is the one with sandy blond hair. He's Dylan's cousin, Jared, from Detroit."

"Detroit? Hard pass." The sarcasm rolls off my tongue. "I'm not looking for a long-distance love. But have no fear, I'll definitely scope out the other two. I'm not opposed to meeting the future Mr. Catriona Masterton tonight."

She beams. "People often meet their future spouses at weddings. It's a thing."

"So, it's got to be my turn, right?"

Jazz playfully punches my arm. "That's the attitude I love! I just wish you were walking down the aisle with me."

I call out to Jennifer, our assistant, "Make sure you pack up all of Jazz's stuff and take it over to her suite at the hotel. Oh, and before you go, tell Elaine to get the limos turned around out front to transport the wedding party to the reception once the ceremony ends."

In addition to being best friends, Jazz and I own a much sought-after event-planning business in Manhattan. We're the go-to duo known for stylishly executing even the trickiest parties—like weddings where the groom was once married to the bride's sister—without a hitch.

I turn to the current bride. "I wish I were walking down the aisle with you too, but someone has to make sure this shin-dig of yours goes off perfectly. There's a ton of potential business out there, so we have to make sure this is our best party yet. Now, hustle, the bridesmaids are already upstairs, and their procession starts in …"—I check my watch— "two minutes, which only gives you seven before it's your turn."

I pick up my friend's chapel-length train to keep it from getting dirty on the stairs. "Let's go, lady; your happily-ever-after awaits."

We arrive upstairs in the entrance of St. John the Divine Cathedral just as Emily, the last bridesmaid, starts her goosestep down the aisle. Jazz and I stand side-by-side watching her go. As Emily takes her place in the front of the altar, the first strains of Trumpet Voluntary fill the atmosphere like a heavenly serenade. Chills race through my body as I kiss my friend's cheek and hand her off to her father who will deliver her to her destiny, one Dylan Finch.

Once the ceremony is over and the reception is in full swing at the St. Regis Hotel, I take off my party-planner hat and put on my dancing shoes. It's go time. I have my eye on a particular groomsman, whom I've met on a couple other occasions. He's sweet and shy, but super easy on the eyes. I'm not sure we're destined for matrimony, but a couple of dances would be fun.

I straighten the skinny navy skirt of my evening dress and prepare for the chase. I take a step forward and wind up doing an unexpected split to the ground. *Ouch!* The waiter rushes over to clean up the spilled drink I inadvertently stepped in, and before I can begin the process of restoring my dignity, a pair of shiny, black shoes shows up next to me.

A manly hand stretches out and a deep voice inquires, "May I be of assistance?" He introduces himself. "Ethan Crenshaw, lifelong friend of the groom." I recognize him from the rehearsal dinner, but I didn't get a chance to talk to him. Not only is Dylan's friend chivalrous, but he has gorgeous green eyes that remind me of Maeve's, my childhood cat.

I take his hand. "Thank you. That's very kind."

"Let me help you to a chair and then I'll get some ice for your injury. It'll keep the swelling down," he announces.

Once I'm positioned at table fourteen in the main ballroom, I watch Ethan walk to the bar. He looks good in a way that suggests he's comfortable in formal wear, like James Bond. And bam, just like that, I realize I had totally forgotten about the cute groomsman.

When my knight in shining armor—a.k.a. a black tuxedo—

returns, he helps prop my foot up on a chair and states, "There's a nine percent chance of getting injured at a wedding reception."

As far as opening lines to, it's not the best. Yet, his previous gallantry more than makes up for it. "That seems to be an awfully high number," I reply. "I've been to almost two hundred weddings so far and this is my first injury. If my calculations are correct, that puts my risk at point five percent, nowhere near your estimate."

"Two hundred weddings? You must be quite a popular friend."

I inform him, "I'm a party planner. I'm Jazz's partner."

"Ah, well then, surely you've had a blister, a burnt finger, or a stiff neck?"

I laugh. "If you're going to include all the mundane discomforts, I'd think you'd be more accurate to say there's a hundred percent chance of getting injured at a wedding."

He shakes his head. "No, only nine percent, unless my research is wrong." With a pointed look he adds, "Which it never is."

What kind of person researches injuries at weddings? So, I ask, "What exactly do you do for a living?"

"I'm an actuary. Certainly, not as glamorous a profession as party planning, but it pays the bills."

I've heard the job title, but I have no idea what it entails. Kind of like an ornithologist. I know it's something. I just don't know what. At my confused look, he explains, "Insurance companies and brokerage firms hire actuaries to assess the financial risk of investments and people. I currently work at an insurance company and help set rates, based on the statistical probability of natural disasters hitting certain demographics. For instance, earthquake insurance in the Midwest costs you next to nothing compared to what it does in California, for a reason."

"Huh." I can't seem to think of any other response.

"It sounds like a job that could bore the paint off the walls, doesn't it?" he laughs.

I flirt, "Lucky for me, I like numbers."

Ethan sits with me for the next three hours while I ice my ankle, ten minutes on and twenty minutes off, as per his suggestion for the best healing effects. As we get to know each other, I watch Jazz flirt and dance with the man who just promised to love her forever.

Dylan is hands down the sweetest, funniest, and most devoted man I've ever met. He adores my friend with his whole being and treats her like delicate china, even though she's not the kind of woman you'd want to sneak up on in a dark alley. Jazzy is one hundred percent Amazon with a touch of Xena Warrior Princess. She and Dylan are perfect for each other.

I was once in love with a man very much like Dylan and it didn't turn out well, which is why I'm currently in the market for someone more practical. I'm less concerned with grand gestures and flowery compliments, than in a reliable partner who will be there when the chips are down.

Throughout the reception, not only do I discover that Ethan adheres to a strictly regimented life, but I also learn he's a lovely man. He even offers, "Would you like me to see you safely home? No ulterior motives, I promise."

"It's kind of early to leave, don't you think?" And while he claims no other motivation, I wouldn't be opposed to a little romance.

He looks at his watch and explains, "I promised my neighbor, Mrs. Fein, I'd look in on her cat while she's away. Apparently, Fifi suffers from separation anxiety and needs someone to bat her toy mouse around with her before she can go to sleep."

As the party is winding down, and I can see the staff has everything well in hand, there's nothing more for me to do. I allow Ethan to escort me home. True to his word, he doesn't try any funny business. He just gives me a sweet kiss, leaving me wanting more, and asks, "When can I see you again?"

The Courtship

When my doorbell rings, I quickly apply a fresh layer of lipstick and grab my purse. Tonight, we're celebrating our first anniversary, which happens to coincide with Jazz and Dylan's first anniversary. I'm wearing a cerulean-blue wrap-dress that compliments my blond hair and blue eyes. I bought it especially for this occasion.

Ethan greets me with a bouquet of long-stemmed white roses. "For my beautiful lady."

I pull him in and give him a proper kiss of appreciation. "These are perfect, thank you." Even though red roses are meant for lovers, Ethan's favorite are white ones. He claims they're pure and untarnished, like me. Swoon, right?

Our dating experience has been perfect. There's no rush to jump into bed and burn ourselves out having wild monkey sex six times a day. That's not to say there's isn't any chemistry. There definitely is. It's just not some uncontrollable chemical explosion guaranteed to fizzle once the initial throes of passion are spent. It would be more accurate to conclude we're committed to an adult relationship that involves a lot of other aspects of our union, in addition to the physical. It's exactly what

I'm looking for. I've reached an age where I'm no longer interested in unpredictable and spontaneous men.

Ethan and I have a nice routine together. We eat out twice a week, taking turns picking the location. Sometimes it's breakfast, sometimes dinner, but it's always twice a week. I change up my location depending on what the buzz on the street is. I'm always on the lookout for a new adventure. Ethan seems content to stay with the same handful of locations, which is fine. There are plenty of new things for me to try, though he seems to favor a few select menu items.

We watch television two nights a week and go to the movies on Sunday. I stay over at his apartment twice a week and he stays the same number at mine. All in all, we spend a lot of time together. We also seem to have a thing for the number two.

I put the roses into a vase and inhale their fragrance deeply before saying, "We'd better run. Our reservation is at seven."

"I changed it to seven thirty. I didn't want to run the risk of being late and losing it," he replies.

That's Ethan in a nutshell. He thinks things through and always has a plan. In a world where people constantly fly by the seat of their pants, I think this is a refreshing way to live. "Perfect. Would you like a glass of wine before we leave?"

He holds out his hand. "No. We can always get one at the bar if we're early. I asked the Lyft driver to wait for us."

As we walk out the door of my Chelsea apartment, the world is my oyster. I'm celebrating a year with the same wonderful man, I have a flourishing career, and the air is finally cooling and starting to smell like a New York City fall. Contentment permeates my world.

Ethan and I hold hands in the car on the way to the restaurant. I say, "This is quite a special night, isn't it?" We don't normally eat at restaurants as expensive as Astor Court, but this is a celebration.

"It is. Since we met at the St. Regis Hotel, it's only fitting we return to the scene of the crime a year later."

Ethan guides me from the car into the hotel with his left hand placed gently on my lower back. The lobby is old-world elegant, and I feel like a princess entering a castle.

Once we're seated, our waiter, a middle-aged man wearing black pants with a matching vest and bow tie, greets us, "Mr. Crenshaw, Ms. Masterton, we're so honored to have you dining with us. My name is Frank, and I'll be taking care of you this evening." Wow, that was worth a couple hundred bucks right there. It's the little things like this that make people keep coming back.

Frank pops open a bottle of champagne and pours for us. Ethan has left no detail unattended. He's even requested the same champagne Jazz and Dylan served at their wedding, Veuve Clicquot Rosé.

After our appetizers are ordered—lobster risotto for me, and the caprese salad for him— Ethan surprises me by dropping to one knee beside me. "Catriona ..." My heart starts to beat so loudly I can hear it pounding inside my ears. Before he can say anything else, I start the little camera in my brain clicking away to save this moment for posterity. I never suspected he was going to propose marriage tonight.

I inhale deeply and look up at the mural of a blue sky with white, fluffy clouds painted on the eighteen-foot ceiling. I observe the gold-leaf crown molding and count all six crystal chandeliers. Everything seems to be moving in slow motion.

I always thought that women who claimed they didn't know a proposal was coming were just playing up the drama for the retelling of their story. Turns out, some might really be surprised. I finally look at Ethan and say, "Yes?"

He smiles widely. "Will you do me the great honor of becoming my wife?"

First of all, there's no way I'm not going to say yes. I mean, this is storybook stuff. Secondly, I love Ethan, and thirdly, did I mention the perfection of this night? I semi-shout, "Yes! Yes, I'll marry you!" A crowd of fellow diners give us an encouraging round of applause as the waiter approaches with a ring box on a silver tray.

Ethan opens the lid and removes an emerald-cut diamond from its black velvet pillow. He places it on my ring finger while uttering a heartfelt, "Thank you."

I wish someone was recording this so I could watch it on replay. Even though I'm living it, it feels like it's happening to someone else and I'm sure to forget some detail. Once Ethan gets back into his chair, he announces, "You should move in with me. We'll be able to save more money for the wedding that way."

What he says is true. My thirty-eight hundred dollar a month apartment will add up to a hefty sum for a wedding. I ask, "When would you like me to do that?"

"I've been thinking about it since I bought the ring, and decided if you said yes, you should move in right away. I know your lease is month-to-month, and as this is the last week in the month, how about over the weekend?"

And just like that, my life as a single woman in New York City comes to an end. I've never lived with a man, and suddenly I feel quite grown up. I mean, sure I'm thirty, and have a successful business, but now I'm an engaged woman to boot. If you had told me last year that this would be happening, I would have never believed you.

One Year Later

"Catriona, would you please pass the No-Salt?" Ethan never calls me Cat.

Despite the fact that he's been asking for that god-awful substitute for the year we've lived together, I can't help but crinkle my nose. Still, I hand over his salt replacement and ask, "Why do you insist on using that?"

Over the top of his glasses, he explains, "Based on my heredity, there's a thirty-eight-percent chance I will develop high blood pressure by the time I'm forty. By not using salt to season my food and by doing a minimum of thirty minutes of cardio a day, I reduce my chances to a mere twelve percent. Those are odds I can't afford to ignore."

This is the kind of information Ethan is known for. It's a bi-product of his job, and while I suppose he's right, I'd personally rather die five years early and really enjoy my food than put up with the weird aftertaste of the fake stuff.

If we can ever get confirmation on our preferred wedding venue, I'm fully prepared for an all-out battle about serving real salt at our reception. For me, this is a non-negotiable point.

"Our flight to Chicago leaves at five thirty tomorrow night."

I say this as I grind some pink sea salt onto my scrambled eggs.

"We should have a car pick us up at eleven fifteen, then."

I perform an internal eye roll. I don't care how early Ethan leaves for the airport when he's traveling alone, but I absolutely refuse to spend my life anticipating the worst and winding up sitting at JFK for three hours before getting on a plane. "I have a lunch meeting tomorrow, so I'll have to meet you there—if you insist on going early, that is."

He gives me the look, one that suggests, "Aren't we being a little frivolous?"

I cut him off at the pass before he has a chance to say it. "I'm meeting with the Vanderhauffers, of Vanderhauffer Jewels on Fifth Avenue, about doing their daughter's wedding. The kind of money and exposure we're talking about will more than make up for the extra car fare."

I'm actually not meeting the Vanderhauffers tomorrow; I'm meeting with them today. I have a massage scheduled for tomorrow to preemptively defeat the incoming stress of Thanksgiving. I don't usually lie to Ethan, but sometimes it's just easier than having to explain myself. Also, it avoids a heated disagreement, which I'm against, as a rule.

Plus, let's be honest, there is no way Ethan will appreciate the eccentricities of my family. I firmly believe there is a widely accepted range of behavior—from straight and stodgy to certifiable—that all humans exhibit from one degree to another. Fortunately, or unfortunately, depending on how you look at it, my family is firmly lodged in the quirky range.

Take my mother, for instance. She's plagued by a disorder where kitchen gadgets actually talk to her and beg her to take them home. During my childhood, she would drag me from one garage sale to the next just to see what treasures people were getting rid of. God forbid it was a shortbread pan in a shape she didn't have or some kitchen wonder that promised to peel, slice, dice, or waffle cut any vegetable you could imagine.

She's currently the proud owner of twenty-nine shortbread pans that form every shape from flower bouquets, to hearts, to the Loch Ness Monster. In addition, she has a basket of assorted culinary oddities, which she stores in the laundry room. She doesn't know exactly what they do or how to assemble them. She just knows they might come in handy one day, and God forbid she not have them when they're needed.

Also, my mother is the only human being alive who knows how to properly load a dishwasher—knives down, forks up, and no spoon caught spooning with another, ever. Even if you follow every one of her dictates to the letter, you will still inevitably do it wrong. "Forks up only on the first twenty-two days of the month and never on a full moon!" You think I'm kidding? Don't get me started on what happens when Mercury is in retrograde.

My mother's idiosyncrasies used to bug the absolute crap out of me until I decided to find them charming. Now when she tells me about a new shortbread pan she's found or complains that after thirty-five years of marriage, my dad still doesn't know how to load the dishwasher, I just smile. I'm never going to change her, and darn if I'm not going to miss these conversations someday.

Then there's my nan, who is happily still alive at eighty, and living with my parents. She developed something like Tourette syndrome when I was eight. Up until then, she was a perfectly normal grandma. Then one day, out of the blue, she snapped.

We had all been sharing a pew at the First Presbyterian Church on Easter morning. I couldn't wait to get home and bite the head off my solid chocolate Godiva Easter Bunny, but in the meantime was covertly popping jelly beans into my mouth, slowly sucking off the semi-hard candy coating before letting the delicious gummy center melt on my tongue.

I'd just eaten two pink ones, two white ones and had started on my two yellow, when Pastor Abernathy's wife walked by us. Nan shouted out as loud as you please, "Twat!" You've never heard such silence. The entire congregation was not only rendered mute, but totally immobile by the epithet hanging in the air above them.

Mrs. Abernathy had stopped dead in her tracks, slowly turned around, and scowled at my grandmother—a woman she'd known since they were in elementary school together. She had stared her down in such a way a lesser mortal would have succumbed to the arctic exposure of her glare.

My grandmother, on the other hand, had merely smiled and greeted, "Dorcas, how are you this fine Sunday?" It effectively left everyone wondering if they'd really heard what they thought they heard or if they'd all been victims of some strange audio hallucination.

The doctor hadn't been able to pinpoint the exact cause of her change, but guessed it was the result of a series of small strokes that effectively killed the governor living in her brain. After the incident at church, Nan became proficient at saying whatever she was thinking, wherever she was thinking it. Most people decided to act like they didn't hear her. It was a weird truce between the citizens of our little town and an old lady seemingly bent on offending everyone she came into contact with.

If a proliferation of shortbread pans and curse words weren't enough, my father's quirk is a love of dead rodents. No, I'm not kidding. I only wish I were. He has other peculiarities, but this one stands out as the most glaring.

My brother, Travis, is plagued by overt-selfishness and an inability to grow up. At twenty-nine, he's unemployed, living in my parents' basement, medicating his angst over life not turning out the way he expected with anything he can get his hands on—scotch, pot, Benadryl, sleeping pills. You name it, if it can alter his consciousness in any way, he's all over it like flies on a cow pie.

Why am I telling you all of this? Because up until this point, I've managed to keep Ethan from ever meeting my family. Even with us in New York City, and them in Illinois, it hasn't been easy to keep them apart. Now that we've been official for over a year, and Thanksgiving is just around the corner, Ethan has decreed he *will* meet my family, regardless of any excuse I come up with to keep that from happening. He's also invited his mom and dad along so that we can share our wedding plans with both sets of parents at the same time.

I can only hope my particular quirk, which is an almost mystical belief that all things work out as they should, is less a Pollyanna-ish pipe dream and more a fact-based reality. Otherwise, there's no way I can see this weekend going well for any of us. Is it any wonder I'll be spending two hours with a hulking masseur? I'll probably need another two when we get home.

Available Now!

Made in the USA
Middletown, DE
03 February 2021

33033391R00176